Resoundi

Antl

MA

and

HANNAH IVES

"A writer to watch."

Laura Lippman

"A writer and a character we want to see again—and soon."

Washington Times

"Hannah Ives is an appealing, believable heroine who would rather face a killer than her own post-cancer emotions, and Marcia Talley perfectly catches her ambivalence."

Margaret Maron

"[Characters] so real they must exist somewhere beyond the page."

Anne Perry

"Talley's thoughtful handling of Hannah's bout with breast cancer and the emotional and physical recovery . . . add depth. . . . [Her] characters shine."

Ft. Lauderdale Sun-Sentinel

"[Her] characters are well drawn and the dialogue sparkles."

Baltimore Sun

Hannah Ives Mysteries
from Marcia Talley

THROUGH THE DARKNESS
THIS ENEMY TOWN
IN DEATH'S SHADOW
OCCASION OF REVENGE
UNBREATHED MEMORIES
SING IT TO HER BONES

MARCIA TALLEY

Through the Darkness

A HANNAH IVES MYSTERY

AVON BOOKS
An Imprint of HarperCollins*Publishers*

This is a work of fiction. Names, characters, places, and incidents are products of the author's imagination or are used fictitiously and are not to be construed as real. Any resemblance to actual events, locales, organizations, or persons, living or dead, is entirely coincidental.

AVON BOOKS
An Imprint of HarperCollins*Publishers*
10 East 53rd Street
New York, New York 10022-5299

ISBN-13: 978-0-06-058741-3
ISBN-10: 0-06-058741-5
www.avonmystery.com

First Avon Books paperback printing: September 2006

Printed in the U.S.A.

10 9 8 7 6 5 4 3 2 1

For my daughters,
Laura Geyer and Sarah Glass

Jesus, tender Shepherd, hear me,
bless thy little lamb tonight;
through the darkness be thou near me,
keep me safe till morning light.

Through this day thy hand has led me,
and I thank thee for thy care;
thou hast warmed me, clothed and fed me,
listen to my evening prayer.

Let my sins be all forgiven,
bless the friends I love so well;
take me, when I die, to heaven,
happy there with thee to dwell.

MARY DUNCAN, (1814–1840)

ACKNOWLEDGMENTS

Thanks . . .

As always, to my husband, Barry, for the galvanized stomach that gets him through the fast food stages of my peripatetic writing life.

To the Rev. Margaret Waters, priest, longtime friend, and ought-to-be-published novelist, for keeping me straight, liturgically speaking.

To Special Agent Marina Murphy, Federal Bureau of Investigation, Annapolis Regional Authority, who answered all my questions about FBI policy and procedures with intelligence and sensitivity.

If I got it wrong, it's entirely my fault, not theirs.

To Perverted-Justice.com, *Dateline NBC*, and reporter Chris Hanson, whose "To Catch A Predator" television specials both inspired and informed this story.

To the National Center for Missing and Exploited Children, Nation's Missing Children Organization, Child Quest International, Beyond Missing, America's Most Wanted, Laura Recovery Center, The Polly Klaas Foundation, The Jimmy Ryce Center for Victims of Predatory Abduction, the Maryland Center for Missing Children, and similar organizations throughout the United States and abroad who work tirelessly to make the world a safer place for our children.

To Linda Jones of Bedford, England, massage therapist extraordinaire, whose hands ought to be insured by Lloyds of London; and to Barbara Holderby, for a truly inspirational "Girls Day Out" at the Spa at Pinehurst in North Carolina.

To my writers groups—Sujata Massey, John Mann, Janice McLane, and Karen Diegmueller in Baltimore and Janet Benrey, Trish Marshall, Mary Ellen Hughes, Ray Flynt, Sherriel Mattingly, and Lyn Taylor in Annapolis—for tough love.

To my amazing editor, Sarah Durand; her excellent assistant, Jeremy Cesarec; my can-do publicist, Danielle Bartlett; and everyone at HarperCollins who makes it such an incredibly supportive place for a mystery writer to be.

To my web diva and lunch buddy, Barbara Parker. Come see what Barbara can do at *www.marciatalley.com.*

To Erika E. Rose, attorney at law, whose generous bid at a charity auction sponsored by the Friends of the Annapolis Symphony Orchestra earned her a starring role in this book.

And to Kate Charles and Deborah Crombie, without whom . . .

Through the Darkness

CHAPTER 1

Crickets. Twittering birds. The patter of rain, gen-tle as springtime, on a tin roof. Somewhere a violin, electronically enhanced, swooped and soared.

"Relax, Hannah."

I melted, boneless, into the warm flannel sheets. "Ummmm."

Fingers, soft, smooth, and sure circled my breast—the good one—compressing here, releasing there. I suppressed an insane urge to giggle. "This feels weird," I said.

Garnelle continued working in silence, her fingers gently kneading, stroking, gradually converging on my nipple. As she worked, she'd glance at me from time to time through a waterfall of blunt-cut silver bangs. "This forces toxic fluids out through your lymph nodes."

"That feels so good, it should be illegal."

Garnelle grinned. "In some states, it is." She paused, let her fingers linger briefly against my skin, then raised them, gracefully, like a pianist from the keyboard as the last note of a Beethoven sonata faded away.

"Ah," I breathed.

Garnelle drew a corner of the flannel sheet up to

cover my newly pink and tingling breast. "Now for the other one."

"Hah!" I snorted, shifting my buttocks, the only part of me that wasn't naked, into a more comfortable position on the massage table. "Fat lot of good it'll do. It's a fake, you know. I haven't had a lymph node on that side since my mastectomy."

Through her bangs, Garnelle studied me as if I had two heads. "Haven't you heard of adhesions?" she asked. I lay still as she peeled the sheet away from my right shoulder, revealing my reconstructed breast in all its lopsided glory. "Regular massage can minimize adhesions."

She resumed work, using the same circular motion as before. "You should do this yourself, Hannah. Here." Garnelle extracted my hand from where it rested, warm and secure under the sheet, and guided it up to my pseudobreast, a flesh-covered mound bisected by a faint scar, with a nipple tattooed on top. "Feel that?"

I nodded.

"That tissue's mobile." She moved my fingers a centimeter closer to the scar. "That's not."

I was surprised I hadn't noticed the difference before, but when I did my monthly self-exam, I was looking for lumps, not adhesions.

"If you don't watch it, girl, that boob will get hard as a rock."

"Wouldn't want that," I said, tucking my arm back under the sheet. I closed my eyes and tried to concentrate as Garnelle instructed me on how to stroke, lift, and roll the scar. I wondered if Paul might like to volunteer to work on my adhesions. My husband was a pretty helpful guy.

"How long's it been?" Garnelle asked a few moments later as her hands began a slow cha-cha-cha along my upper arm.

"Six years, three months, and . . ." Beneath the sheet I tapped my fingers one by one against the leather. ". . . and seven days."

"But who's counting, right?"

I opened my eyes and grinned up at her. "Oh, but I do. Every day's a blessing."

"My aunt had breast cancer," Garnelle said, working my elbow. "Said chemo was the pits, what with the nausea and all."

"Can't say I'd recommend it, either," I muttered, "but if it puts her into the 'cured' category like me, then all the barfing will have been worth it."

"Three years out for her."

"That's *so* good," I moaned.

"What? My aunt's continuing good health, or the effleurage?"

I opened my mouth to answer, but by then Garnelle had turned her attention to my neck and head, her long fingers moving expertly along my scalp, drawing any thoughts I might have had completely out of my brain. "Ummmm."

"Shhhh."

Never let it be said that I don't know how to follow orders.

As Garnelle's gentle fingers moved along under my hair, I lay still, half listening to the new age music that drifted at low volume from speakers mounted flush into the walnut cabinets high on the wall. Something by Sayama, I guessed, having pawed through Garnelle's CD collection a while earlier, with flutes and gongs and tinkling temple bells. If I were wrong, though, and it turned out to be one of her other titles, like *Time*

Temptress, or *Spirit of the Wolf,* I would be out of there the minute the panpipes kicked in.

Breathe in, breathe out. In. Out. Nothing existed for me but Garnelle Taylor's amazing hands and the calming scent of the essential oils she favored, a subtle mix of sandalwood and patchouli, with a touch of bergamot.

In. Out. Pachelbel's canon with the ocean crashing on a distant shore. Something by Enya, lyricless and soothing. I was so far away that they'd have to send out a search party to find me.

Then, out of the speakers, an acoustic flute sustained a note so high and impossibly long that if it had been produced by a human being rather than a synthesizer, the player would have passed out cold a long time ago.

"Nice trick," I sighed.

"You can do this yourself, too," Garnelle said, misinterpreting my remark. She cradled my head in both her hands and rocked it gently from side to side, stretching the muscles along each side of my neck.

"What?" I asked, still worrying about the poor flute player.

"Massage."

"Why would I want to," I asked, "as long as I have you?" My eyelids fluttered open. "Would you cut your own hair?"

"No, I wouldn't," she chuckled.

I chuckled, too, feeling stupid. Except for her bangs, Garnelle hadn't cut her hair in years. She wore it today as I suspected she always had, in a single long braid, brown and streaked with silver, down her back. A child of the Woodstock Nation, you might think, but you'd be wrong. Just under forty, Garnelle was far too young for Woodstock or the Summer of Love. If you quizzed her on it, she'd probably guess that Jefferson Airplane was an upstart, cut-rate airline.

I studied Garnelle's face hovering upside down over mine, her braid flopped casually over one shoulder, and fantasized about grabbing a pair of scissors, hacking it off, and dragging her down the hall to the salon for an expert cut and blow dry. I'm a sucker for those makeover shows on TV. I imagined the "reveal," the camera zooming in on all her friends clapping their hands to their cheeks and screaming, "Ohmahgawd, ohmahgawd, you look ten years younger."

"Ever think of cutting your hair?" I ventured.

Garnelle wriggled her fingers. "I'm like Sampson," she quipped. "It'd sap my strength, destroy my powers."

I smiled and closed my eyes, so a few minutes later I only sensed it when Garnelle moved around the table to begin working on my ankles, the arch of my foot, and, incredibly, little-piggy-went-to-market-like on my toes. "This freebie is just a preview of coming attractions, then?" I asked, praying it would be so. "When the spa actually opens, you're going to stay?"

"Dante hired me yesterday," she replied.

At the mention of my son-in-law, my eyelids flew open and I stared at the ceiling where track lighting with pink bulbs suffused the room with warmth, making the walnut paneling—the best that Dante's major investor, Phyllis Strother's money, could buy—glow. Shelves surrounded a porcelain sink that was made, I swear, from an ancient Chinese bowl. With the exception of the exotic oils stored in dark brown bottles that ranged along the shelves, the massage room could just as easily have been the library of a corporate CEO, minus the executive desk and all the leather-bound books.

And Paradiso had three more rooms just like it, each situated at the end of a short corridor—north, south, east, and west—off the spa's focal point, a Roman-inspired Natatorium that featured an Olympic-sized swimming pool.

"Bravo for Dante." If my hands hadn't been trapped underneath the towel, I would have applauded.

Somewhere, a power saw screamed as if hitting a nail. Garnelle squeezed my little toe. "Sorry," she said. "I'm still not used to all the construction, and that saw, it's like fingernails on a blackboard." She began again, working on my other foot. It felt so divine, I wished I had three feet to offer her.

"Do you think he's going to make it on time?" Garnelle asked, referring, I knew, to the gala opening of Paradiso, scheduled for the following Saturday, barely a week away.

"He has to," I told her. "The invitations are already out. Everyone's RSVP'd, even the mayor."

"So, who's catering?"

"Nobody. Dante's hired a chef, thank God. Frank Lesperance, a guy he knew at Haverford College."

"Ah, yes, I think I met said chef when I went scouting for a bottle of water in the kitchen. He was checking out the walk-in freezer." Garnelle patted my foot and covered it up with the blanket. "Except he introduced himself as François."

"Viva la difference," I said, thinking about the other new hire I'd just met, Wally Jessop, the nail artist. With a name like Wally, I expected somebody butch. Hah! Eyebrowless Wally of the gleaming scalp and multiple piercings would probably do a bang-up job on sculptured fingernails, I supposed, if he didn't expire in a hissy fit every time the water in the pedi-spa got one degree hotter than 143. I lay on the table and wondered how long any spa could survive being staffed by a ragtag band of former classmates of a guy who was born Daniel Shemansky but always wanted to be called Dante. Just Dante. Like Cher or Madonna or Elvis.

Dante's Paradiso. The spa had been a dream of my son-in-law ever since he dropped out of Haverford a year before graduation and eloped with my daughter, Emily, to Colorado. Out West, he'd studied massage as seriously as if it were nanophysics, then apprenticed at the Golden Door before moving east to the New Life Spa in the mountains of Virginia. There, his charm, impeccable manners, and talented fingers had developed such a following that it wasn't long before grateful clients began urging him to open his own establishment. Some, like Phyllis Strother, putting their money where their mouth was. Paul and I had enough confidence in the enterprise to invest in it, too, although our piece of the corporate pie amounted to the size of a broom closet.

Listening to the sawing and banging going on outside the room, I wondered if Dante were regretting his decision to venture out so soon on his own. His talented fingers hadn't touched a client for months, except to shake hands with a new employee or sign a work order for one of the contractors who had been transforming what had once been a restaurant into Dante's Paradiso, a twenty-thousand-square-foot luxury day spa.

When I tuned in again, Garnelle had picked up the flannel sheet and was holding it in front of her face like a mother playing peekaboo. "Turn over," she instructed. Pleased with the way she respected my modesty, I obeyed, settling my face comfortably into a padded doughnut that surrounded a hole cut into the massage table.

Garnelle's fingers pressed into the muscles of my shoulder, forcing my face further into the doughnut that cradled it. "What have you been doing? You're tight as a drum, right here. All knots."

I opened my eyes, but instead of a flowering meadow, I stared into the quiet mauve of the carpet where Garnelle's toes, painted acid green, peeked out from the ends of her Birkenstocks. "Moving furniture," I moaned. "Oh God, your fingers are magic. They should be insured by Lloyds of London."

Garnelle's big toe twitched. "Speaking of London, it's that personal trainer with the British accent that I'd like to get my hands on."

"You mean Norman Salterelli?"

"Uh-huh. Abs from here to Christmas."

"He's a former trainer with the U.S. Olympic team."

"So I noticed."

"He's also married."

Garnelle shrugged. "So what?"

"With kids."

"Rats."

Thinking about kids reminded me of my daughter, who had been working flat-out for days on Puddle Ducks, the day care center that would tend to the children of clients while they were being pummeled and steamed and exfoliated. Surprisingly, Puddle Ducks had been Dante's idea. Providing day care was a necessity if one wished to attract younger clientele, the yummy mummies who had left their high-salaried corporate positions to devote themselves full-time, and with every bit as much attention as they had formerly given to corporate America, to raising their children. As if he knew I was thinking about him, I heard Dante's voice ricocheting off the hand-painted Mediterranean tiles that decorated the Natatorium just on the other side of the door.

"The exercise equipment! Thank *gawd*! Where the hell are you, dude?" Dante seemed to be on his cell phone, shouting directions. "You're way off! Turn your rig around and get yourself down Forest Drive toward Bay Ridge. Right on Herndon. When you get to the water, look right and you're there. Ask for Emily. She'll show you where the stuff goes, get you a cup of *cawfee*."

After six months living north of the Virginia border, the slight drawl Dante had affected while working in the Blue Ridge Mountains was slowly giving way to his native New Jersey twang.

"Oh, Emily will know where it goes, all right," I muttered to the floor. "But if she has to keep taking up the slack for her husband, she'll never get the day care center done."

Like a good employee, Garnelle ignored my remark. "I almost didn't come, you know," she commented softly a few minutes later.

"That would have been tragic," I said, meaning it to the tips of my well-massaged toes.

"When Dante first called about the job, he told me the spa was going to be built down Indian Head way. Frankly, I didn't think you'd get a whole lot of business down in that neck of the woods, if you know what I mean."

"That's what Mrs. Strother's market analysts advised. The golf club was gorgeous, but after they conducted a series of focus groups, they decided to look for property around Annapolis instead. Better demographics. I'm not complaining, mind," I said. "I enjoy spoiling my grandchildren rotten, and for the first time, I won't have to drive three hours to do it!"

"I love it here," Garnelle commented as she kneaded my left bicep. "The view of the water from the front porch is fantastic. You can see all the way to the Bay Bridge."

"I know. Before it became Paradiso, this was the Bay View Inn, a pretty classy restaurant. I can't tell you how many wedding receptions I attended here over the years. It's really strange to see Jacuzzis installed in the middle of what used to be the main dining room."

"Do *you* think we'll be fully staffed by the time we open? Officially, I mean, for the clients?" Garnelle asked, drawing the sheet back over my right arm, and a few seconds later drawing the opposite corner back to expose my left.

Under her hands, I shrugged. "I don't know, but I certainly hope so. When I went by the office a few minutes ago, every chair was full, and there were a couple of people sitting out in the hallway."

"So, he's still interviewing? I thought he was finished with that."

"He's looking for an accountant. And I think there are still a couple of openings for guides." Even as I said it, the word seemed ridiculous, but that's what Dante's ad on Monster.com had said:

Spa guides for upper-demographic, full-service spa near Annapolis, MD. Responsibilities of this role include receiving members at front desk, scheduling services, program registrations, payment processing, and telephone reception. Day, early morning and weekend hours; flexible time schedules available.

" 'Guides'? For a spa? What's the world coming to?" Garnelle tut-tutted. "It's bad enough when 'associates' are bagging your groceries."

"They'll be competent, but decorative, too, I suspect, although Emily nixed the skimpy white uniforms that Dante had in mind. Everyone's going to be wearing khakis and forest green polo shirts embroidered with the spa logo." Paul's artist sister, Connie, had designed the logo, a stylized *P* that morphed into a semireclining female form.

Garnelle sniffed, then picked up my hand and massaged my fingers, one by one, as I lay, limp as a cooked noodle, on the table.

"Not there, you idiot!" Dante was disrupting my *wah* again. Judging by the *beep-beep-beep* of a truck backing up, the main doors to the spa must have been propped open and my son-in-law had to be directing traffic somewhere along the serpentine drive—laid out by my older sister, Ruth Gannon, and echoing (she said) the natural movement of *chi*—that led visitors up a gentle slope to the main entrance of the spa. Ruth was probably, even as we spoke, out with the gardener feng-shuiing the heck out of the place.

Garnelle's fingers slid away, and for a few delicious seconds hovered over mine, which tingled almost as if a charge of electricity was arching between us. "Shhh . . ." she whispered. "Stay here for a while and rest. I'll be waiting by the sauna when you're ready."

Garnelle drifted away, her sandals silent on the plush carpet. I sensed rather than heard the door close behind her.

Alone, as I struggled to tune out the construction and feel the ocean waves roll out of the speakers, washing over me like a blanket, I made a mental note to speak to Dante about the importance of better soundproofing.

Outside the room, two people began arguing. Dante, for certain, and unless I missed my guess, Emily was the other. Dante spoke too intensely and Emily too quietly for me to make out what they were saying, but from the rise and fall of Emily's voice, I could tell she was unhappy about something.

A prolonged scraping sound, followed by a splash, and someone shouting *shitfuckdamn.*

Something had fallen into the swimming pool, something big, but locked in the peaceful embrace of the sea, I was too far gone to care.

CHAPTER 2

When I padded out of the sauna half an hour later, flushed from head to toe, my hair curling damply against my cheeks, and sipping the fresh strawberry smoothie that Alison, one of the guides, had whipped up for me, I immediately ran into Dante. Still as tall and rail thin as he had been when he married my daughter almost eight years ago, my son-in-law was directing the retrieval of a lounge chair from the deep end of the swimming pool. Ben Geyer, the pool boy, had stripped down to his khaki Bermuda shorts and was poking ineffectually at the submerged piece of furniture with a long aluminum pole. He'd already shed his shoes. Next to the shoes, a sodden green and white striped cushion silently drained onto the tiles.

"I think you're going to have to get in," Dante told the young man.

Ben scowled. Clearly, retrieving furniture from swimming pools hadn't been mentioned in his job description, but he stripped off his belt, draped it over his shoes, shrugged, and jumped into the pool.

Ben had his work cut out for him. The redwood lounge chair, heavy under normal circumstances, would be completely waterlogged. Barring the eleventh-hour arrival of a Navy scuba team, I predicted a swim in Dante's future.

With a smile and a wave, I left the guys to it and headed off to help Emily.

I found her in the former club room, which was rapidly being transformed into Puddle Ducks. Surrounded by boxes, Emily was unpacking a pint-sized table and chair set painted in bright primary colors. Three wooden puzzles were already arranged on an identical table set up near a picture window that comprised one entire wall.

Behind Emily, my sister-in-law, Connie, stood on a step ladder, dabbing blue paint onto Jemima Puddle Duck's paisley shawl. Jemima, in her sky-blue poke bonnet, curled her webbed feet over the chair rail and seemed to be speaking with Kip the collie dog about her lost eggs. Still wrapped in my spa robe, I stood still sipping my smoothie, admiring Connie's handiwork. "That's really cute, Con!"

Connie turned and sent a thousand-watt smile in my direction. With her copper curls, checked gingham shirt, and a dab of blue paint on her nose, she looked like Raggedy Ann all grown up. "It is, isn't it?" Connie gestured with her paintbrush. "What do you think about that one?"

I turned to consider the mural on the wall behind me: Flopsy, Mopsy, Cottontail, and Peter were picking blackberries in Mr. McGregor's garden.

"Peter didn't get any blackberries," I corrected. " 'First he ate some lettuces and some French beans; and then he ate some radishes; and then, feeling rather sick, he went to look for some parsley,' " I quoted, the story still fresh in my mind from the number of times I'd read it to Chloe. "Peter got a dose of chamomile tea, if I'm not mistaken. 'One table spoonful to be taken at bedtime.' "

Connie waved a brush. "Poetic license. I'm an artist, not a novelist."

I was still admiring the botanical accuracy of the mural when I noticed Ruth chugging down the hallway, both hands jammed into the pockets of the lightweight blue cotton sweater she usually reserved for working in the garden. She'd gathered her abundant silver hair into an untidy bundle on the top of her head, and secured it there with a pencil. "I told him and told him, but did he listen? No," Ruth muttered before her foot had even crossed the threshold.

Emily looked blankly at her aunt and shrugged. "Told who what?"

"Dante! It's poor planning, Emily. The day care center should be on the *east* side of the building, not the north. The Palace of Beijing put the little princes in the east. North is so dark, and negative." Ruth lowered her voice. "It's evil and calamity, too. Can't you do something about it, Hannah?"

"Shut up, Ruth," I hissed. That last remark was going too far, even for someone as militantly new age as Ruth.

Emily wasn't having any of it, either. "That is such *bullshit*, Aunt Ruth."

"Two thousand years of Chinese civilization can't be wrong," Ruth said.

"But in feng shui," I pointed out, "there's always a remedy, right?" I'd been around my older sister long enough to pick up on the lingo.

"Well, yes." Ruth favored me with a smile, as if I

were a prized pupil. The awkward moment passed. "And that fabulous mural's certainly a good place to start."

I sensed a *but* coming, and Connie must have sensed it, too, because she pasted on her brightest, most disingenuous smile and waited.

"Your children will be playing here, Emily, don't forget," Ruth said, as if ours were the only children who mattered.

My granddaughter Chloe, at six, was in first grade. Jake, just turned three, attended nursery school, but would be joining his baby brother, Tim, at Puddle Ducks each afternoon once the spa opened for good. At the moment, Tim, the baby brother in question, was the center of attention, occupying a gleaming white playpen that had been set up near the French doors leading out to the patio and the Japanese garden beyond. Adorably dressed in a blue and white striped Petit Bateau coverall I'd splurged on at Madeleine's Boutique on Maryland Avenue, he didn't seem the least concerned about the elements of feng shui, or Jemima Puddleduck's lost eggs, or anything else for that matter. He sat contentedly in his playpen, gnawing on a wooden block.

"*I'm* running the day care center, Aunt Ruth," Emily said. I half expected her to add *and not you*, but I'd brought my daughter up with better manners. "And I'm certainly willing to listen to anything you have to say, but you have to realize that it's too late to change it now!"

"You're right, of course," Ruth admitted. "But it's just so frustrating! If Dante had listened to me in the first place, Puddle Ducks would have been built where the gift shop is now."

I was about to put in my two cents about conversion plans as recommended by highly paid D.C. architects who were *not* disciples of the Compass school of feng shui—naturally, they'd given the east side of the building, with its expansive view of the Chesapeake Bay, to the spa's dining room—but thankfully, Ruth had already moved on.

"We can add a light fixture over there. . . ." She gestured toward the west wall. With a wink at me, she added, "Phyllis can certainly afford it!" Without drawing a breath, she forged on. "And maybe a mobile. Something light and a bit whimsical. I think I know where to get one."

"Okay, Aunt Ruth."

Hands on hips, Ruth turned, scrutinizing the room. "You should put the stereo equipment on the northeast wall," she said, waving her hand in a vague, northerly direction, "and it'd be better if you moved the tables and chairs closer to the east wall," she said. "Wisdom and education go there."

"Okay." Emily, again, being diplomatic.

"And put that Little Red Hen bulletin board on the south wall!" she finished triumphantly.

"Of course," Emily managed from between clenched teeth.

"I'll ask Dante about the mobile." Ruth wandered over to the windows and adjusted the curtains to admit the early afternoon sun in all its glory. My sister had finally run out of steam.

"I wish you luck getting his ear," Emily said, squinting into the glare, ignoring her aunt's instructions, at least for the moment. "The ad for the accountant came out in Sunday's Baltimore *Sun*. The phone's been ringing off the hook. Dante's got interviews scheduled back-to-back until almost eight o'clock tonight."

"Last time I saw him, Dante was helping Ben fish a chair out of the swimming pool," I offered helpfully.

Connie's paintbrush hovered over a bright green radish top. "What? How'd that happen?"

With a sideways glance at Emily, whose bland expression gave no hint of what I suspected was major responsibility for the "accident" to the chair, I said, "Who knows? When one enters Garnelle's massage therapy room, all brain functions cease."

Ruth grinned. "Thanks, I'll check the swimming pool first, then." She turned on her sensible black heels and started out the door. "A green dragon, Connie," she called back over her shoulder.

"What?" I wasn't sure I'd heard her correctly.

"A green dragon on that east wall." She pointed.

Back on her stepladder, Connie rolled her eyes.

"And a white tiger over there. Those children need some guardians." And then she was gone.

Once Ruth was out of earshot, Connie said, "A tiger? What do you think Beatrix Potter would say if I painted a tiger stalking among the cabbages in Mr. McGregor's very proper British garden?"

"It never bothered Rousseau," I commented dryly, dredging up a factoid from an Art History course I'd taken at Oberlin. "Remember his jungle paintings? Rousseau let on that he had firsthand knowledge of the jungle from time spent in the army, but I'm quite sure he never left Paris. He once painted a Native American, headdress and all, fighting off a gorilla. And I remember a painting of monkeys with back-scratchers and a milk bottle."

While Connie and I nattered on about art, working our way through the decades to Jackson Pollock and Willem DeKooning and wondering how anybody in their right mind could call those splattered canvases works of genius, Tim had tossed the block aside and pulled himself to his feet. He clung to the playpen railing with both hands, making cheerful grunting sounds while his untrained legs wobbled unsteadily beneath him.

I saw the problem at once. Lamby, his well-loved plush toy, lay spread-eagle on the carpet. I retrieved Lamby, handed it back to him. My grandson promptly plopped to his well-padded bottom and began chewing on Lamby's tail.

Having exhausted the topic of modern art, I concentrated on helping my daughter fold, crush, and stuff boxes and packing material into an oversized trash can. Still worrying about the argument I'd almost overheard, I asked if everything was all right between her and Dante.

"Of course!" she insisted, dismissing my concerns.

"Emily?" I prodded.

She laid a reassuring hand on my arm. "Everything is *fine*, Mom. We're just under a lot of pressure right now. Besides, we're always snapping at each other. It's just our way."

If Emily and Dante's recipe for successful marriage had always included lighthearted bickering, I wouldn't have known. This was the first time since they'd left college in Pennsylvania that our daughter and her family had lived close enough for Paul and me to play a significant role in their lives. Frankly, bickering or no bickering, I was relishing it.

After a bit, I said, "Thanks for being patient with

your aunt. I love Ruth, but sometimes she can be a royal pain in the ass."

"You noticed? I half expected her to whip out a deck of tarot cards and offer to tell our fortunes."

I chuckled. "Do you think marrying Hutch will settle her down any?" After three years, Ruth and her live-in boyfriend, a prominent Annapolis attorney, had set a date for the following November.

"I don't know, Mom, but taking on a moniker like Mrs. Maurice Gaylord Hutchinson the Third would certainly slow *me* down!"

"Speaking of husbands," Connie said as she stepped down from her stepladder, wiping her paintbrush with a dry cloth, "I promised Dennis I'd meet him for a late lunch."

"Call the *New York Times*!" I said.

Connie finished cleaning her brushes, slipped them into a wooden box, and began closing up her paints. "They've made an arrest in the Bailey homicide, Hannah. Finally the good lieutenant will get an afternoon off."

"Until the next case comes along."

"Let's pray for a crime-free weekend, then," Connie said, shutting the lid on her paint box. "There are a lot of things that need doing on the farm."

"As soon as we get the spa on its feet, I'll come help," I promised, feeling a genuine pang of guilt for neglecting Connie, who was more than a sister-in-law; she was my best friend.

"How are you at roofing barns?" Connie teased.

"I let my fingers do the walking through the yellow pages, just like everyone else," I said.

I was hugging Connie good-bye when Dante

stomped into the room wearing a fresh blue oxford cloth shirt, his ponytail dripping.

"Can you give me a hand, Emily?"

I prayed it wasn't with the lounge chair, but from the sodden looks of him, Dante had that situation well under control.

Emily glanced from her husband to the playpen where Tim had picked up the block and was pummeling Lamby with it. "What's wrong?"

"Don't worry about the baby," I cut in. "I'll be happy to watch him."

"On that note, I'm outahere!" Connie blew everyone a kiss and disappeared.

Emily checked her watch. "Tim will be wanting to eat in a few minutes."

I knew better than to volunteer for *that*. Emily was breast-feeding.

Dante still looked dark, angry. "Hauling that chair out of the pool put a deep scratch into it, right across the logo."

Emily winced.

Those chairs had cost a pretty penny. Paradiso hadn't opened yet, and already the snake had entered the garden. "Throw a Paradiso towel over it the night of the opening," I suggested. "No one will ever notice."

Dante threw me a half grateful smile. "That'll have to do. Come on," he said to Emily. "You need to sign something. It'll only take a minute."

"Go ahead," I told my daughter. "Tim's not going to starve to death in the time it takes you to sign a few papers."

To tell the truth, ever since I entered the room, I'd been longing to pick up and cuddle my grandson, but since he had been happily entertaining himself, I knew Emily wouldn't have seen the point of it.

Once Emily and Dante were gone, though, I leaned over and lifted Tim from the playpen, adjusted his legs until he was comfortably straddling my hip, and carried him over to the French doors. A squirrel, looking thoroughly out of place in the Japanese-style garden, dropped from the branch of a fir tree and scampered across the flagstones.

"That's a squirrel," I told my grandson as I opened the doors and carried him outside into the spring sunshine. "Can Tim-Tim say 'squirrel'?"

Tim's tiny brow furrowed. *Who is this person and why is she talking so goofy?* But when he caught sight of the squirrel, Tim stretched out his arms and squealed in sheer delight. His smile lit up my heart.

What is so special about grandchildren? I wondered. I loved my daughter, of course, but I was absolutely *crazy* about my grandkids. Was it because I felt a sense of failure in raising Emily? Emily had been a sullen and willful child, leaving home after college for a life on the road, incommunicado, learning everything the hard way—from her mistakes, and there had been quite a number of them. Maybe with this child, Tim—or with her older ones, Chloe and Jake—I'd have a second chance.

Tim wrapped his chubby hand around my finger and latched on tightly. He had bright green eyes and a fuzz of fine, peach-colored hair, inherited, I'm proud to say, from my side of the family. Our baby sister, Georgina, had been blessed with hair like that: it was the color of buttered sweet potatoes. I kissed the top of his head thinking, *And just as sweet-smelling, too.*

A Welsh poet once said that perfect love sometimes

does not come until the first grandchild. As Tim and I stood in the doorway watching that squirrel scatter a family of sparrows into a clump of ancient boxwood, flapping and cheeping, I knew exactly what that poet meant.

CHAPTER 3

Paul extracted the business section from the Sun- day *Capital,* smoothed it out, rested his elbows on the table and began reading. "Well," he said, glancing from the paper to me over the top of his reading glasses. "It looks like Paradiso's grand opening was an unqualified success."

I turned the burner under the oatmeal to low and wandered over to check out the paper. Unbelievably, the *Capital* had devoted almost the entire front page of the section to Paradiso's debut. In addition to the article, the editors published three pictures, all in color, all above the fold.

Dante and Kendel Ehrlich, the wife of the Maryland governor, looking radiant as usual, cutting the ribbon.

Emily and Dante grinning broadly, raising glasses of champagne with a group that included Annapolis mayor Ellen Moyer.

A shot of the swimming pool, sparkling like topaz, surrounded by dozens of tuxedo- and evening-gown-clad partygoers.

"That wide-angle lens makes the pool look big as a football field," I commented.

"It *is* big as a football field," Paul snorted. "Glad I don't have to maintain it."

I tapped Dante's photo with my fingertip. "Our son-in-law looks handsome, doesn't he? Black tie was a good call." I probably sounded smug. Black tie had been my idea.

"Apparently."

"It was a *fantastic* party." I sighed, remembering.

"Dante's investors have deep pockets, Hannah."

Indeed, they had. The guests at the elaborate, invitation-only gala had spilled over from the open bars and hors d'oeuvres tables that surrounded the swimming pool, flowed into the elegant, wood-paneled reception area, and trickled into the gift shop where Alison, Ben, and some of the other guides had taken turns handing out souvenir mugs, pocket calendars, and gold mesh bags of sample-size beauty and health-care products, all emblazoned with the spa logo.

On the veranda, using a sauté pan over a gas ring, François cooked up tortellini to order. Next to him, the sous-chef carved wafer-thin slices of prime rib, turkey, and ham for the guests, who could eat on the veranda, if they chose, or amble down to the beach, where tables and chairs had been set out. At surfside, illuminated by luau torches, another of François's acolytes prepared Mongolian barbecue, using oversized chopsticks to toss personalized meat and vegetable mixtures over a sizzling grill, all to the appreciative oohs and ahs of the hungry crowd.

On the day before opening, though, I feared it would never come together. For weeks the concrete slab had been ready for the gazebo, but it wasn't until late on Friday that a tractor-trailer delivered it—in four parts.

Dante freaked when he saw the pieces until the workmen demonstrated how easily the whole thing could be assembled. By the time Tuxedo Junction arrived late Saturday afternoon, set up their instruments, and swung energetically into "String of Pearls," the orchestra had no clue that the gazebo they were playing in had been moldering in the rose garden for years. And how they played! Big Band music drifted out over the Chesapeake Bay until one o'clock in the morning. Paul and I were among the last to leave the dance floor.

In the photographs, you couldn't see the tool chests, of course, or the table saws, sanders, and routers, or the scaffolding that had been taken down and stashed in the garden shed. And the reporter hadn't stopped to wonder about the locked door marked STAFF, behind which the paint cans and drop cloths had been hastily stowed prior to the party.

You couldn't see me in the pictures, either, thank God. At the last possible minute, after what seemed like hours of indecision in front of my closet, Paul had zipped me into a blue taffeta evening gown that was eight years too old and a half size too small. I hadn't had time to shop for anything new.

As if reading my mind, Paul grabbed my hand and pulled me into his lap. "You looked gorgeous," he whispered into my hair.

"Hah!" I looked like a bridesmaid at a cut-rate wedding.

"I mean it. I always liked you in that dress." He kissed me on the mouth. "The last time you wore it, I believe I got laid."

"If you don't stop right now," I warned, "your cereal will get cold."

"I can eat breakfast later," he said, nibbling on my earlobe.

"But, it's almost eight. We'll be late for church."

Paul ran a finger along my cheek, down my neck, and hooked his finger in the V of my knit top. "Why don't we go to the eleven o'clock service, Hannah?"

"I just *love* cold oatmeal," I said.

The oatmeal *was* cold, but the microwave fixed that.

And as it turned out, we didn't miss the coffee hour between services, either. Finding a parking space had been a problem, though, so by the time Paul and I straggled into the fellowship hall at St. Cat's, we were breathing hard.

Erika Rose was manning the door. "We missed you at eight-thirty," Erika said in the same disapproving voice she probably used on her children, if she had any, or on the hapless litigants she faced every day in a Baltimore courtroom. Erika thumbed through the name tags in the slotted tray, located ours, and held onto them for a few seconds, as if our tardiness required an explanation before she'd turn them over.

I glanced at Paul and rolled my eyes.

"Running late today," Paul muttered as he pinned the name tag to his lapel.

"Big party last night," I added while attaching my name tag to my scarf.

"I figured," she said. "Sorry I couldn't make it. Had a deposition that kept me at the office until nearly midnight. Who knew the latex glove business could be so litigious?"

I was trying to remember if Erika Rose had actually been on the guest list, all the while thinking up something witty to say about latex, gloves or otherwise, when Pastor Eva rescued me. "Good to see you both!"

Evangeline Haberman had been rector of St. Catherine of Sienna Episcopal Church on Ridgley Avenue for less than a year, but she had already won the hearts of parishioners by her open and caring manner, not to mention her ability to deliver a cogent, yet motivational ten-minute sermon. "Running late this morning?" She looked at me suspiciously, one dark eyebrow raised.

" 'Morning, Eva." I felt my face flush. Was my hair standing on end? My lipstick smeared? Nothing seemed to get by the Reverend Evangeline Haberman.

Eva winked. "You two must have been partying until the wee hours of the morning. Please thank your daughter for inviting us, by the way. Roger could have boogied on until dawn, I think, but, alas, we had to leave early. I had a sermon to tweak."

Indeed, Pastor Eva had come to the party wearing a slinky red number as far removed from her usual clerical garb as Times Square is from Paducah, Kentucky. I'd caught glimpses of Roger but hadn't spoken to him.

"Sorry I missed chatting with Roger," I said.

"He was perfectly charming, Eva," Paul said. "I introduced him to Mongolian barbecue and the mayor of Annapolis, in that order. When I last saw him, they had their heads together, discussing bus routes."

"What's going on today?" I asked. "We had to park *miles* away and walk," I added, hoping that would help explain my less than put-together appearance.

"We have a visiting choir from Atlanta, Georgia. You probably noticed the bus in the parking lot."

I nodded. The darn thing had been taking up six parking spaces.

" 'Ezekiel Saw the Wheel' proved a little too much for some of the seniors at the early service, but I certainly enjoyed it. Blew the steeple clean off the roof." Eva laid a hand on my arm. "When the psalmist wrote about making a joyful noise unto the Lord, I doubt he had short-circuiting hearing aids in mind!"

"I'll look forward to it," I said, although my taste in church music leaned more toward Bach, Mozart, and William Byrd. A *lot* more.

Eva grinned. "You know me! Always like to shake things up a bit." Dark, shoulder-length hair swinging, she turned to grab the upper arm of a kid who rocketed into the fellowship hall, making a beeline for the chocolate covered doughnuts. "Where's the fire, Michael?"

"Sorry, Pastor Eva." And he departed for the refreshments table at a more leisurely pace.

"Eva!"

A woman I didn't recognize came toddling toward us across the parish hall. Her hair was streaked with so many different shades of blond that it was impossible to tell what the original color might have been. It curled under her ears like a badly thatched roof.

Eva greeted the woman warmly, then turned to us. "Hannah, Paul, I'd like you to meet Cassandra Matthews, Roger's boss at Eastport Yacht Sales."

"Wonderful party!" Cassandra said. "Thanks for including me."

Another person I'd missed among all the merrymaking. I was glad Cassandra was feeling singled out for special attention, but in point of fact, Dante and Emily had invited just about anybody associated with the sailing industry in Annapolis, figuring that where there's sailing, there's money.

Sailboat: A hole in the water where you throw your money.

That's what *The Sailors' Dictionary* tells us, anyway. Its authors, Beard and McKie, also define "crew" as "heavy, stationary objects used on shipboard to hold down charts, anchor cushions in place, and dampen sudden movements of the boom," which pretty much summarized my sailing expertise.

"It's a wonderful facility, Hannah," Cassandra was saying when I tuned back in. "You must be awfully proud of your son-in-law."

"We are," Paul said.

"And our daughter, too," I hastened to add. In just eight short years, Dante had clawed his way up from college dropout to spa owner, an incredible feat. But it wouldn't have happened without the unflagging support of our daughter, Emily.

"Gotta run," Eva said. "But take my advice, boys and girls, and hold onto your hats! The service is going to be a doozy. See you in the narthex afterward."

But after the service, our ears literally ringing with the joyful noise of a rousing gospel rendition of "When the Saints Go Marching In," Paul and I steered clear of the narthex and headed for the south door, so we could make a quick escape to Paradiso in time to help with the cleanup as we'd promised.

We were too late.

At Paradiso the Dumpster was full, the floors

swept, Party Perfect was just departing with the tent, tables, chairs, and luau torches, someone from Cheryl's Chalets was busily forklifting deluxe Porta-Potties onto a flatbed truck, and half the Paradiso staff was sitting on the veranda, sipping iced tea out of tall glasses.

"Iced tea?" asked Emily.

Paul squeezed my hand. "Your mother and I would love some tea, Emily."

While the sous-chef—whose name, I learned, was Jimmy George—went to fetch our tea, Dante offered me his chair.

"The calm before the storm," he said as he held the back of my rocker with one hand while dragging another one over with his left.

"Why?" Paul asked. "It's Sunday. A day of rest. What's on tap for today?"

"Magazine interviews." Emily dumped the contents of a pink packet into her tea and stirred it with a straw. "We've been rushing around like maniacs all morning because the photographer from the *Washington Post* magazine is due at two—"

"And *Baltimore Magazine*'s sending someone at three-thirty," Dante cut in.

"And we still don't have an accountant, Dad."

Paul raised a hand. "Don't look at me! If I were a plumber, would you ask me to fix the pipes? Just because I teach math . . ." His voice trailed off.

"Oh, no." Emily set her glass down on the table, grinned broadly and leaned forward. "We've got a much more interesting job for you, Dad, if you're willing."

"As long as it doesn't involve heavy lifting, I'm all ears," Paul said, reaching for the tea Jimmy had magically produced from the kitchen. "Thanks, Jimmy."

Balancing his tray on one hand, Jimmy bowed deeply. "My pleasure."

"So," I said, sipping. "How can we help?"

Emily glanced at her husband, and when Dante nodded, she continued. "We'd like you to take a typical journey."

"Where will I be going?"

"Nowhere!" Emily laughed.

François's elbow caught Jimmy in the ribs, and both men chuckled.

The tips of Paul's ears turned pink. "I haven't cottoned on to the lingo yet, I see."

"A typical spa guest journey, I mean." Emily grinned. "It's like a test run, part of staff training. The receptionist will greet you and introduce you to spa staff, who'll take you on a tour of the spa, and explain the spa menu du jour."

"We give all new guests a complimentary massage," Dante cut in.

"And clients are encouraged to share their personal goals so that we adjust future treatments and schedules accordingly," Emily added.

Paul turned to me. "So, what are my personal goals, Hannah?"

I studied my husband, who was tall and lean, but not the least bit skinny. Since early spring, Paul had joined me on a daily jog around the Naval Academy sea wall, something I'd been in the habit of doing every since my late friend Valerie had turned me on to it. Paul's thighs and glutes were in great shape; his pecs and abs incredible. The man was ripped. I could think of only one area—his back—that needed work. He'd injured it in a farm accident many years ago.

"More flexibility in your back?" I suggested, thinking that if Garnelle's fingers couldn't work miracles on his creaky vertebrae, nobody's could.

Paul patted his face. "How about doing something about these wrinkles?"

He was joking, but Emily didn't get it. "Yes! We can schedule you for a chemical peel!"

Paul waved a hand. "Hold on! Let's just stick with the massages for now. Do real men get facials?"

Dante looked shocked. "Of course."

Emily pressed her palms together. "Good! A massage and a facial, then. And you'll want to spend some time in the steam room."

"The steam room's divine, Paul," I said. "I can vouch for that. And when you come out, you can hit the Jacuzzi, or the pool. There's a refreshment station where they've got springwater with lemon slices and herbal teas." I reached out and squeezed Paul's knee. "And if you ask very nicely, one of the guides will bring you a smoothie."

Paul consulted François. "Peach?"

"Any flavor you want, Professor."

"Then after you're done," Emily rattled on enthusiastically, "one of the guides will help you plan your next visit, take you back to the receptionist for scheduling, and then they'll thank you and escort you to the door."

"To the gift shop," Dante corrected.

Emily grinned. "Oh, right. To the gift shop, then."

Paul leaned back in his chair. "A massage and a facial. Sounds like a real hardship."

"Can you come when we open tomorrow?"

"How about right now?" Paul asked.

Emily shook her head. "We gave almost everyone the day off."

"I have to teach first thing in the morning. How about we show up around lunchtime?" Paul raised an eyebrow in my direction. "No sense bringing two cars all the way out here."

When I nodded in agreement, Emily said, "Okay. I'll put you down for an appointment. And remember, Dad, the staff aren't supposed to know you're a ringer."

"So," I asked, "when do you start getting real customers instead of guinea pigs like me and your father?"

"Tomorrow." Emily rose from her chair to check on Tim, who had awakened from his nap and was fussing quietly in his car seat, tugging on the seat belt, trying to worm his way out of the contraption. "We started taking appointments by phone yesterday morning," she said brightly, "and by the time the party was over, we were seventy-five percent booked for the first month."

In spite of his wife's cheerful optimism, Dante looked worried. "After the party, I thought we'd be at one hundred percent." He relaxed into the cushion and laced his fingers behind his head. "What we need is some sort of publicity stunt."

"Don't be silly," Emily said. "The opening attracted lots of attention. Calls are still coming in."

Dante continued as if his wife had never spoken. "Remember when we filled Founders Green with plastic lawn ornaments the day before graduation?"

François threw back his head and laughed. "God, that was a riot!"

"Remember the 'Fords who stole the sacred statue of

Athena from the Great Hall at Bryn Mawr, and managed to knock her head off?" Dante chuckled.

He was referring to Haverford College, where he and François had sown a goodly number of wild oats.

Emily, a 'Mawrter, was clearly unimpressed. "That was so low-brow," she sniffed. "Paradiso's much more upmarket than that."

"Yeah," François said. "Don't be an asshole, Dante."

Ever since my daughter eloped with Dante, my relationship with my son-in-law had been an up and down thing. Just when I was growing to like the guy, he'd pull some bone-headed stunt and I'd find myself wondering what Emily saw in him all those years and three children ago.

I wasn't even entirely convinced that the two were officially married. The only proof I had of the ceremony was a photograph of the happy couple in front of a wedding chapel in Las Vegas, sent via e-mail attachment. I had a picture of myself with Princess Leia cinnamon buns clapped to my head, helping Han Solo blast the bejessus out of the Death Star, and I'd never even met Harrison Ford, so what did that prove? Only that the computers in the photo booth at King's Dominion can work wonders, that's what.

"I think you should concentrate on the here and now," Paul said reasonably. "Do you think you'll be ready for tomorrow, Dante?"

Dante shrugged. "We've gotta be."

"Except for the nursery," Emily corrected. "That opens next week."

Speaking of the nursery reminded me that I hadn't seen Chloe or Jake since we arrived. "Where are the children?" I asked.

Emily unstrapped Tim, lifted him out of the car seat,

and settled him on her hip. She flapped her free hand in the direction of the beach.

Down by the breakwater, I caught a glimpse of Chloe's blond ponytails and Jake's curly mop bent over something on the sand. As I watched, Jake began stabbing at the mystery object with a blue plastic shovel. I shaded my eyes against the sun. "Who's that looking after them?"

"Alison Dutton, one of the guides. She just loves the kids. I don't know what I would have done without her the past week. Jake's always been a picky eater, you know, but he'll even eat François's spinach quiche if Alison feeds it to him, and it's got feta in it."

"Alison's supposed to be taking care of *clients*," Dante grumbled. He drew breath to elaborate when his cell phone erupted, bringing a welcome end to that topic of conversation. We watched Dante check the caller ID. "Sorry, guys. Gotta take this call." We waited politely while he hit Talk, pressed the phone to his ear and wandered to the far end of the veranda, where he parked a hip on the railing and spoke quietly to whomever was calling.

Emily, who half a minute earlier had been shooting daggers at her husband, relaxed. "And you can help, too, Mom."

"How's that?"

"You used to screen candidates when you worked at Whitworth and Sullivan, right?"

I nodded, almost afraid to admit it, because it didn't take a Mensa membership to figure out where this conversation was going. "And you'd like me to look over some résumés?"

"Would you? You're an angel!"

As simple as that, I had volunteered.

"Dante's doing all the interviews, but if you could pull out the good ones and set up appointments, that would be great."

Tucking his cell phone back into its holster, Dante rejoined us. He squeezed Emily's shoulder. "I'm sure your mother has better things to do, Em."

Emily blinked, bit her lower lip. I'd seen that look before. Emily hated being squelched.

I quickly jumped to her rescue. "I'm more than happy to help out, Dante. Bring on the résumés." Then, to Emily, I said, "What positions are we talking about?"

"The accountant you know. But we're also looking for a certified aesthetician."

I groaned. "I'm not even sure what an aesthetician does!"

"Skin care, facials, manicures, pedicures, hair removal—"

"For the beauty parlor?"

François gasped theatrically and pressed a hand to his chest. "Oh God, don't let Wally Jessop hear you. *'Bellissima, s'il vous plaît!'* " he drawled, imitating the dubious French accent Cleveland-born Wally had been trying on lately. "Zee salon de bow-tay she eez called Bellissima."

I'd chatted with Wally, and I suspected that the closest he ever got to France was the French bread bin at our local Whole Foods market. "But 'Bellissima' is an Italian word, surely?"

François grinned. "Of course, but Wally's a continental kind of guy."

"So you'll do it, Mom?"

"Okay, I'll do it," I said, "but I'd rather take care of the children."

"Don't be silly, Mom. That's my job."

How I wish, now, that I had insisted.

CHAPTER 4

Late Monday morning I dropped Paul off at Recep-tion, leaving him in the capable hands of Heather, one of the female guides, looking sturdy and persuasively Teutonic in her polo shirt and shorts. In a former life, Heather could have been a hostess on QVC selling Handcrafted Tiffany Style Pet Bobble Head Accent Lamps to third-world villagers. She'd nearly signed me up for a tourmaline facial and a warm stone rubdown before I came to my senses and remembered that I'd promised to help Dante review résumés, and made my escape.

I found Dante hanging massage school diplomas on his office wall, the largest of three adjoining rooms in the elegantly furnished, walnut-paneled suite. He looked spiffy and very much in charge in his Perry Ellis, four-button pinstripe suit. In answer to my "Hi," Dante laid the hammer on the credenza next to a bronze bust of Dante Alighieri and greeted me warmly. "Thanks for coming, Hannah."

"Nice suit."

He smiled. "I wasn't so sure about the buttons, but Emily liked it. So either I'm way out of style or I'm starting a trend."

"Where did that come from?" I asked, pointing to the bust of the poet. I was certain it hadn't been there the last time I'd visited the office.

"It was my grandmother's," he said, resting a hand on the statue's head. "It used to glare at me from on top of the bookshelf in Grandfather's library, daring me to leave before finishing my homework."

Four-year-old Dante had been staying with his grandparents the weekend his mother and father died of carbon monoxide poisoning on a camping trip to the Santa Cruz Mountains. His grandparents had raised him, but both were gone now. Everytime I found myself getting annoyed with Dante, I remembered this, and tried to focus on his strengths rather than his shortcomings. We were the only family the poor boy had.

"What happened to the rest of your grandmother's things?" I asked.

Dante hugged himself, as if trying to compensate for his loss. "We auctioned everything off," he said. "Emily and I sank it all into the business."

"I'm sure your grandmother would have approved," I said, meaning it.

"Yes. Well, let me get you started." Almost absent-mindedly, Dante gathered up some plump file folders from his desk and led me into the adjoining office. Through the plantation-style shutters the sun drew railroad tracks of light on the polished desktop. A flat screen monitor sat to the right, a telephone to the left.

Dante switched on the overhead light, a blaze of crystal prisms the size of a basketball. "This is where our business manager will hang out, whenever we hire one, that is."

I stood there like an idiot, admiring the decor. *Must be nice.* When I managed the Records Department at

Whitworth and Sullivan, I had been assigned to a cubicle so deep within the bowels of the building that when I ventured out for lunch, it took me five minutes to find a window to look out of to see if I needed to take an umbrella.

Dante laid the folders on the desk and flipped one of them open. It contained several dozen envelopes.

"Have you opened them yet?" I asked.

"Not yet. The postman brought them this morning."

I groaned.

Dante chuckled, flipped the folder closed and handed me another one. "Let me give you this one instead. These are the folks who are coming for interviews this afternoon. I'd appreciate your feedback."

I hefted the folder, weighing it. "Oh, this will cost you big, Dante."

His eyebrows flew up. "I told Emily we couldn't afford you."

I laughed. "But I'm so easily bribed. Say, with lunch?"

"No problem, then. When you're ready, just call François in the kitchen and tell him what you're in the mood for."

"Deal." I walked to the window, raised one of the slats and peeked out into a glorious expanse of . . . parking lot. Clearly, Ruth and her Japanese gardener friend hadn't made it around to this side of the building.

"Let me leave you to get on with it, then." A few seconds later my son-in-law poked his head back around the corner. "If you need me, I'll be in the conference center." He checked his watch. "I've got an interview with *Shape* magazine at eleven-thirty. Wish me luck!"

And before I could say "Break a leg," he was gone, leaving me alone with the folders.

It didn't take me long to discover that in the world of job applications, at least, not much had changed since I left Whitworth and Sullivan. Dante's ad had plainly stated "list salary requirements," but three of the first five applicants whose résumés I reviewed had failed to do so.

Yet, I didn't want to eliminate an otherwise qualified candidate simply because he or she couldn't follow directions.

Or maybe I did.

Someone rapped smartly on the door, and I looked up with some relief from the employment history of Claudia Marie Harris, who evidently thought that printing her résumé on paper the color of Pepto Bismol would get her noticed. An attractive brunette about Emily's age stood in the doorway, looking damp and frazzled.

"Sorry to interrupt," she said, "but can you tell me where I could find Dante?"

"He's in the conference room," I told her, "but he's busy with interviews at present. Have you checked in with reception?"

"No."

"That would be your best bet, then."

"Thanks."

After the woman had gone, I returned to Ms. Harris. I learned that she was a cosmetologist and a "rabid typist." I filed her résumé in the trash.

Stephen Davis had taken "curses in accounting" at Anne Arundel Community College. Circular file for Stephen, too.

laura elizabeth barnes kept all the books for garner, butters and aaronson in chestertown, maryland, and offered to revolutionize accounting for dante's paradiso, but not, I thought, until she got her shift key repaired. Toss, rim shot, ker-plunk.

And how could you take seriously any applicant who used teeny-tiny type, or really weird fonts, or an e-mail address like kissmygrits@yahoo.com?

Suddenly, I needed a drink.

Tucking a handful of résumés under my arm, I wandered into the Natatorium, homing in on the refreshment center at the far end. I passed half a dozen clients who were stretched out on the lounge chairs surrounding the pool, each wearing the spa's distinctive terrycloth robe—pink for women and lime green for men, with the spa logo embroidered on the left breast pocket. Several other clients were perched on the edge of the pool, their legs dangling in the water.

Feeling out of place in my chinos and T-shirt, thinking, *Damn, I'd rather be swimming,* I thumbed through the box of Tazo tea, and selected a China Green Tips packet. I tore open the packet, dropped the tea bag into my mug, pumped in some boiling water, and carried the mug over to a lounge chair, thoughtfully dunking.

The résumés I'd brought with me weren't much better. One guy had a three-year gap in his employment history that made me wonder if he'd been doing time up at Jessup State Detention Center. Another closed his cover letter with: "Thank you for your time. Hope to hear from you shorty."

I sighed and sipped my tea, finding it hard to believe that Dante had preselected these losers and was actually planning to interview them. Maybe I'd picked up the wrong folder.

I turned the pile over and started at the bottom.

Ah, this was more like it. Karen Barton, like Dante, had attended Haverford College, but unlike my son-in-law, she had graduated, with a B.A. in anthropology. Apparently the job market for anthropologists had dried up because Karen had gone on to earn an advanced degree in aesthetics and cosmetology from Spa Tech Institute of South Portland, Maine. Karen's hobby was knitting. I liked the girl already.

Roger Haberman was next. Now, that was interesting. The only Roger I knew was married to our priest, Evangeline Haberman. I checked the heading for an address, and saw that Roger lived on Monterey, the same street in West Annapolis as the parsonage. According to his experience block, before their move to Annapolis from California, Roger had been a CPA but was now working as a bookkeeper at Eastport Yacht Sales. Eva's Roger all right.

None of the applications included photographs, but I'd been introduced to Roger when Eva got the call to St. Cat's, and I'd caught glimpses of him at the party, looking stiff and uncomfortable in a rented tux. I remembered Roger as about five-foot-ten, handsome in a rugged, outdoorsy sort of way, with dark wavy hair, combed straight back. We hardly ever saw him at church—Eva often joked that her husband was a Methodist. Roger'd popped into a vestry meeting once, whispered quietly into his wife's ear, then just as quickly popped back out again. His infrequent appearances at St. Cat's gave new definition to the term "low profile."

I checked Roger's salary at Eastport. No wonder he was looking for a new job. For someone with his experience, which included an MBA from Boston University, Eastport Yacht Sales was paying peanuts. Clearly Eva was the breadwinner in the family.

Feeling confident that Dante had at least two viable

candidates to interview that afternoon, and lulled by the lyrical strains of a Mozart symphony wafting down from the speaker over my head, I leaned back in the lounger and closed my eyes.

I was hovering on the fringes of sleep when somebody bumped my chair.

"Sorry, ma'am. I was just collecting your mug."

"That's okay," I said dreamily, looking up at the young man and trying to focus. "Is that a menu?" I asked, pointing to the gold-embossed, green leather-bound folder under his arm.

"Right. I'm Steve. What can I get you?" he asked, handing it to me.

I took a few moments to drool over a list of delicious-sounding selections. Although sorely tempted by the Fruited Chicken Curry Pita and the Turkey Wraps with Apples and Cabbage, I finally ordered a sensible pear salad, and asked that it be delivered to the office.

Back in the office, somewhat reluctantly, I had just started opening envelopes, scanning résumés, and sorting them into piles by job title when Alison popped in carrying my salad on a tray, along with a side of Parmesan Pita Crisps and something aggressively orange in a tall glass. "Was just on my way to the gift shop, so François asked me to deliver this," she said, setting the tray down on the desk.

"What's that?" I asked, pointing to the glass.

"Papaya drink," she told me. "That was my idea."

The drink turned out to be heavenly, and the salad—a confection of Anjou pear with arugula, bleu cheese, and cinnamon-roasted pecans—equally divine. I was noisily sucking the last of the payaya drink up through a straw when Emily poked her head into the room.

"Mom, is Timothy with you?"

"No. I thought he was in the nursery."

"Have you seen Alison?"

"She just left. She brought me a salad, then said she was going to the gift shop. Wait a minute." I picked up the phone and dialed the two digit extension for the gift shop. Alison picked up. "Alison, you don't happen to have Tim with you, do you?"

"Sorry, no." Alison paused to speak to a customer. "That'll be ninety-eight fifty, Mrs. Lewis." I heard electronic beeps as Alison ran the purchase through the credit card machine. "Is there a problem?" she asked.

"I'll let you know," I said, hanging up the telephone. I looked at Emily and shook my head.

"Could he be with Dad?"

"I doubt it." My stomach lurched. Something was terribly wrong. "Your father's with one of the new girls, getting a massage and a facial. How about Dante?"

Emily grabbed onto the door frame for support. "No, I checked the conference room first. He's still talking to that woman from *Shape*." Suddenly, she slumped over, resting her hands on her knees, and began to sob. "Oh my God, oh my God, I left Tim alone in the nursery for just a minute. He was napping in his playpen. I came back, and he's gone!"

I took a deep breath, struggling to stay calm. Somebody had to, because my daughter was coming unglued. "C'mon." I grabbed Emily's hand. "Let's look again."

Emily and I tore down the hall and burst through the doors of the day care center. Never had the room looked so vast and so empty. Tim's playpen sat where it always had, but except for Lamby and a half-consumed formula bottle of orange juice, nothing. Our little boy was gone.

"Do you think Tim learned to climb out of the playpen?" I panted. "Kids can surprise you. Maybe he climbed out and crawled away?" Even I knew I was grasping at straws.

Emily shook her head miserably. "I've checked everywhere. The bookshelves, the closet, the toy box, under the slide. I was only gone for two minutes, Mother, I swear!"

"Where the hell did you go, Emily? The restroom?"

The creases deepened on Emily's brow. "God, noooooh! Somebody called from the office and told me that Dante needed me out on the loading dock to sign for some exercise bikes. Tim was sleeping so soundly, I didn't want to disturb him, so I ran out to the loading dock, but by the time I got out there, the truck was gone. Two minutes!" she wailed. "Where could a baby have got to in two minutes?"

I helped Emily into a chair, then checked the French doors that led to the patio. They were firmly closed. If Tim *had* managed to escape his playpen and crawl away, he hadn't left the nursery that way.

The only other door led into the main hallway. I looked at Emily and we both had the same thought. "The swimming pool!" I yelled.

Emily knocked over her chair in her rush to get out of the room. When I caught up with her, she was standing at the edge of the pool, staring into the water. Except for gentle ripples generated by two women swimming lazy laps, the water was crystal clear. No floundering child. No small, lifeless form lying on the bottom.

Emily was crying now, big heaving sobs. "What kind of a mother am I? How could I have been so stupid?"

Close to tears myself, my heart pounding in my ears

so loudly I could barely think, I tried to sort it out. Emily'd left Tim alone for two minutes, maybe three. Add the time to find me, call Alison, and search the day care center, another five minutes, tops. If somebody'd snatched little Tim, they might still be in the building.

So I did the only sensible thing.

I pulled the fire alarm.

CHAPTER 5

The state of Maryland can fine you up to five thou-sand dollars for calling in a false alarm, but it was a price I'd gladly pay if it helped find Timmy.

The clock was ticking for my grandson, so I didn't waste a moment waiting for the fire brigade. With the klaxon relentlessly hooting, I grabbed Emily's hand and raced from the day care center into the reception area, where, like some deranged Pied Piper, I picked up Heather, then hurried across the lobby to the gift shop where Alison was frantically closing up.

"Forget that," I said. "There's no fire. Timmy's missing!" I snatched the cash drawer from under Alison's arm and tucked it beneath a pile of fleece hoodies that had been arranged for sale on a nearby display table. "Alison, I need you to go out to the parking lot. Grab everyone coming out the exits from the kitchen and the fitness suite. Herd them together and keep them in the parking lot until . . . well, I don't know until when, just do it! And when Norman Salterelli shows up," I called after Alison's departing back, "tell him to get down the drive to the main gate and don't let anybody leave until I say so!"

I turned to Heather. "You do the same thing on the

patio for the folks coming out of the swimming pool exits, okay?"

"Right!" Heather turned smartly on the toes of her brand new athletic shoes and chugged out of the shop. On her way, she laid a hand on Emily's shoulder. "We'll find Tim, don't you worry."

Emily wiped her eyes with the back of her hand, bobbed her head, and forced a smile. "Thank you."

After Heather left, heading into the Natatorium against the flow of people hustling in the opposite direction, I gathered Emily into my arms. "We will find him, Em. I promise." Still holding my daughter by the shoulders, I stepped back and looked deeply into her troubled, red-rimmed eyes. "But you need to be strong. Not only for Timmy's sake, but also for Chloe and Jake."

Under my hands, Emily shivered. "Chloe and Jake! I almost forgot! I have to pick them up from school at three!"

On the wall over Emily's head the hands of a brass ship's bell clock pointed to 1:25. Paul and I had picked it out at the Midshipmen's Store as our "housewarming" present for the spa. Then, I had thought it was beautiful. Now the clock ticked at me accusingly, each tick reminding me that another second had passed, and Tim was still missing.

A tendril of hair had escaped from Emily's braid and was plastered damply to her cheek. I smoothed it back gently. "Don't worry about the children, honey. We have plenty of time. I'll take care of them," I said, not having the slightest idea how that would be accomplished, but reasonably certain that the school wouldn't chuck my grandkids out on the street if Emily didn't show up at three on the dot. "Now, come with me."

A few seconds later I stationed myself just outside the main doors of Paradiso. As clients streamed out the door—dripping wet from the pool, or sweating from exercise, some still tying their robes around them—I scanned each face, looking for a sign, but I saw nothing but confusion, fear, and panic that mirrored our own.

"Yes, yes, everything's fine," I shouted over the deafening sound of the klaxon, all the time wondering, *Where the hell is Paul?* "Yes, the firemen are on their way. Please, move on. We're to assemble in the garden."

At some point Emily left my side and began grabbing at shirtsleeves, tugging at robes, her eyes wide with panic. "My son is missing! Has anyone seen a ten-month-old boy?"

The sad shake of a head. "No."

A concerned smile. "I'm so sorry."

While the crowd in the garden grew.

I had no idea there had been so many people in the building. François, Jimmy, and the kitchen staff would be out back, of course, but Wally and his two shampoo girls, the bikini wax specialist, a half-dozen guides, the guy who'd been introduced to me as Julio the Pilates instructor, and three massage therapists including Garnelle, were already congregating in and around the gazebo, reassuring clients and awaiting instructions.

I felt a hand on my shoulder, the familiar voice of my husband in my ear. "Hannah. What's going on? I don't smell any smoke."

An elderly woman stumbled as she stepped over the threshold. I grabbed her elbow, steadying her, then directed her to the gazebo before turning to face Paul. "There isn't any fire," I said. "Tim—" I choked on my grandson's name.

Paul's dark chocolate eyes searched mine for clues.

Until he wiped my tears gently away with his thumb, I didn't realize I had been crying. "What, Hannah? What about Tim?"

"He's missing, Paul. We think someone snatched him from the nursery."

Paul sucked air noisily through his teeth. "Are you sure?"

"Would I have pulled the fire alarm if I wasn't?"

"My God, Hannah." He wrapped an arm around my shoulder and pulled me to him. I turned, buried my face in his chest, and began to sob. *Paul's here now. He'll take this burden away. Everything will be fine.*

"Where's the goddamn fire?"

I raised my head, focusing through my tears on my son-in-law as he stood in the doorway, pointing the business end of a large red fire extinguisher in our direction.

Paul grabbed his arm. "Put the extinguisher down, Dante, you won't need it. Hannah pulled the alarm. Tim is missing."

"What?" Dante gasped as if he'd been struck in the stomach. "Where's Emily?"

I nodded to my right, where Emily was leaning against a pillar, her head bowed.

Dante cast the fire extinguisher aside and yelled, "Emily, what the hell?"

Emily looked up miserably, tears streaming down her cheeks, too choked up to say anything. I answered for her. "When Emily went to sign for the exercise bikes like you asked, Tim disappeared."

"What do you mean, he disappeared?"

"He was napping in his playpen. Five minutes later, he wasn't."

In four long strides Dante crossed the veranda. Before I could intervene, he grabbed Emily by the upper arms with both hands and started shaking her. "You left Tim alone? You stupid *bitch!* How could you do that?"

Emily threw back her head and wailed like a lost soul. Her cries cut through me like a hot knife. *My child is in pain.*

Paul, too, was struggling for control. He had been hugging me so tightly I could barely breathe, but Dante's outburst seemed to galvanize him, because he suddenly released me, crossed the porch, clapped a firm hand on Dante's shoulder and snarled under his breath, "This is your spa; you are in charge here. Now act like it!"

Paralyzed by shock, or grief, or fear, or shame—perhaps all of the above—Dante simply stared at his father-in-law. Paul jerked his head toward the spa employees and clients huddled in the garden. "Well?"

Dante didn't move.

Paul waited a moment more, then strode to the end of the veranda, stood on the top step, bathrobed and barefooted, and gazed out over the crowd like a Roman orator.

"Okay, everyone, look around you. Is anyone missing?"

A low murmur drifted up from the garden, like a theater audience in the opening moments before the curtain rises.

"Okay, then. Everybody stay put until the fire trucks get here. If you need anything . . . Wally?"

From the shade of a sculptured lime tree, Wally, dressed in tight black jeans and an equally form-fitting black T-shirt under his Paradiso smock, stepped forward. "You rang?"

The crowd tittered uncomfortably.

"If you need anything, talk to Wally here," Paul instructed, wisely ignoring Wally's quip. He crooked a finger at Julio, then turned his back on the crowd. "Dante, Emily, come inside with me." When neither showed any sign of movement, he added, "Now!"

While we waited in the elegant reception area for Paul to collect Julio, Dante tried to pull Emily close, but she shoved him away so hard that he stumbled.

"Em! I'm sorry. I was upset. I didn't mean what I said out there!" Dante had to shout to be heard over the klaxon.

"You did, too!" she screamed back. "I told you we should wait until everything was ready before opening the spa, but you wouldn't listen to anyone but your precious Mrs. Strother. Yes, Phyllis. No, Phyllis. Anything you say, Phyllis. Kiss my butt, Phyllis. You make me *sick*!"

"Em—"

"You *knew* I had too much on my plate, but it was always Emily come here, or Emily do this, or Emily do that." She took a deep breath, winding up to launch another verbal assault at her husband.

I had to step in. "Stop it, both of you! Fighting with one another is not going to help us find Tim, and the sooner you pull yourselves together, the better."

"Do you know how to shut that damn thing off?" Paul shouted as he walked, still barefoot, into the reception area, both hands clapped over his ears.

"No," Dante said simply, a blush of embarrassment reddening his neck.

"Okay, then, I guess we'll just have to live with the noise until the firemen get here. In the meantime, we're going to search this place. Thoroughly. We're going to look into every room, every closet, every cupboard, every toilet and shower stall, every nook and every cranny, anywhere a child could hide. Or be hidden," he added, ominously.

"Julio, you take Hannah and Emily and search the women's wing. Dante and I will do the men's. We'll meet back here when we're done. Got it?"

Still separated by several car lengths, Emily and Dante nodded mutely.

Paul approached our daughter, cupped her chin in his hand and tipped her face until he could look directly into her sad eyes. "It's going to be all right, Emily."

From one of his pockets, Dante produced a tissue, and handed it to his wife like a flag of truce. She took it from his fingers without comment and snuffled into it.

"Okay," Paul said, tightening the sash of his bathrobe. "Let's go."

The search was fruitless.

Back in the reception area, discouraged and exhausted, I sat on an upholstered bench next to my daughter and tried to comfort her.

"Emily . . ." I began, struggling to find the right words.

Emily leaned her head back against the wall. "It's past his feeding time. He'll be hungry, and scared." She pressed her hands to her breasts, where a wet stain was rapidly spreading, darkening the bright pink of her shirt. "Oh, God, just thinking about Tim and my milk lets down. Who will feed my baby now, Mom? Who? Who?"

"Whoever stole Tim took a very big risk," I said. "If there's to be a ransom, he'll want to keep Timmy alive, and will take good care of him."

"But what if they took him for . . . ?" Emily shuddered. "What if a sexual predator has Timmy? If he's hurt, I'll kill myself. Oh, God, please don't let anyone hurt my little boy!"

Emily hugged her chest tightly and began rocking back and forth. "Oh, God, Mom, it aches. It aches so much. What am I going to do?"

"Here comes your father," I said, standing. I raised a hopeful eyebrow, but Paul simply shook his head. Dante drooped behind him, and Julio looked ready to punch the lights out of the next person who looked at him cross-eyed.

"So, Tim's really gone?" I asked.

Emily began to whimper. Her whole body shook. Dante, having come to his senses at last, rushed to his wife's side and folded her into his arms, where she buried her head in his chest and wept uncontrollably.

"What do we do now?" I whispered.

Paul's face had turned to stone. "We call 911."

CHAPTER 6

"Where are they? What's keeping them?"

Paul squeezed my hand. "It's been less than five minutes, Hannah. They'll be here soon."

Less than five minutes. It had seemed like hours since Paul punched 911 into his cell phone, then dragged me out onto the veranda of Paradiso by the arm, insisting that I get some fresh air.

"Emily needs me—" I began.

"Right now, I think she needs her husband more."

Just moments before, while Paul changed back into his street clothes, I'd persuaded my daughter to lie down on the massage table in Garnelle's studio, where Garnelle had placed a cool, aromatic compress on her forehead. We'd left Dante sitting on a chair next to the table, stroking Emily's hand. Every time she struggled to sit up, he'd gently force her to stay put.

"I can't believe this is happening, Paul. Emily knew I was working in the office! Puddle Ducks has a telephone. Why didn't she call and ask *me* to watch Timmy for a few minutes?"

Paul wrapped his arms around me, drew me close and rested his chin on the top of my head. "Emily will probably never stop asking herself that question. But at this point, I can't think of anything more counterproductive. She didn't, so you couldn't, so here we are."

My cheek felt hot against the cool, clean-smelling fabric of his shirt, until I began to dampen it with a fresh waterfall of tears. I couldn't help it. Images of Timmy kept flashing through my mind like a slide show: Timmy's mischievous green eyes; the white stub of a tooth just breaking through the gum on his lower jaw; his gurgly laugh. "I'm crazy about that little boy!" I sobbed. "If anyone hurts Timmy, I'll kill them. I swear to God I'll rip them apart with my bare hands!"

Paul's arms tightened around me. "And I'll help you to it. But let's cross that bridge when we come to it, Hannah. Let's pray the police can find Tim and bring him safely home."

I dabbed at my eyes with the sleeve of my shirt and stared out over the Chesapeake Bay, but the calm beauty of the sun-dappled water, the cloudless blue sky, and even the gulls reeling leisurely overhead failed to soothe me as they usually did.

Farther down the drive, I could see Norman Salterelli guarding the gates as I had asked him to, a formidable mountain of muscle and sinew barely contained by the black spandex workout clothes he wore. "Do you think they got past Norman?" I wondered aloud.

Paul grunted. "Nobody gets by Norman."

In point of fact, nobody—not spa employees nor their clients—seemed anxious to challenge the body builder. Perhaps drawn by morbid curiosity, several dozen folks still lounged about the garden, milled around the patio or loitered on the beach, showing little inclination to go back inside and fetch their things. If anybody wondered why they couldn't see flames or smell smoke, they didn't mention it.

The parking lot remained full, too. I noticed several individuals hanging around their vehicles, as if waiting for the alarm to stop ringing and the all clear to sound so they could get on with their business.

A clean-cut military type, wearing his tools as proudly as a gun belt, paced next to a green and white van marked THOS. SOMERVILLE CO. François told me he'd been waiting for a repairman to fix a malfunctioning thermostat in the dishwasher, so I figured that had to be the guy. "H2O Tommy" waited, too, the five-gallon bottles of springwater he had been planning to deliver staying cool in his truck.

A twenty-something gal wearing a blue windbreaker and tennis togs, looking wholesome in a L.L. Bean sort of way, sat sideways in the driver's seat of a Volkswagen Jetta with the door open, her feet resting on the ground on either side of her gym bag. I glared at her suspiciously. Wasn't that bag big enough to hide an infant the size of Timmy? I had just made up my mind to ask Paul what he thought about her when the young woman shrugged out of her jacket, leaned over, unzipped the bag, and stuffed the windbreaker into it. Then she stood, stretched, and plopped the gym bag on top of the VW. I sighed. Not a kidnapper. Just a ding-aling who was going to drive off and forget about that bag sitting on her roof. In my youth I'd lost a fancy new camera that way.

A Toyota Camry and a BMW wagon's distance away from the Jetta, another man who looked vaguely familiar rested his backside against the hood of a late model, gold Chevy Malibu. I'd been wondering about him for a while, too, and just as I heard the wail of the first siren, the penny dropped. It was Eva's husband, Roger Haberman, who had arrived for his interview. I hoped Roger would be happy with his job at the marina a little while longer because he sure as hell wouldn't get hired at Spa Paradiso today. Maybe not any day, the way things were going now.

"Looks like the police beat the fire brigade," Paul murmured into my hair as a two-toned blue Anne Arundel County police car sped up the drive. It was followed by a second patrol car, lights flashing and sirens screaming. Seconds later a ladder truck from Eastport wheeled up the drive and, hot on its tail, the three-thousand-gallon water supply tanker engine the county keeps at the city's Forest Drive facility.

Paul kissed my hair, then released me to lope down the steps and speak to the officer. The officer, in turn, jogged down the drive to consult with the firemen, several of whom had already dismounted from their trucks dressed in full fire-fighting regalia. After a few moments the driver of the tanker engine removed his fire hat and set it on the seat of the vehicle, then accompanied Paul and the police officers up the drive, zeroing in on me as if they knew I was the guilty party who had called in the false alarm.

"I'm sorry," I said before anyone could admonish me. "It's my ten-month-old grandson who's missing. Pulling the alarm was the only way I could think of to flush everyone out of the building so we could search for him." I was already feeling a twinge of regret for all the man-hours I wasted when a white and yellow EMS vehicle pulled in next to the ladder truck, adding to the blockade, and my vague sense of remorse. "It seemed like a good idea at the time."

One of the policemen stepped forward. "We've met before, Mrs. Ives. I'm Ron Powers, and this is Officer

Will Dunham and Captain Tom May of the Annapolis Fire Department."

"Of course, I remember you," I said, extending my hand. The last time I'd seen Officer Powers, he'd rescued me from a wrecked van after some crooks had taken me and my friend, Naddie Bromley, on a high-speed chase up Interstate 97. I recognized the serious gray eyes, but Powers had shaved his mustache since we'd said good-bye to one another in the emergency room after the crash, and somewhere along the way his chin had acquired a half-inch scar that only emphasized the resolute squareness of his jaw.

"So, there's no fire." It was a statement, not a question.

"No fire."

Powers turned to Captain May. "The ladder and the tanker can head back, Tom, but we may need an EMT, so ask them to stick around, will you? Is there someplace inside where we can talk?" he asked, addressing Paul rather than me.

"They have a conference room."

"That would be fine."

As I led the officers into Paradiso, Powers asked, "You said it's your grandson who is missing. Are you his caretaker?"

"No, my daughter and her husband run this spa. Timmy disappeared from the day care center when my daughter stepped out of the room for a minute."

Disappeared. I couldn't bring myself to use the word *taken.* Even then, as irrational as it seemed, I must have harbored some small hope that Timmy had escaped from his playpen, crawled off on some private infant adventure, and would be found napping quietly behind a curtain, say, or nestled comfortably in a pile of towels. But it was going on an hour past his feeding time, in which case Timmy—never one to pass up a meal—would most certainly have been howling from whatever hidey hole he'd gotten himself into.

"Has anyone been in the day care center since your daughter found the child missing?"

"No, just me. Emily . . ." I started to explain about Emily being called away to the loading dock, but what would that have accomplished? Making lame excuses for my daughter wouldn't bring Timmy back. I lowered my eyes to avoid Ron Powers's unblinking, uncompromising gaze. *Don't these people read the newspaper? Watch television?* His eyes were accusing. *Never leave a child unattended. Never!*

"Would you like to see it?" I asked.

Powers nodded, then turned to Paul. "Mr. Ives, while your wife takes me to the day care center, will you show Officer Dunham to the conference room, then locate the child's parents and have them meet me there in, say, ten minutes?"

Reluctantly, or so it seemed to me, Paul released my hand. His lips brushed my cheek. "Are you going to be okay?"

"I think so, Paul. I'm doing something, at least. That helps a little."

Two minutes later I wasn't so sure. I escorted Officer Powers to Puddle Ducks, but once there, I found I couldn't go in. Even though the lights were on and the afternoon sun streamed through the French doors, the nursery seemed dark, the cheerful murals making a mockery of the playpen, its vast emptiness burning like a hole in the center of the room.

Officer Powers produced latex gloves from his pocket and slipped them on. He circled Timmy's playpen, bent at the waist and peered into it, but didn't touch anything. "Is that Timmy's toy?" he asked, pointing a latex finger at Lamby.

"Yes. He won't go to sleep without . . ." I paused, too choked up to continue. I turned my head away, concentrated on the painting of Jemima Puddle Duck, and fought back my tears. *Dear God, let us find Timmy. Let him sleep in his own crib tonight, with Lamby by his side.*

Powers crossed over to the French doors. "Were these doors locked?"

"I don't know. They were closed, though. I'm sure of that."

Powers straightened. "They aren't locked now."

Did I imagine it, or was there disapproval in his tone, an unspoken *but they should have been*?

"Does Spa Paradiso have a Code Adam in place?" Powers asked as he gazed through the windows to the patio and the woods beyond.

"Code Adam?" It wasn't until I said the words aloud that it occurred to me what they meant. Code Adam. Adam had to stand for Adam Walsh. "Is it named for that child who was abducted in Florida?"

"Right."

Six-year-old Adam Walsh had been found murdered. Every parent's nightmare, a horror too terrible to contemplate. "What exactly is a Code Adam?"

"Best thing ever to come out of Wal-Mart," Powers explained as he opened the door to the supply closet and peered in. "Now more and more stores are following their example. When a customer reports a missing kid to a store employee, they get a description and broadcast a Code Adam over the P.A. Everything stops while they look for the kid, and employees monitor all the exits to keep the kid from leaving the store." He shut the door firmly. "A Code Adam foiled a kidnapping out at the Barnes & Noble in Harbour Center last month," he added.

"I think that's what I had in mind when I reached for the handle on the fire alarm," I said, not the least bit apologetically. "I know the contractor has installed the equipment and the wiring for a P.A. system in the spa, but I don't think they've finished with it yet."

Officer Powers's index finger swung in an arc from one corner of the room to the other, pointing out a pair of surveillance cameras that I hadn't noticed before. "Are those working?"

My heart, quite literally, skipped a beat. If someone had snatched Timmy from his playpen, what a godsend those cameras would be! But I didn't hold out much hope of that. The same outfit that installed the public address system was supposed to be installing the monitoring station for the surveillance cameras, and as late as last week, Dante had told me they had been waiting for parts.

"I don't know, Officer Powers. You'll have to ask my son-in-law."

Powers grunted, then circled the room once again, more slowly this time, checking out the furniture and the toys and the games while the second hand on the clock ticked relentlessly on. It was maddening how slowly the man was moving.

"We'll need to seal off this room until the evidence technicians can get here," he said at long last. "Can this door be locked?"

"Emily has a key."

"Good. Why don't you go get it, then. I'll wait here until you get back."

Grateful that something was going to be done that involved the active collection of evidence, I hustled off to the conference room, where I found only Garnelle and my daughter. Emily was sitting bolt upright in a chair, stiff as a poker and about as responsive. From her ramblings, I deduced that the key was in her purse, but she didn't have the slightest idea where that purse might be.

"Where's Dante?" I asked Garnelle, who was standing at the refreshment station, fixing a mug of coffee. "And my husband?"

"Outside with Officer Dunham." Garnelle added a generous amount of milk and two packets of sugar to the coffee, stirred, and brought it over to Emily. "Here you go, honey. Drink some of this."

Emily wrapped both hands around the mug but made no move to drink it.

"They're taking down names, addresses, and telephone numbers," Garnelle added. "Then Dunham says they'll start letting people go home."

As if they knew we were talking about them, Paul and Dante suddenly appeared, followed by Officer Dunham. "Reinforcements have arrived, thank God," Paul announced, coming to stand by my side.

"Officer Powers needs to secure the nursery," I informed my son-in-law. "Can you take him a key?"

Dante executed a rapid U-turn and left the room.

A few minutes later he was back, accompanied by Ron Powers. "Everyone take a seat," Powers ordered, taking charge.

"Coffee?" asked Garnelle.

"Yes, thank you. That would be nice. Black, no sugar . . . Okay," he continued, accepting the steaming mug from Garnelle. "So, who was the last person to see the child?"

Emily blew her nose noisily into a tissue. "The child's name is Timmy."

"Sorry. Timmy. Who was the last person to see Timmy?"

"I was," Emily snuffled.

"And that was, what time?"

"Five minutes after one."

I glanced at my watch. Two o'clock. Timmy had been missing for nearly an hour.

Powers looked up from the notes he was scribbling with a ballpoint pen into a slender, flip-top notebook. "Anybody else see the little, uh, Timmy, in the nursery?"

Emily shot out of her chair. "What difference does it make who else saw him? *I* saw him!"

I started to say that I had seen Timmy, but then I remembered that I hadn't. I'd accompanied Paul to reception, then gone straight to Dante's office. I'd not stopped by the nursery at all, knowing that I'd be going there later to play with Timmy.

Powers turned to my son-in-law and asked, "And where were you between one and one-thirty this afternoon, Mr. Shemansky?"

Dante bristled. "Surely you don't think that *I*—"

"I'm just trying to establish where everyone was at the time Timmy disappeared," Powers insisted. "I'll be asking everyone the same question."

Dante looked only slightly mollified. "I was right here, being interviewed by a reporter from *Shape* magazine. Hope Katz. Last time I saw her, she was heading for the garden with everyone else."

François appeared at the conference room door carrying a fresh carafe of coffee and a plate of sandwiches. He paused on the threshold, as if waiting for permission to enter. "I thought you could use something to eat."

When nobody said anything, François crossed the room and placed the plate of sandwiches on the credenza next to me. I recognized his turkey wraps with apples and cabbage; his sweet potato and portabella wrap; his famous crustless, almond-butter finger sandwiches. My stomach lurched, and I pushed the platter away. If I took a single bite, even of one of François's delectable sandwiches, I knew I'd throw up.

"And you are?" Powers asked, his eyes following the platter.

François favored the officer with a withering glance. He flourished the carafe, the hot liquid slopping dangerously close to its lip. "Do you mind if I set it down first?"

Powers flapped his hand dismissively, waiting.

François exchanged the full carafe for the empty one, then pulled himself up to his full six-foot-two. "I am François Lesperance, executive chef at Spa Paradiso."

"And where were you, Mr. Lesperance, between one and one-thirty today?"

"In the kitchen, supervising the lunch preparation. You may check with my staff."

Powers scribbled something, then turned to Paul, one eyebrow raised.

Paul alibied for Garnelle and vice versa.

Dante, who had been growing increasingly red-faced as he sat in a corner, fidgeting with a pencil, suddenly erupted. "What the hell does any of this have to do with finding Timmy, you asshole! The longer you screw around with us here, the farther away the SOB who took Timmy can get with him."

Emily chimed in. "Other than wasting time asking us damn fool questions, what the hell are you doing, anyway?"

I sighed. At least they were agreeing on something.

If Powers was upset by their insults, he didn't show it. "Let me assure you that we're doing everything within our powers to return your son to you," he said calmly. "There's only one road in and out of the Bay Ridge community. The minute we learned the nature of your 911 call, we set up a roadblock at the entrance. We've been stopping every car coming out of your community."

"Aren't you going to issue an Amber Alert? Whoever took Tim could be miles away by now!"

Powers shifted uncomfortably from one foot to another. "Once we determine that an abduction has occurred—"

"What?" I thought Dante would fly across the room and attack the man. "Of course an abduction has occurred, you moron!"

Paul laid a restraining hand on Dante's arm. "It won't help to insult the officer."

Dante's eyes blazed. "This is such bullshit!"

Emily glared. "They always suspect the parents."

I waved both hands in the air. "Time out!" When I had everyone's attention, I turned to the officer and said, "I know you're just doing your job, Officer Powers, and that you have to eliminate us as suspects, but I think I speak for everyone in this room when I say that we're all willing to take a lie detector test to prove we had absolutely nothing to do with Timmy's disappearance. Once that's out of the way, you can move on to other more promising suspects."

"Test me right now," Emily insisted. "Get the guy with the polygraph down here right now and let's do it!"

"I'll arrange it," Powers said. "In the meantime, do you have a recent picture of the chi—Timmy?"

A worried glance passed between Emily and Dante. "We've just moved here, and most of our pictures are still packed."

I reached into my purse and pulled out a wallet-sized photograph of my grandson. "I took that picture last week," I said, handing it over, feeling a deep sense of loss as Timmy's image slipped from my fingers to his. In the photograph, Timmy was dressed in a white and blue sailor suit, posed next to Coco, their chocolate Labradoodle. Coco wore Tim's sailor cap lopsidedly between his floppy ears. "Can you crop out the dog?"

Powers nodded, and tucked the photograph carefully between the pages of his notebook. "If, as I suspect, Timmy was taken away in a vehicle, it would help if we had a description of that vehicle." He turned to face Dante. "I notice you have security cameras both inside and out. Are they working?"

Tears pooled in Dante's eyes, overflowed, and spilled down his cheeks. "They're coming to install the monitors this weekend."

"That would be no?"

"No."

"He was trying to save money," Emily snapped. "He hired some cut-rate outfit run by a friend of his just to save a few bucks. I told you we weren't ready to open yet! Ooooohhhh . . ."

"Did anyone notice anything suspicious today?" Powers continued, interupting my daughter's rant. "Any vehicles that didn't belong, or ones that were parked too close to the building?"

Everyone simply stared.

"Did anyone show any unusual interest in the child? Give him gifts?"

Emily said, "Everyone loved Timmy, Officer Powers. But I don't remember anyone paying more attention to him than they would to any other cute baby."

Powers tucked the notebook into his pocket. "Okay, here's what we're going to do. Since we don't have a suspect vehicle, we can't post anything to the changeable message signs on the highway that allow us to communicate with motorists. But we'll issue a 'Be on the Lookout,' and we can prepare a description of Timmy and the circumstances of his disappearance and fax it to the media. They'll put the BOLO out on all area radio, TV, and cable systems, where it will be seen and heard by millions of listeners."

I'd seen those messages before—other people's children, never ours—sad details about their abduction crawling along the bottom of our television screen. A school picture, a candid photo of the child, slightly out of focus. I wondered how many of those stories had happy endings.

"And we're bringing in a tracking dog from Baltimore County."

"What kind of dog?" Paul wanted to know.

"We've requested a bloodhound. Bloodhounds will be able to pick up Timmy's scent even if he was carried away in somebody's arms."

"What good will that do?" Emily was sobbing again. "If the kidnapper took Timmy away in a car, the trail will stop at the parking lot, right?"

"Bloodhound noses are many times more sensitive than German shepherds'," Powers pointed out. "It was a bloodhound that tracked Laci Peterson's scent down the center of a highway, if you remember, proving she left the house in a vehicle, not on foot, as her husband had claimed."

Laci Peterson. Another victim who didn't make it. This wasn't encouraging.

Dante slouched in his chair, hands pressed tightly between his knees. "You know what really bothers me?" he told the officer. "I never asked Emily to sign for anything today. As far as I know, there was no delivery."

Emily looked up, face blotched from crying. "Then who . . . ?"

"You didn't recognize the voice on the telephone?" I asked.

Emily bit her lower lip. "Just a woman's voice. I assumed it was one of the staff."

"Hey, everybody!" The head of a white stuffed tiger lunged into the room, followed immediately by the equally white head of my sister, Ruth. "What's with all the police cars, anyway? I had to sneak in through the loading dock. Look what I brought for Puddle Ducks," she chirped, not pausing long enough for anyone to answer her question. She galloped the super-sized toy along the chair rail. "This will solve the problem."

CHAPTER 7

Greeted by a silence so heavy it was palpable, still cradling that ridiculous white tiger, Ruth froze. "What? What did I say?"

"Timmy's missing," Dante snapped.

Ruth looked from Dante to the tiger and burst into tears.

I wasn't due at Hillsmere Elementary to meet Chloe until three-ten, but I decided I couldn't bear another torrent of tears when I could barely control my own. "I need to pick up Chloe and Jake," I announced, suddenly rising from my chair. I was desperate to get outside. Maybe breathing the fresh salt air would revive me. I consulted Officer Powers. "Is that okay?"

"Who are Chloe and Jake?" he wanted to know, as if they were suspects he needed to add to his interview list.

After I explained that Chloe and Jake were my grandchildren, he nodded permission. With a reassuring squeeze of my hand from Paul, and a barely audible thank-you from my son-in-law, I managed to escape the spa.

Getting out of the grounds wasn't as simple. As I stepped onto the concrete apron that surrounded the parking lot, someone said, "It's Hannah, isn't it?"

I turned. Roger Haberman.

I had been charting a course straight for my trusty LeBaron, and I didn't want to be delayed by Roger Haberman or anyone else.

"Is everything all right?" Roger asked, his face scrunched up with concern. "I beg your pardon, but you look terrible."

No doubt my face *was* a mess, whatever makeup I'd managed to dab on that morning long since washed away by torrents of tears. "No, Roger, everything isn't all right. Our ten-month-old grandson appears to have been snatched from the day care center. That's why the police are here."

Just sharing the bad news with Roger started me off on another crying jag. Roger waited until I had more or less gotten myself under control, then laid a gentle hand on my arm. "I'm *so* sorry. Are the police organizing a search? Where do I sign up?"

"Timmy hasn't learned how to walk yet, so they don't think he wandered off into the woods on his own." I pulled a ragged tissue out of my handbag and dabbed at my eyes. "Honestly, Roger, if I thought that chopping down every tree in Bay Ridge would find him, I'd grab a chain saw and turn the whole neighborhood into a pile of kindling."

A sudden thought occurred to me. "You've been out here for a while, haven't you?"

Roger nodded. "I was just arriving for an interview when all hell broke loose."

"Did you notice anything out of the ordinary?"

"I'm afraid not. Just your usual to-ing and fro-ing, like that water truck over there."

It occurred to me that if Roger had been entering the gates just as the fire alarm went off, he might well have passed the kidnapper as he or she was making a getaway on Herndon, the narrow, two-lane road that led directly from Paradiso on Kimmel Lane down to Bay Ridge Road. "How about on the way here?" I asked, my hopes rising.

Roger thought for a moment. "There was a car behind me. That one," he said, pointing to the girl in the Jetta, who I now realized must have been coming to the spa rather than going away from it. "And I'm sure I passed a few cars on the way here, but I don't remember any car in particular."

"*Think,* Roger," I urged. "Close your eyes and try to picture those cars."

Roger closed his eyes as instructed. "Two cars, I think, and an SUV definitely."

"What kind of cars? Did you notice the make of the SUV?"

Roger grimaced. "Sorry. The cars were just cars, and all SUVs look the same to me. Big and ugly."

"Oh." I felt like I'd been punched in the stomach.

"The SUV was brown, though. I remember that. Or it could have been gold. Looked like one of those vehicles you take on safari."

"Oh, Roger, bless you! The police are inside Paradiso right now, interviewing people. Please tell them exactly what you've just told me. Make sure to ask for Officer Powers."

"I wish I could be more helpful." He tapped his temple with a forefinger. "Old noggin ain't what it used to be."

Two cars and a brown SUV, I thought, mulling it over. Pitifully little to go on, and Paradiso wasn't the only establishment at the end of Herndon Road. The vehicles could just as well have been heading back to Annapolis from the Chesapeake Bay Foundation, a brand new facility built on property adjoining Paradiso. Nevertheless, Roger's information might help narrow the field if a list of suspects was eventually identified.

"I'd be happy to help search," Roger said, returning to an earlier topic.

"Thanks, Roger, but the police are bringing search dogs in pretty soon. Officer Powers thinks the dogs will confirm that somebody picked Timmy up and walked away with him."

"I see." Roger scowled. "It's a terrible thing to harm a child." His face softened. "Eva and I were never blessed with children, so I can only imagine what you must be going through. And the child's parents, too," he added quickly.

"Thank you for your concern, Roger."

"If there's anything I can do, anything at all . . ." His voice trailed off.

At that moment all I wanted was to get away from Roger Haberman and be by myself for a little while. If I could concentrate on things that needed to be done, perhaps it would keep my mind from drifting off into the terrifying, dark corners of my imagination.

I had taken several steps in the direction of my car, but turned back. "Do you think Eva will be in her office tomorrow morning?"

"She's up by seven, and usually in the office around nine," Roger told me. "Would it help if I mentioned that you might drop by, or would you rather call her yourself?"

Just thinking about picking up the telephone and talking about Timmy made me ill. With Roger to give Pastor Eva a heads-up, at least when I saw her, I wouldn't have to deal with her initial shock and surprise, which would set me off crying again for sure.

"Thank you, Roger. That would be a real kindness. And if she can't see me at nine, perhaps she could give me a call at home and we'll work out another time." I dredged up a smile from somewhere and pasted it on my face. "Now, if you'll excuse me, I need to go, or I'll be late picking up my grandchildren."

"Of course," Roger said. "Take care."

He was still looking after me like a kindly uncle when, two minutes later, my LeBaron and I pulled out of the parking lot and headed down Kimmel Lane.

Step one accomplished.

Step two. I had to make my way past the police who were guarding the gate to Paradiso. Norman Salterelli, the body-builder, was still on duty, lounging against the gatepost, beefy arms folded over equally beefy chest, chatting with the officer.

I rolled down my window to identify myself. To his credit, the officer punched a number on his Nextel and checked out my story with Powers before motioning me through.

For a split second I entertained a fantasy of peeling out of Paradiso in a roostertail of flying gravel, until Norman squashed the idea by resting his hairy forearms on the roof of my car and leaning into my open window. "You take care, Hannah Ives, and if there's anything I can do for you, just let me know."

"Thanks, Norman. You've been a real star."

He patted the top of my convertible with the flat of his hand. "Go with God."

"Thank you." In spite of myself, I smiled.

Step three.

I'd forgotten about step three. True to his word, Ron Powers had ordered a roadblock at the gates that once upon a time had guarded the entrance to the Bay Ridge community. Drumming my fingers on the steering wheel, I waited at the end of a long line of cars for my turn for inspection. The police were thorough, thank goodness, checking front and back seats, and asking everyone to pop open their trunks, too. I didn't think I could endure one more sympathetic look, so when it was my turn, I simply let the officer check my car for Timmy, thanked him, and drove on.

At the light at Arundel on the Bay Road, I turned left. Hillsmere Elementary School, where Chloe attended first grade from 8:55 to 3:10, was almost immediately on the right, a modern brick building, typical of Anne Arundel school architecture in the 1970s. I was early, so I pulled around a queue of school buses with their engines idling and into a parking space marked VISITORS, where Chloe would be certain to see me.

Because Dante and Emily lived in Hillsmere Shores, Chloe could have ridden the bus, of course, but Emily had to drive Jake to preschool at St. Anne's Day School just a quarter of a mile farther down the road, so she preferred to drive the children herself. Fortunately, I was on the schools' lists of approved "picker uppers" so I wouldn't have any trouble driving away with the children.

Neither had Timmy's kidnapper.

That thought stung. I wanted the world to stop—the cars on the road, the birds in flight, even that stray dog trotting down the road—I wanted them to stop, look my way and say, "I feel your pain." But even the day refused to go into mourning: the sun shone in a cloudless sky, a gentle breeze blew. I sighed, and because I knew the children would approve, I reached up, released the levers, and powered down the top on my convertible. No matter what I did, life would go on.

I leaned my head back against the headrest, closed my eyes and let the sun shine directly on my face. The sun must have jump-started my brain, too, because I sat up so suddenly that I bumped my head on the sun visor. Dennis! Dennis Rutherford, Connie's husband, my brother-in-law, my *police lieutenant* brother-in-law from Chesapeake County. He'd know what to do.

I rarely called Dennis on his cell phone, except in case of emergency. After the last time he'd galloped to my rescue, he'd programmed his number into my phone as a joke. "Here," he'd said, handing it back to me. "Don't bother with 911. Just call me."

If this wasn't a 911, I didn't know what was.

I scrolled down to DENNIS and pushed the Call button. After two rings his message machine kicked in. *Damn damn damn*. I left word that I needed to talk to him and pressed End.

Something in the recording of my voice must have given him a clue to my state of mind, because Dennis rang back almost at once. When I told him that Timmy was missing, he exploded. "Jesus Christ, Hannah, how long ago was that?"

"Two hours."

"Two hours." He repeated my words in the same tone of voice he might have used if I'd said "two days" or "two years." Two of anything was clearly too long. "Tell me you've called the police."

My throat felt raw, but I managed to croak, "Of course we called the police. They're at Paradiso right now. I had to leave to pick up the kids."

"Tell me what Anne Arundel County is doing."

"Wait a minute." I rummaged under the passenger seat and came up with a bottle of springwater that had been rolling around on the floor since Valentine's Day. I twisted off the cap and took a long drink, trying to soothe my aching throat before continuing. I explained to Dennis what I knew about the investigation so far, about the BOLO and the Amber Alert, while Dennis made attentive listening noises—*uh-huh, right, okay*. From his reaction, I assumed he didn't think we were dealing with rank amateurs.

"Who's in charge?" he asked after I wound down.

I told him what I knew about Ron Powers.

Dennis mentioned that he'd met the guy, then reassured me by adding, "Sounds like Powers has a good handle on it, Hannah, but I want you to check on a couple of things." He paused. "Are you up to this, or do you want me to do it?"

I found myself nodding, which was ridiculous since Dennis couldn't see me over the cell phone. "I can handle it, but I think it might be better if you call Paul's cell. He's at Paradiso right now, and he can put you through directly to Powers. I can't imagine that Powers has let anyone go home just yet."

"Right." Dennis hesitated for a moment, and his phone went *beep-beep* in my ear. "Okay, good. I've got Paul's number programmed into my cell."

"What do you want Paul to do, Dennis?"

"Unless I'm very much mistaken, Anne Arundel County hasn't had a noncustodial kidnapping in years, so I'm not sure they're completely up to speed. Did anyone call the FBI?"

"My God! Should I have? I thought that was the cops' job."

"Absolutely, it's their job, and I imagine they'll do it, but we should make sure it happens, sooner rather than later. The FBI has the resources to help us find Timmy, and time is generally not on our side in cases like this."

"Won't Powers feel like we're stepping on his toes if we insist on bringing in the FBI?"

"I don't give a damn about his *feelings*, for Christ's sake, and neither should you. Law enforcement agencies cooperate to the fullest when a missing child is involved." He drew a long breath. "The first thing we need to do is get information about Timmy up on NCIC. Sorry, that's the National Crime Information Center's missing persons' file."

Dennis didn't need to explain about NCIC, the database maintained by the FBI to track information about crimes and criminals. My name and vital statistics had been added to that database a year ago when I'd been falsely accused of murder. I hoped the negative information about me had been purged when all charges against me were dismissed, but I knew better. Old data never died. All of it was archived somewhere in that great big CPU in the sky. In addition to my rap sheet, anyone with a computer and Google or Ask.com could see how I felt about libraries, fair use, and other relevant provisions of the Copyright Act of 1976 way back when I worked as records manager at Whitworth and Sullivan.

"I gave Powers a picture of Timmy, and Emily gave him a description, so that NCIC business may already have been done."

"Good, good. But we should check on that. Where are you now?"

"Waiting at Chloe's school. Then I'll swing over to St. Anne's and collect Jake. After that, I'll stop by their house and pick up a few things so they can spend the night with us." Until I said the words, I didn't know I already had a plan.

"Good." Dennis paused. "Look, Hannah, unless they find Timmy right away, things are going to get frantic. Once the word gets out, people will crawl out of the woodwork volunteering to help. The press will show up on Emily's doorstep. They'll camp outside the spa. We're going to need a family spokesman. Do you think Dante is up to it?"

"Frankly, no. I'd do it, but if I'm watching Chloe and Jake . . ." I took a deep, steadying breath. "We should ask Paul."

"Good idea. I'll suggest it."

"Oh, Dennis, what am I going to tell the children when they ask me about Timmy?"

"If they ask, you tell them the truth. But keep it simple."

"Easier said than done."

"Hang in there, Hannah." And the line went dead.

The opportunity to tell the truth came sooner than I expected. Chloe came loping down the sidewalk, bent like a Sherpa under the weight of an oversized backpack.

"Grandma!" She wiggled out of her backpack, letting it drop to the sidewalk with a thud. I noticed that Emily had taken the time to braid Chloe's hair into neat French braids that morning. My heart turned over. *Emily* is *a good mother.*

"Can I ride in the front?"

"Of course," I said, without thinking. Then I remembered the airbag. "But only if we slide your seat *way* back." I unfastened my seat belt, leaned over the console and eased the passenger seat back as far as it would go. Then I waited until Chloe had hoisted her backpack into the car, crawled onto the seat, and we both buckled ourselves in before shifting into gear.

"Where's Mommy?" she asked as I pulled away from the curb.

"Your mama's really busy at the spa," I answered, "so she asked me to come get you. Is that okay?"

"Sure." Chloe folded her hands primly in her lap. "K-E-W-L," she added.

I flipped up my turn signal. "Kewl?" I pronounced the word. "Oh, I see! Cool!"

Chloe's head bobbed up and down. "Kewl."

"I hope that wasn't on your spelling test this week, Chloe."

"You're silly, Grandma. I know how to spell. I get A's on my spelling tests. N-B-D."

I turned right onto Arundel on the Bay road. "What's N-B-D?"

"No big deal."

"I see. Where did you learn that, Chloe?"

"It's computer talk."

"Do you do your homework on the computer?" I asked, thinking that the world was far too serious a place if six-and-a-half-year-olds were required to know Word and PowerPoint to produce their book reports.

"Sometimes. I like games, too."

"What games do you play on the computer?"

"I like Zoboomafoo. Harry Potter's cool, too."

I thought a website featuring Harry Potter and his gang might be a little too advanced for a child Chloe's age, but after further conversation, it turned out that the website's main attraction was Hedwig, Harry's snowy owl that whoo-whooed through a clever opening sequence.

"Sometimes after school I get to play games at Sammy's house," Chloe said seriously. "That's funner, because Sammy doesn't have P-O-S."

P-O-S? I considered the possibilities. Point of sale? Pepsi on sofa? Pigs on steroids?

"Okay, I give up. What's P-O-S?"

Chloe's shoulders shot up, nearly touching her ears. "Dunno."

I made a mental note to ask Emily about this Sammy person, but not just that minute. Emily had far more important things on her mind.

"Is Sammy a boy or a girl?" I asked, trying to distract my granddaughter, who had turned on the radio and begun punching buttons, changing the station from classical to all news to country and back to classical again.

"Sammy's mother calls her Samantha," Chloe said, punching another button, tuning into WETA just as the news on the half hour began.

"Anne Arundel County Police are asking the public's help in finding a young Annapolis boy who was abducted from—"

I slammed my thumb down on the power button, and the radio fell silent. *Oh God, it's for real.* Riding in the car with Chloe, chatting with her about mundane things like spelling tests and computer games, I could almost convince myself that Timmy's kidnapping had never occurred. Hearing those words tumble so matter-of-factly out of my car radio turned the knot in my stomach to stone. Timmy was really gone.

"Samantha is a nice name," I stammered, gripping the steering wheel tightly, trying to keep my hands from shaking and the car squarely on the road as I rounded the curve at Old Annapolis Neck Road. A few seconds later I turned into the drive at St. Anne's

School and slotted the car into a parking spot. I rested my forehead on the steering wheel for a moment, breathing deeply, feeling as exhausted as if I'd just completed an obstacle course.

"You tired, Grandma?"

Without lifting my head, I studied Chloe sideways. "A little bit, pumpkin. C'mon, let's go get your brother."

Officially, Jake attended school from eight-fifteen to noon, but until Puddle Ducks opened for good, he'd been taking part in Afternoon Enrichment, followed by Extended Care, which allowed Emily the flexibility to leave him there until six if necessary.

I checked in at the office to let someone know I had arrived, then went to track down Jake. We found him in a classroom with four other children, working seriously on a drawing with a fat brown crayon.

"What's that?" I asked, studying the amorphous brown blob taking shape on his paper.

Jake exchanged the brown crayon for a black one and drew a small black circle within the brown blob. "It's Coco."

I squinted at the masterpiece. "Right," I said, more to myself than to Jake, who was now adding the dog's lolling, red tongue to his drawing. "I'd forgotten about Coco."

The teacher helped Jake slide the drawing into his book bag, and located his sweater. "See you tomorrow, Jake."

I managed an anemic grin. "Come on, guys and gals. We're going to pick up Coco, and your pjs, and we'll all have a slumber party at Grandma's house. Anybody up for pizza?"

"Pizza! Yay!" shouted Chloe.

"Pizza!" echoed Jake.

Skipping down the hall with the children, thinking about pizza, did nothing to lighten my spirits. In three years, Timmy would be old enough to attend St. Anne's Day School.

Would I ever get to skip down the hall with Timmy?

Chloe tugged on my sleeve. "No pepperoni, Grandma."

I blinked back tears.

Would Timmy's kidnapper give him the chance to grow up and hate pepperoni, too?

I smiled down at Chloe, my heart nearly breaking. "No pepperoni, I promise."

CHAPTER 8

I was so proud of myself. I stayed cheerful and grandma-lovey all evening. I didn't even cry when we watched *Finding Nemo* for the umpteenth time. By the time we went to bed, I still hadn't needed to tell the children about Timmy.

Tuesday morning I staggered out of bed, let Coco out to do her business in the yard, stumbled through breakfast, and supervised the children's face washing and tooth brushing while gulping down copious amounts of strong black coffee. I usually spiked my coffee with half and half, but I didn't want to dilute the caffeine that I was counting on to jump-start me out of a semicoma so I could drive the kids to school without running the car off the road. Paul would have helped, of course, but earlier, after hugs all around, he'd hurried off to the Academy to make arrangements for someone to take his classes. He promised to meet me back at Spa Paradiso as soon as he could get away.

At St. Anne's Day School, after Chloe and I escorted Jake to his classroom, we stopped by the office, where I intended to explain about Timmy. As it turned out, no explanation was necessary. The school secretary, normally a relentlessly cheerful sort, wore such a long face that I could tell she already knew.

"Is there any news this morning?" she asked.

Struggling for control of my emotions, I shook my head.

"Chloe? Do you want to sit down for a minute?" I directed my granddaughter to one of two chairs arranged at right angles to an end table in a nearby corner. "Do you have a library book in your backpack?"

Chloe nodded, her ponytails bobbing. I was never any good at French braids, a failing that had marked me as a Bad Mother when Emily was going through the Terrible Twelves.

"Why don't you get out your book and read it while I go to that little room on the other side of the desk and talk to the principal. Okay?"

I left Chloe pawing through her backpack. When I returned five minutes later, though, she wasn't reading a book. She was out of her chair, kneeling on the floor in front of the end table where a copy of the Baltimore *Sun* lay open. Timmy's picture was on the front page.

"That's Timmy, Grandmother!" Chloe said, looking up from the paper with excitement dancing in her eyes.

"I know."

"Is Timmy famous?"

I sat down in the chair next to her, my heart pounding. "Yes he is, Chloe."

Any doubts I had about whether Chloe had actually read the article vanished when she asked, "Grandma, what does 'abducted' mean?"

"Abducted means stolen."

Chloe's pale eyebrows disappeared into her bangs. "Somebody *stole* Timmy?"

"I'm afraid so, Chloe. But, your mommy and daddy, and your granddaddy and I, are trying very hard to find Timmy and bring him back home."

"My mommy says that stealing is very bad."

"Your mommy's right. That's why the police are helping us find the person who took your little brother away."

Chloe hung her head, then studied me sideways through her eyelashes. "I stole a candy bar once at the grocery store. Daddy made me take it back and say sorry."

"And the police are going to make the person who took Timmy bring him back and say sorry, too."

Chloe's worried frown vanished. "I'm gonna tell about Timmy at Show and Tell!"

I tugged lightly on the end of one of her ponytails. "Maybe we can keep it a secret for just a little while, Chloe. When Timmy comes home, *then* you can tell. Okay?"

"Is Timmy coming home today?" she asked as I helped her shoulder her backpack.

"I don't know, pumpkin, but I hope so."

"Is he coming home tomorrow?"

Conversations with Chloe had a way of spiraling out of control. She was perfectly capable of trotting out every day of the week between now and the Fourth of July, so I quickly changed the subject to a trip we'd taken to Disney World the previous year, and we chattered about Pirates of the Caribbean and Thunder Mountain as we walked hand in hand down the sidewalk to the parking lot.

At Hillsmere Elementary five minutes later, Chloe's teacher was waiting for us in the school office. Again, no explanations were necessary. While Mrs. Rogers escorted Chloe to her classroom, the school principal urged me to allow my granddaughter to chat with the school psychologist, a plan I vaguely agreed to, thinking I should have asked Emily about it first.

By the time I got to St. Catherine's on the corner of Ridgley and Monterey, the caffeine had kicked in. I felt wired, every nerve in my body bristling with electricity. I hadn't been so juiced since Oberlin, when I pulled two all-nighters in a row writing a term paper on Stendahl. If I had run into Timmy's kidnapper at that moment, all the police would ever find of him would be bones and occasional pieces of skin.

I parked near the parish hall, cut the motor, and looked around. I was the only car in the lot.

I fiddled with the radio. I organized the glove compartment. I cleaned old Exxon receipts out of the console. Finally, I went looking for Eva, thinking that perhaps Roger had dropped her off on his way to work at the marina in Eastport.

Pastor Eva's office was in the parish hall, through a door and to the left, just off a Plantation-style breezeway that joined the parish hall to the church proper. I jiggled the doorknob, but the parish hall was locked. A note taped to the window told me Eva'd been called to Anne Arundel Medical Center to pray with a patient about to undergo emergency surgery and I should wait for her in the garden.

Taking my time, I wandered back along the breezeway and stepped into the garden, the soles of my boat shoes scrunching comfortably on the graveled path. *This is a* real *garden,* I thought. It was filled with lilac, sweet william, mint, and such an abundance of flowers that it invited butterflies and hummingbirds that wouldn't have been caught dead flitting about one of Ruth's sterile, sculptured creations. Later in the summer zinnias and milkweed would be in full bloom at St. Catherine's, and after that, sunflowers. In the fall, asters, phlox, purple cornflower, and goldenrod would turn the garden into a riot of Technicolor, a sight so beautiful that even parish asthma sufferers had not dared to complain.

I sat down heavily between two deep pink azaleas on a bench dedicated to a parishioner who had been killed in the explosion of Pan Am flight 103 over Lockerbie, Scotland. With my back to the plaque, I tried to put all thoughts of death out of my mind.

The sun was just inching over the trees, touching the garden here and there, awakening the butterflies that clustered on fence posts and flat rocks, sluggishly stretching their wings, preparing for a busy day gathering nectar. On my right, a hedgerow of forsythia was a blaze of yellow, separating me from the traffic whizzing by on Ridgley Avenue.

Bathed in sunlight, I closed my eyes, wincing as the inside of my eyelids scraped over my eyeballs like dry sandpaper. In spite of all the caffeine I'd consumed in the previous twenty-four hours, I felt I could fall asleep on this bench, uncushioned hardwood and all. I could sleep here for days and days and days. Yet I had to keep going, do whatever it took, for Timmy's sake.

"Hannah?" Eva's voice spiraled down, as if through a tunnel, to wherever it was I had gone. "Hannah, it's Eva."

I felt a hand on my shoulder and dragged myself into consciousness. "Eva, I'm sorry. I was somewhere in La-La Land." I rubbed at a crick in the back of my neck.

"I hated to wake you."

I managed a weak smile. "It's so peaceful here in the

garden. Sitting here, a gal could almost pretend she didn't have a care in the world."

"Would you like some coffee? I just put on a fresh pot."

"Thank you, yes. Although I'm pretty wired."

"Come."

Although Eva wore black slacks and a rose-colored short-sleeved silk blouse with a clerical collar, something about the way she stood there with her arms extended, palms up, reminded me of a picture in a book of Bible stories I'd had as a child. *Suffer the little children to come unto me.* My head swimming, I rose from the bench, staggered, and grabbed her hands for support. "He's just a little boy," I sobbed. "He's only ten months old. How could anybody . . . ?" Eva folded me into her arms, and I began to weep, refusing to be comforted. I threw back my head and screamed to the sky, "Why, God, why?"

Eva shook me gently, peering deep into my eyes as if searching there for my lost faith. "It's all right to be angry. Yell at God if you need to. God is not afraid of *you,* Hannah Ives."

Quietly, holding me close, Pastor Eva waited me out.

"I don't think I have any more tears left." I pulled a tissue out of a fresh packet in my handbag and blew my nose. "And damn, now I've got the hiccups."

"Roger told me about Timmy," Eva said. "And of course, we heard it on the news."

"I kept the TV turned off." I scrunched the tissue into a ball and stuffed it into the pocket of my jeans. "We watched *Finding Nemo* instead. My grandchildren are staying with me," I added by way of explanation.

"You know," I said as we strolled side by side down the path toward her office, "*Finding Nemo* used to be one of my favorite cheer-up flicks, but last night while I was watching it with the kids, every time I laughed, I was faking it."

"Roger took me to see the movie when it first came out," Eva said, smiling slightly. "And he bought the DVD when it came out, for St. Catherine's nursery, or so he said. Roger's particularly fond of the seagulls going 'mine, mine, mine.' "

"I used to think it was hysterical, too, until last night, and it hit me like a ton of bricks. *Finding Nemo* is all about a kidnapped child! Think about it. Marlin watches helplessly as a diver scoops up his son, Nemo, who ends up held captive in the aquarium of a sadistic dentist."

"I never thought of it like that, but you're right." Eva held the door open for me, and waited until I stepped inside. "But it has a happy ending, doesn't it? Marlin and his friends rescue Nemo. Perhaps we should focus on that." She took a deep breath. "How's your daughter?"

"Not good. Dante said she'd taken a handful of pills from a bottle in the medicine cabinet, then when the police showed up to search Timmy's bedroom, she took a handful of something else. He thought he might have to take her to the emergency room to get her stomach pumped, but then she threw it all up.

"They couldn't stay in the house," I continued, "and if they stayed with us, it would be too upsetting for the children. Paul got them situated in a room at the waterfront Marriott. Although I don't think they'll be appreciating the view."

"If Timmy disappeared from the spa, why are the police searching his bedroom?"

"I don't know exactly. But they took away his hairbrush, and some of his toys in Ziploc bags."

Eva nodded. "Scenting objects, I suspect. They must be bringing in the dogs."

I nodded. "Sometime this morning. They're waiting for a bloodhound from Baltimore. They're the best at this kind of work."

Eva fished a key ring out of her pocket, located a key, and unlocked the door to her office. "And how's Paul?"

"Hanging in. We've appointed him family spokesman. He's at the Academy now, making arrangements to be away."

"Did he get any sleep?"

"Not much. The bags under his eyes are even darker than mine, if that's possible."

Eva's office was a small but agreeable twelve by twelve. When she pulled aside the drapes, I saw that the window overlooked the garden. "Lovely," I said. "If this were my office, I wouldn't get much work done."

"That's why God invented draperies," she said, indicating a chair at a round conference table in the corner.

While Eva puttered—closing the door, turning off the telephone so it wouldn't ring during our visit—I paced, studying her walls. The wall to my left was covered with photographs and framed diplomas. In addition to a B.A. from Wellesley, Eva had earned a Th.D. at the Church Divinity School of the Pacific, and was ordained from St. James Church in Los Angeles. The wall to my right was hung with wooden, brass, and ceramic crosses, several dozen of them. In addition to the familiar Latin cross, I recognized a Jerusalem cross, a Greek cross, the cross of St. Andrew, one Maltese, several Celtic.

"What's this one?" I asked, pointing to a cross that appeared to be an *X* superimposed over a *P*, or vice versa.

"It's called a Chi-Rho," she said, pulling out one of the chairs. "Do you know the story?"

"Tell me," I said, sitting down in the chair opposite her.

"Chi and rho are the first two letters of the Greek word for Christ. They're also similar to the pagan emblem used as a standard by the Roman cavalry. Constantine was the chief priest of the pagan Roman religion, so when he converted to Christianity, it's easy to see why he chose the Chi-Rho for his emblem.

"It's a warrior's cross," she continued. "It urges us to follow Christ's example, to wage war on terror, persecution, oppression, and all forms of evil. And the surest thing to overcome evil is love."

"How can I feel love toward Timmy's kidnapper?" I scoffed. "All I feel is a dark, gut-wrenching hate."

"I can understand that."

"And God's on my shit list, too. I'm falling seriously out of love with a God who could allow such a thing to happen to an innocent child."

Eva smiled and patted my hand. "God is with us, Hannah, but he may not always be in control."

I sat quietly for a while, mulling over what Eva had said, staring at her bookcase through a film of tears. Office bookshelves have personalities, I always thought, personalities defined by that curious mix of books needed for the job and those photographs and tchotchkes that remind workers that they actually have private lives. Eva's shelves contained Bibles in many versions, Greek and Hebrew lexicons, commentaries, concordances, and collections of sermons. On one shelf, the Quran was sandwiched between the Book of Mormon and the Egyptian Book of the Dead, and on the shelf below that, next to the Bhagavad Gita, stood a Barbie doll dressed in an alb, cincture, and pure white stole.

I had to smile. "Since when did Barbie become a priest?"

She chuckled. "My sister made it as a gift for my ordination. Liturgically correct, with stoles for every feast day and liturgical season. Barbie's usually wearing green, but we're coming up on the sixth Sunday in Easter, so the stole is white."

"Think she'll ever be Bishop Barbie?" I mused, thinking about the stained-glass ceiling Eva, and female priests like her, kept bumping into.

"Your mouth to God's ears." Eva reached across the table and slipped a business card out of a plain wooden holder. She scribbled something on the back of the card before handing it to me. "This is my home number, and my cell phone number. If you, or anyone in your family, needs anything, at any time, just call."

I accepted it gratefully, finding comfort in the knowledge that I'd be able to reach my pastor—and friend—whenever things started coming unglued.

"We haven't seen Emily for a long time, Hannah. Is she attending another church?"

"Emily's left her faith so far behind that only God knows where it is."

"And her husband?"

"Dante, too. He believes that religion is simply a crutch."

Eva raised an eyebrow. "I'd like to tell Dante that there's no shame to using a crutch if your leg has been broken."

"I'm afraid for them, Eva. Aside from Paul and me,

they only have each other, but instead of bringing them together, this terrible situation seems to be driving a wedge between them."

Eva stared out the window thoughtfully, then asked me for Emily's address. Somehow I knew that in addition to a personal note of support from her former pastor, Eva was likely to sic the Daughters of the King on my wayward daughter, dedicated churchwomen all, who would serve up a nightly succession of hot casseroles along with their quiet evangelism.

"With your permission," she continued, "I'll go ahead and e-mail our prayer chains, get them going on prayers for Timmy's safe return. And we'll add his name to the Prayers of the People on Sunday, of course."

"Thank you," I whispered, taking both her hands in mine and squeezing, hard. "But let's pray he'll be home long before that."

"I will lift up mine eyes unto the hills, from whence cometh my help . . ." Eva began, and I felt a wave of comfort wash over me. We bowed our heads and Eva prayed in soft, soothing tones for Timmy's safe return, for courage, for peace, and for the police who were working so hard to find my grandson. When we joined our voices in the Twenty-third Psalm—*I will fear no evil, for thou art with me*—I felt better armed for what I knew would be difficult days ahead.

Eva accompanied me out to the parking lot. "You know, if the Psalms don't work for you, there's always Dory," she mused as we approached my car.

"Dory?" I wasn't following her.

"From *Finding Nemo*," she reminded me. "Dory is relentlessly optimistic in spite of overwhelming obstacles. She never loses hope, does she? And without hope, we cannot survive."

While I climbed into the driver's seat and fastened my seat belt, Eva stared into the woods as if what she were about to say were carved into the bark of one of the trees. "What's that line? Ah, yes, 'Hey there, Mr. Grumpy Gills. When life gets you down, do you wanna know what you've gotta do? Just keep swimming. Just keep swimming.' "

CHAPTER 9

Spa Paradiso is closed until further notice. We are sorry for any inconvenience.

The sign had been freshly painted in black letters on white metal, and hung from the gatepost on a triangle of stout wire. I imagined Phyllis Strother and her investors spinning in their Guccis over the inconvenience of the closing, all the while reassuring Dante that, okay-fine, under the circumstances, what could one do?

The police had established a perimeter approximately fifty yards from the gates, completely blocking Kimmel Lane.

Kimmel Lane. I had to smile. Like Puddle Ducks, the name was the invention of my son-in-law. Every street in the Bay Ridge community had been named after a naval hero, like Mayo, Bancroft, Wainwright, and Decatur. Rear Admiral Husband E. Kimmel, on the other hand, a 1904 Naval Academy grad, had been a scapegoat, summarily relieved of his command after the Japanese attack on Pearl Harbor. History had long since cleared his name, but the Department of Defense had not. It's not often one gets to thumb his nose at the DOD, and Dante enjoyed making his point.

Keeping my head low, I aimed my LeBaron at the gap between the gateposts, navigating my way around three television trucks from Baltimore and Washington, affiliates of the major networks, their communications stalks extending high into the sky, and running a gauntlet of unmarked vehicles parked higgledy-piggledy along the shoulder of the narrow road, probably by reporters and curiosity seekers.

I identified myself to the police officer on guard, who scrutinized my driver's license and wished me well before waving me through into the grounds.

To my great relief, Paul's Volvo already sat in a far corner of the parking lot, as did my sister-in-law Connie's red Ford pickup. I didn't have to wonder why they had parked so far away: the section of the lot nearest the main entrance to the spa had been cordoned off for use by the police, including three patrol cars, a pair of dark-colored Crown Vics, and—a welcome sight—the blue-striped, white SUV that belonged to the Baltimore County K-9 unit.

A uniformed officer was just unfolding her legs from the driver's side of the SUV. I squinted at the vehicle, hoping to catch sight of the dog, praying that they brought a bloodhound, but, alas, the windows were tinted.

I pulled in next to Connie's pickup and turned off the ignition. When I went to drop my keys into my handbag, I discovered that my hands were shaking so badly I could barely operate the toggle that secured the flap over the pouch. My heart was doing flip-flops in my chest, and I was short of breath from the simple effort of tugging at the flap of my handbag.

It's the caffeine. Surely, it's the caffeine. You'll have to knock it off, Hannah.

I pulled on the flap until the snap gave, leaving four neat holes in the leather. The snap ricocheted off the steering wheel, pinged on the console, and dropped onto the passenger side floor mat. Damn! Not an auspicious omen for the remainder of the day.

Tucking the ruined bag under my arm, I stumbled up the drive and onto the porch. A police officer I recognized from the day before—Duncan? Dunham?—greeted me at the main door and directed me to the conference room where, he said, everyone had gathered for a briefing. I hustled along in that direction, but when I got to the reception area, I froze.

CRIME SCENE—DO NOT CROSS. The yellow tape stretched forebodingly from the door of the gift shop, along the paneled wall, and across the double doors that led into Puddle Ducks. I closed my eyes and took several deep, steadying breaths, but my heart continued to pound in my ears and my head swam. If I didn't find a place to sit down soon, I'd keel over.

When I got there, the door to the conference room was closed, but through a garland etched in the glass I could see Paul and Connie seated next to each other at one end of the polished mahogany table. Next to Connie the sleeve of a pink sweater I recognized as Emily's rested on the table; she must have been just out of sight to Connie's right. I assumed Dante would be there somewhere, possibly seated next to his wife, and perhaps others, law enforcement types, would be in attendance, too. I rapped on the door, turned the knob, and went in without waiting for anyone to say "Come in."

Dante was there, indeed, sitting between Emily and a

pudgy, white-haired guy in a gray suit. A plainclothes policewoman stood at the head of the table, and seemed in charge of the proceedings.

"Sorry to interrupt." I felt my face grow hot as I lurched toward the vacant chair next to my husband. "I'm Hannah Ives," I began, before realizing that the woman I was addressing needed no introduction to me.

FBI Special Agent Amanda Crisp of the Annapolis Regional Authority hadn't changed much since early last year, when I'd come so close to eluding her at the Ballston Metro station. Her honey-blond hair had grown out, and she'd gathered it neatly into a bunlike coil at the nape of her neck, but otherwise I would have recognized her anywhere. Same dark gray pantsuit and crisp white shirt. Same telltale bulge under her jacket. Same highly polished shoes. Besides, you tend not to forget people who roust you out of bed at five-thirty in the morning and haul your ass off to jail.

I grabbed the back of my chair for support. "Agent Crisp! Quite frankly, the last time we were together, I hoped it would be the last. No offense."

"None taken."

"I hope you'll believe me when I tell you how very glad I am to see you," I added. "In spite of all the unpleasantness last year, I have a very high level of confidence in the FBI."

"Thank you."

Was it my imagination, or was there a hint of a smile? Just as quickly as it came, the smile vanished. "Chief Sheldon has asked us to coordinate the investigation into Timmy's disappearance."

"So soon? We're so grateful." I was thinking that Chief Sheldon probably had precious little to do with it. Lieutenant Dennis Rutherford had friends in high places, and his fingerprints were all over Crisp's current assignment.

The white-haired guy in the gray suit stirred. "Special Agent Norm Brown here, Mrs. Ives. Normally we wait at least forty-eight hours before we get involved in a kidnapping, but we're working under the assumption that Timmy might already have been taken across state lines."

How well I knew. It was one of the thoughts that had kept me tossing and turning the previous night. Annapolis is only thirty minutes from Washington, thirty-five from Virginia, an hour from Delaware, and an hour and a half, max, from the West Virginia, Pennsylvania, or New Jersey state lines. It had been twenty-four hours since we'd last seen our baby. He could be virtually anywhere.

"Has there been any ransom demand?" I asked as Paul helped me into a chair, a worried frown creasing his brow.

"Not yet. But we've put a tap on the switchboard here at the spa, and on the telephone at the Shemansky home."

Emily had been slouched in her chair, staring at her thumbs, but she raised her head fractionally to ask, "Shouldn't there have been a ransom demand by now?"

"Children are taken for many reasons, Mrs. Shemansky. We're trying to take all those possibilities into account."

I watch television, I read the newspapers. I knew

what some of those possibilities were, and it made my stomach clench.

"Who could do this?" Emily wailed, rocking back and forth in her chair. "Who? Who? Who?"

"We don't know, but as we gather the evidence, we'll be turning it over to a behaviorist from the Behavioral Sciences Unit at the FBI Academy in Quantico, Virginia. He'll sort it out and give us his evaluation."

"Behavorist?" Dante snorted. "You mean one of those profilers? One of those mental giants who announced that the D.C. sniper was a local boy, an angry white man, working alone? So it turns out we have two black guys from Washington State. *That* was taxpayer money well spent."

Emily bowed her head and began to sob quietly.

Trying to turn the discussion in a more promising direction, I said, "When I drove up, the K-9 unit had just arrived. What can you tell us about that?"

Crisp's face brightened. "Good. I imagine they'll be running the dog shortly." She tipped her head toward her colleague. "Agent Brown, would you locate the handler? Ask him to check in with me?"

Agent Brown scooted his chair back and stood up. "Right." He strode out of the conference room, hitching up his pants by the belt, and I realized that in spite of the abundant white hair, he couldn't have been more than forty.

"Will they be using bloodhounds?" Connie asked after the door closed behind Brown. "I understand bloodhounds are the best for tracking on the ground." I wondered if Connie had fessed up to being the wife of a cop, or whether she had identified herself simply as great-aunt to the victim.

"We've brought the best."

"May we watch?" Connie wanted to know.

"I don't want to watch," Emily whimpered. "I just want my little boy back."

"If you stay outside the perimeter tape," Agent Crisp said, focusing on Connie, "it shouldn't be a problem."

Dante turned to me. "Before you showed up, Hannah, Agent Crisp was telling us that she's heading the crisis negotiation team the FBI has assigned to our case. They're setting up a command center at our house."

Emily's eyes grew wide with panic. "But, we're all here! What if the kidnapper calls the house and there's nobody there to answer the phone?"

"We have an agent at the house, Mrs. Shemansky," Crisp said, "and we've already patched the phones through. If the phone rings at the house, it rings here." She indicated the telephone sitting silently and ominously on the credenza.

Paul swiveled in his chair to face me. "We've called our first press conference for two o'clock this afternoon."

"At Dante and Emily's?" I asked.

"That's right." He paused. "Hannah? Are you all right? Your face is red as a beet."

I put a hand to my cheek. It was burning with fever. But if I were coming down with something, I didn't want to know about it.

"I'm fine, Paul," I lied, dismissing his concerns. I forced a smile. "That's a good plan," I pointed out. "The children will still be in school."

"We thought that, too."

I knew from previous, sad experience that by meeting with the press at two, we might assure a spot on the early editions of the evening news. And by setting a time, we might limit the size of the press corps camping out on Emily's lawn at other times of the day.

Thinking of the rabid horde of reporters already clustered at the gates of the spa, and of all the April weekends Paul had helped Dante fertilize and seed his yard, I said, dumbly, "They'll ruin the lawn."

Dante grimaced. "Fuck the lawn."

We were saved from further comment by the arrival of a red and tan bloodhound about the height of a coffee table. Yoda, as she was called, was blessed with muscular shoulders and a deep chest. At 135, I probably outweighed the dog by only five or ten pounds. Yoda's eyes were set deeply into her oversized head; her floppy ears, wrinkled face, and drooling, drooping lips gave her a morning-after look. Yoda looked like I felt.

Hung over.

Yoda was followed into the room by her handler, a young officer introduced to us by Agent Brown as Barbara Helm. Carrying Yoda's leash loosely in her hands, Officer Helm explained that Yoda was a man-tracking dog. She'd be taken to the nursery where she'd be given Timmy's sccnt, and then we'd see where she took us.

"I don't want to get your hopes up," Helm added, smiling at Yoda with obvious pride, "but this bloodhound has proven herself able to track the faint scent of the victim coming out through a car's ventilating system."

"How is that possible?" Connie asked, genuine amazement in her voice.

Officer Helm laid Yoda's leash across the arm of a nearby chair. "Since 1978, all American cars are required to circulate the inside air while the motor is running to protect people from getting carbon monoxide poisoning."

Across the table, I saw Dante flinch.

"The fan forces air out through the air flow system," Helm continued, "leaving a faint trail of scent, even when the car windows are closed."

I turned to the dog, who sat modestly next to her handler. "So, Yoda, what's it like having such an incredible sense of smell?"

"It's like this," Barbara Helm explained. "When you or I walk in the front door, we take a whiff and can tell that spaghetti sauce is cooking." She jerked her head toward her dog. "Whereas Yoda here, she smells that same sauce, and knows how much salt's in it, how much pepper, whether it's fresh or canned tomatoes, how much oregano, how much basil, how much garlic, and whether you're using a Calphalon or copper-bottom pan."

Supernose stared at us balefully, a string of drool hanging from her lip.

Helm picked up the leash. "So, Yoda, do you wanna work?"

Yoda still looked like she was having an Alka-Seltzer moment, but her tail thumped against the carpet and she threw back her head and answered, *Rooooooooo!*

"C'mon, slobber snout."

Straining at her harness, Yoda dragged Officer Helm out the conference room door. We followed at a discreet distance.

"Yoda's a working dog, not a pet," Agent Crisp cautioned. "Please do not interact with her in any way."

At the door to Puddle Ducks, Agent Crisp removed the crime scene tape and unlocked the door. She passed a Ziploc bag to Yoda's handler. We stood in the hallway and watched as Officer Helm accompanied the dog into the room, removed Lamby from the plastic bag and thrust the toy under Yoda's nose. Behind me, Emily began to whimper.

The dog dug her nose into Lamby, taking a good sniff.

"Search!"

Yoda's nose shot to the ground. She circled the playpen in an ever widening circle, then made a beeline for the patio doors. With Helm holding onto the leash for dear life, Yoda flew through the French doors and out to the patio. She was working fast, sniffing her way over the flagstones, along the path through the garden, across the lawn, moving in the general direction of the parking lot.

A half-dozen yards into the parking lot, Yoda seemed to lose the trail.

"Oh, no," I moaned.

Barbara Helm slowed down to let Yoda work it out, moving her in a wider and wider circle, repeatedly casting the dog off to let her find the scent. Suddenly, Yoda hit it and was on the trail again, straining on the leash, her nose scouring the ground, trotting down the driveway that led to Kimmel Lane.

Although an officer had been sent on ahead to keep the reporters out of the way, at sight of the dog they must have surged forward because I heard Helm yell, "Get those people the hell out of there!" Yoda and her handler charged through the gates, turned the corner and out of sight, followed slowly by the K-9 van.

"What if the kidnapper was on foot, and took Timmy into the woods?" Paul asked Agent Crisp.

"It's even easier to track in the woods," Crisp replied. "And they've got their radios."

Radios. Of course they had radios.

Agents Crisp and Brown excused themselves, leaving us sitting in chairs on the porch, the same chairs where just forty-eight hours earlier we'd been chatting and yucking it up, drinking iced tea.

Nobody spoke, sitting quietly, nursing their own thoughts.

As sensitive as her nose was, I was thinking, it would be something of a miracle if Yoda could follow Timmy's trail along the miles and miles of road the kidnapper might have used while making his getaway. It was not outside the realm of possibility, though. I knew that from a program I'd seen on television, on the crime channel, maybe, or it could have been *Animal Planet*. Trails had been laid in a park, then a fishing contest was held. Over a thousand people attended the event, walking over the trails, driving their cars over them. Some trails were laid over water, and in some cases it had rained. And yet, even after all that, the dogs were able to track and find their targets. And they say animals are dumb.

"Scientists think the drool helps reconstitute the microscopic particles that drop off the victims," Connie commented.

So, she had been thinking about bloodhounds, too. Or else she was a witch, reading my mind.

"Fingers crossed," said Paul.

Ten minutes passed, then fifteen.

Suddenly, Paul stood up. The K-9 van was on its way back up the drive.

I sprang to my feet. "It's too soon, Paul. They're coming back too soon."

"We don't know that."

"No, Hannah's right," said Connie. "They're coming back way too soon."

CHAPTER 10

Paul looked handsome pacing in front of the cam-eras, positively presidential. Wearing a navy blue windbreaker, open-necked shirt, and pressed denims, he appeared more put-together than any of the other members of my family clustered behind that bank of microphones, but it was entirely accidental, I knew, as he'd grabbed the first thing that came to hand in the closet that morning, not giving a moment's thought to how he should dress for a television appearance.

It was 1:55 P.M. The press continued to gather at the end of the driveway in rowdy, fidgety packs. Standing on the sidelines between Connie and Dennis, I watched Paul turn his back on the crowd and speak quietly to Emily.

Dante was otherwise occupied, conversing in hushed tones with Jim Cheevers, our attorney, who had dispensed with his usual trademark tie—tropical fish and Disney characters were among his current favorites—for one in a somber maroon and gray stripe. Recently, Jim had taken over the handling of our legal affairs from our old friend Murray Simon. Murray had been summoned to Washington to head up a presidential task force on Hurricane Katrina relief. Judging from the number of times we'd heard from him since last fall, Murray might as well have been abducted by aliens. One evening I ran into Murray's wife at the symphony. She'd reported a Murray sighting at Christmas, but other than that, claimed not to have seen him in ages.

From my vantage point at the edge of the driveway, with the branches of a forsythia bush periodically stabbing me in the back, I saw Dante's hands flutter.

Cheevers nodded.

Dante raised a finger.

Cheevers shrugged.

For all I knew, they might have been discussing the plays of Monday night's baseball game.

Without warning, an icy hand reached out and seized my heart, squeezing it so hard I could barely breathe. *What we need is a publicity stunt.* My son-in-law's exact words, spoken only a few short days before.

Sweet Jesus. Was the success of Paradiso so important to him that he'd engineer the kidnapping of his own child? It was unthinkable! And yet . . .

"Dennis?" I hissed.

"Shhhh," my brother-in-law hissed back, inclining his head toward mine. "I think they're going to begin."

They'd evidently been waiting for a signal from Agent Amanda Crisp, who emerged from the house and took her place to the left, just behind Emily. Next to Agent Crisp stood Officer Ron Powers. Earlier, Powers had asked if I wanted to be on camera, but I'd politely declined. I had no desire to appear on television—I looked like something the cat dragged in, for one thing—but there was a more practical consideration. If the press conference ran long, I'd need the flexibility to duck out unobtrusively and pick up the children.

That might be easier said than done. Cedar Lane, a

quiet street not far from the entrance to Hillsmere Shores, was now parked wall-to-wall with cars, SUVs, and trucks. The overflow spilled onto Hickory and Pine. I was congratulating myself for taking the precaution of parking out on Edgemere Drive where I wouldn't get hemmed in, when a hush stole over the crowd.

Paul had stepped up to the microphones. Speaking without notes, looking directly into the cameras, he began.

"At approximately one o'clock on Monday, May fifteenth, our grandson, Timothy Gordon Shemansky, was taken from his playpen at Spa Paradiso in the Bay Ridge community near Annapolis, Maryland. Timothy is ten months old. He has short red hair and green eyes, and was last seen wearing denim overalls, a blue and green striped polo shirt with a white collar, socks with Thomas the Tank Engine on them, and black and white tennis shoes. The heels of Timmy's shoes blink red. If you see Timmy, or have any information about his disappearance, please call the Anne Arundel County Police Department or the Federal Bureau of Investigation at the number which is now showing at the bottom of your screen."

At the mention of Timmy's shoes, I reached out and grabbed Connie's hand. I'd bought those shoes for Timmy, and he adored them. He'd sit in his high chair, pounding his heels on the rungs, squealing with delight every time a well-placed kick got them to light up. My heart lurched, remembering.

Paul turned and extended a hand to Emily, who slipped out from under her husband's arm to join her father at the podium.

Emily was a mess. Her eyes were red-rimmed, her lids swollen. Her thick blond hair—normally worn in a single, plump braid—was gathered willy-nilly at the back of her head and secured there with a large plastic clip. Strands of hair had escaped the clip and hung untidily over her shoulders. Had it even been combed? I doubted it. In spite of the warm afternoon, she wore a shapeless sweater over a pair of black jeans with frayed cuffs.

Emily coughed. She cleared her throat. With downcast eyes and her lips close to the microphone she began speaking quietly. "If you have our little boy, please bring him back." Then she raised her eyes and looked directly into one of the cameras. "Timmy, Daddy and Mommy love you very much. I want you to be a brave little boy, to . . . to . . ." Tears leaked out of Emily's eyes and rolled down her cheeks. She sucked in her lips and shook her head from side to side, unable to continue.

Looking gaunt and haunted, Dante stepped to the podium, whispered something in his wife's ear, waited until she had been safely turned over to the care of her father, then bent at the waist so his mouth could reach the microphone.

"Please. If you have children, you know how much Timmy means to my wife and to me. There is a big, deep hole in our hearts that won't be filled until Timmy is back home again. We miss him so much, and so does his big sister, Chloe, and his big brother, Jake." Dante paused, pressing the bridge of his nose between his thumb and forefinger. "If you have Timmy, please, please take good care of him. Please don't harm him." Dante raised both hands, palms out. I'd seen him do that before. He was struggling for control.

You are an idiot, Hannah. How could you doubt this man, even for a minute?

Paul quickly stepped in and continued where his son-in-law had left off. "This is a message to whomever took my grandson. Please, bring Timmy to a police station, or to a hospital. Or take him someplace where he'll be safe, and call 911 and let us know where he is. We bear you no ill will. We just want our boy back."

We bear you no ill will. That was a crock. In my opinion, a sex change operation using a rusty penknife would have been too good for Timmy's kidnapper.

"Thank you for coming." Paul was wrapping it up. "Now, Officer Ron Powers of the Anne Arundel County police will answer your questions."

With Powers in charge of the mikes, all hell broke loose. Until that moment, presumably out of respect for our family, the press corps had listened in polite silence, scribbling notes to the accompaniment of the beeping and clicking of digital cameras. With the police in charge, however, all bets were off. Powers—clearly a pro at dealing with the press—simply stood there saying nothing, waiting them out.

"I have a brief announcement," he said when the crowd grew quiet, "then I will take your questions. Our department is working around the clock to reunite Timothy Shemansky with his family. To that end, we have enlisted the help of the FBI, who have assigned a crisis negotiation team to the case." A brief nod here to Agent Crisp. "Until the child is found, we will be holding a press conference daily at this time and place. If there is breaking news, we will, of course, let you know. That is all."

"Officer Powers! Officer Powers!" The shouts came at him from every direction.

Powers pointed to someone on his right wearing a ball cap. "You."

"Has there been any ransom demand?"

"No." A finger to the left.

"We know you brought the K-9 team in this morning. What did they find?"

"Canine Officer Barbara Helm and her dog, Yoda, working out of the Baltimore County Search and Rescue Center, determined that Timothy Shemansky was taken from his playpen at Spa Paradiso. The kidnapper carried the child to a vehicle in the parking lot, and drove down Herndon Road toward Annapolis. The dog lost the scent at the intersection of Forest Drive and Bay Ridge, which as you know is a busy intersection. There is some indication that the kidnapper may have entered the Bay Ridge shopping center, so we are checking the surveillance cameras there, and will let you know if there's anything to report in that regard."

"Officer Powers!" A reporter in a red windbreaker had sidled up to us where we stood on the fringes of the crowd. "Officer Powers!" He was standing so close to me that I feared for my eardrums if Powers didn't call on the guy soon.

Powers ignored the man and continued. "In addition, we have been conducting a roadblock search at the entrance to Bay Ridge, talking to people who use that route every day to see if we can come up with any witnesses who remember seeing Timmy or any unusual vehicles."

"Sir, sir . . ." The jerk in the windbreaker again.

Powers's head swiveled our way. "Yes?"

"At what time was the child taken?"

"I believe we've already answered that question. Next?"

"How about other surveillance cameras?" another reporter wanted to know.

"The spa has surveillance cameras. We're working on that now."

Dennis's head spun in my direction. *What?* he mouthed.

I shrugged and whispered into his ear, "They're not working. Apparently the FBI doesn't want the kidnapper to know that."

And the FBI seemed to have the situation well in hand. While we stood outside the house listening to Officer Powers answer questions, the FBI's crisis negotiation team was inside, manning the command center. We'd given them complete run of the upper level of the house, including its three bedrooms.

Dante and Emily had checked out of the hotel, but they'd decided to occupy the "mother-in-law" suite of their split-foyer home, a bed, bath, and pocket kitchen combination that had been built into the basement by a previous owner. As for Chloe and Jake, we would try to keep their lives as normal as possible. They'd stay with Paul and me, for the time being, at least.

For one thing, I didn't want the children to witness their mother's inexorable slide into depression. Emily was, completely understandably, going through a wide range of emotions—upset, frightened, and clinging to her husband one minute, angry and argumentative the next, refusing to be comforted, either by Dante or anyone else. In coaching my daughter in how to deal with the kidnappers, the FBI had its work cut out for them. Crisp urged Emily to pull herself together, to be strong to help save her son's life. Emily responded by alternating between screaming insults at everyone and staring at the wall. Once, in exasperation, I'd threatened to drive my daughter back to the Marriott where she could hole up in her room, watch television, and order junk food from room service. She told me to go to hell, but it did seem to calm her down.

While I took care of the children, Connie had been designated community liaison. She would answer the telephone, keep notes, organize the volunteers (who were already starting to call), and decide which visitors to admit to the residence. Taking her responsibilities seriously, Connie had arrived around noon with an assortment of salads and carbonated fruit drinks she'd purchased at the Whole Foods market in Harbour Center. These were sitting in the refrigerator, however, largely untouched, because nobody felt much like eating.

"Officer Powers!" The questions seemed to go on and on. Powers was built like a Sherman tank; he could roll on forever.

"Agent Crisp! Would you comment on . . . ?" Even Amanda Crisp hadn't wilted under the barrage.

Emily, though, was flagging. "Take care of Em," I whispered to Connie. "It's time for me to pick up the children."

Connie nodded, and I managed to slip away without attracting attention.

As I passed Locust Lane on my way to Edgemere Drive, where I had abandoned my car, I ran into the name tag lady from church, Erika Rose. I'd never seen Erika in anything but a suit, so I almost didn't recognize her in khaki pants, a white shirt, and a bright pink cardigan. Mother always told me that redheads shouldn't wear pink, but on Erika, especially with her hair pulled back, the effect was stunning. She was carrying a white and blue casserole dish covered with foil.

I didn't much feel like talking to Erika or anybody else, but since she was chugging in my direction bearing food for my starving children, I really had no choice in the matter.

"Erika! How good of you to come."

She greeted me soberly. "Eva called and suggested I come right over."

"I'm very glad you did," I said, truthfully. "And thanks for bringing the casserole." I gestured back down Cedar Lane. "It's only fair to warn you, though, that there's a press conference going on, and it's a madhouse over there. They should be wrapping up soon."

"Don't worry." She smiled grimly. "I have plenty of experience dealing with the press."

I'll bet you do, I was about to say, remembering that Erika had been all over the news when a firm she used to work for had been defending a Baltimore slum lord against charges of flipping houses. "We could use some advice, I guess."

Erika looked me up and down, taking in my crumpled sweat pants, tank top, and hoodie. "How are *you* doing, Hannah?"

"I'm doing okay, under the circumstances, but I'm really worried about my daughter. The FBI has been trying to prepare us for all eventualities, but some of those eventualities are more than Emily can take. Everything they say just seems to upset her. My sister-in-law is with her right now, but I would appreciate any suggestions."

Erika hoisted the casserole dish. "I'm not sure a turkey-noodle casserole will do much to help in that department, but I'll give it a try." She studied me thoughtfully. "I'm sure you're aware that I do quite a bit of pro bono work."

I wasn't, but didn't want to admit it. "Yes?"

"I'm a passionate advocate for children's rights, for

one thing," she told me, "and fortunately, my firm encourages my efforts. Recently I worked with Amnesty International seeking asylum for a woman who'd fled to the United States with her seven-year-old daughter to prevent the daughter from being subjected to female genital mutilation."

I shivered. Chloe would be seven next year! Just thinking about the torture female children were subjected to in the name of cultural tradition made me ill. And the practice wasn't limited to third-world countries, either, I'd heard. "Tell me you were successful."

"Oh, yes," Erika said, in a tone of voice that suggested that once she was on the case, you'd better lend her a hand, or get the hell out of the way.

"Thank goodness!" I glanced at my watch. "Oh, gosh, it's getting late, and I have to pick up my grandchildren from school."

"Don't let me keep you, then."

I smiled a genuine smile of gratitude. "Thanks, Erika."

She'd taken several steps past me, and then turned back. "Hannah?"

"Yes?"

"I'm sure the police are doing an excellent job with their investigation, but I know from experience that there are other things we can do that might improve our chances of getting Timmy back. And time is of the essence."

"I know that," I said. "And we're prepared to do whatever it takes. *Anything.*"

"Good. Well, you'd better get on with picking up your grandkids, we can talk later. Will you be coming back here?"

I shook my head. "Not tonight. We've decided it's

better for Chloe and Jake to stay with Paul and me." I indicated the bag I was carrying. "Emily picked out some clothes for the children to wear over the next couple of days, but in her rattled state, she didn't do a very good job of it, I'm afraid. It's a good thing I checked, because Emily'd forgotten the socks and the underwear."

"Is anyone with her, then?" Erika took a breath. "A woman, I mean. Husbands aren't always the best choice in times like this, I've discovered."

That was certainly the truth. Dante had been trying to help, Lord knows, but Emily had seemed inconsolable.

"Her aunt is with her," I said.

"Good. Good. Well, I'll see you later, then."

See you later. That, as it turned out, was the understatement of the century.

CHAPTER 11

The next morning, to avoid the press corps that was camped out like Boy Scouts in my daughter's driveway, I parked in the next block, cut through the neighbor's backyard, squeezed under a split rail fence, and let myself in through the back door.

To my surprise, my baby sister, Georgina, was in the kitchen, fixing coffee. I hadn't seen her since her new baby, Tina, was born six months ago.

"Georgina!" I spread my arms wide and gave her a hug.

"Careful, or you'll spill the coffee." She set the grinder down on the counter. "So good to see you, Hannah. I've been trying to get to Annapolis for several days, but with the kids . . ." She shrugged. "I just couldn't bring the kids."

"I understand. How are they?"

"A handful."

"I'll bet." Sean and Dylan, the twins, were nearly nine, and their younger sister, the wise, witty, and wonderful Julie, was seven going on twenty-seven. "And Scott?"

"Bitching and moaning. I simply told him I was

coming down to help out and he would be in charge of the children. It's not like he has to drive to the office or anything."

"I thought he was going to share an office with some other CPAs."

Georgina stuffed a paper filter into the coffee machine and tapped the fresh grounds into it. "I wish. It's always wait until this account comes through, or that one." She sighed. "I'm afraid I'll never get him out of the house."

"You make it too comfortable for him."

"I guess I do. Maybe I should stop cleaning up after him. Once the papers reach his ears, maybe he'd take the hint." She grinned.

I grinned, too, pleased with how normal my sister sounded. Her new shrink deserved a bonus.

"What's happening?" I asked. "Any news?"

"No, and it just breaks my heart. If anything happened to our little Tina . . ." Georgina dabbed at her eyes with the paper towel she'd been using to blot water up from the counter. "I can't imagine what Emily's going through. I took her some hot tea with honey a few minutes ago, and she looked like she'd been run over by a truck."

"I know."

"Dante's with her now, trying to get her to drink some of it."

"Good," I said, somewhat distracted by a noise wafting in from the direction of the driveway. I raised a hand. "What's that?"

Over the gurgle of the coffeemaker, what began as a murmur became a dull roar. One shout, then another, and another. Then silence.

Dante met us coming down the hall. "What the hell? Just as I got Emily settled down." He muscled his way past us to the living room window, drew the drapes aside and peered out.

"What is it?"

"The reporters are talking to somebody."

I hurried to the window and opened the curtain just wide enough so that both Georgina and I could see what all the fuss was about.

The press was interviewing a woman who stood before them, her fingers laced primly together at her waist. She was dressed in a long black skirt, a tailored white shirt, and wore a shawl with a peacock feather design fastened at the shoulder in a bulky knot. Her eyes were just visible under a coarse black fringe that looked like it'd been nibbled by a small and very hungry animal.

"I don't recognize her, do you?" Georgina said.

"No."

"What's going on, then?"

"I don't know, but I'll find out."

I'd just opened the front door and stepped out onto the stoop when the woman extricated herself from the clot of reporters and hurried up the driveway toward the house. As she got closer, I saw that her eyes were rimmed in black. Eyebrows had been painted on generously with a pencil. She had pink cheeks never dreamed of by Mother Nature. Clearly, a woman not in the habit of studying herself in the mirror each morning, wondering if she was wearing too much makeup.

She lifted her skirt slightly as she climbed the steps. "Mrs. Shemansky?"

I had to admit being flattered at being mistaken for my daughter. "No. I'm Emily's mother. How can I help you?"

"Is Mrs. Shemansky in?"

Dante squeezed past me. "*Mr.* Shemansky is in. How can I help you?"

"It is I who can help you," she said, her glossy red lips pulling back over impossibly white teeth. "At least I hope so."

As we stood on the stoop with our mouths agape, she continued. "I beg your pardon. I'm so nervous I forgot to introduce myself. I'm Montana Martin. Perhaps you've heard of me."

From our silence, she could only assume not.

First an author named Nevada, then an actress named Dakota, now Montana? The next thing you knew, some fool would name their daughter Mississippi.

"I'm a psychic detective," she told us. "I've worked with police departments all over the country. Perhaps you've heard of the Lonnie Edwards case?"

Dante shifted his weight from one foot to another. "No."

"Well, it's like this. I see, and talk to dead people."

I didn't know Emily had come out of her bedroom until she screamed. "Oh my God! Timmy's dead!"

"No, no!" Montana shouted, straight-arming her way past Dante and into the foyer, homing in on the woman she had correctly identified as the missing child's mother. "Timmy's *not* dead. That's what I came here to tell you. When I was reading the newspaper this morning and saw his picture, I had a vision about Timmy. I want to share it with you."

"Look, Miss Dakota—" Dante began.

"Montana."

"Whatever. I can't have you barging into my home and upsetting my wife."

"I have a gift, Mr. Shemansky. I use it to help people." She raised a white and ringless hand. "I don't want any money. Just listen to what I have to say, and then either believe me or not."

"Let her in, Dante. It can't hurt to listen." To Montana Martin, Emily said sweetly, "Please, let's go somewhere and sit down."

"Wait a minute," Agent Crisp interrupted just as we were getting settled in the living room. "I've heard of you and your work, Ms. Martin, but it's only fair to warn you, as I'm sure you're already aware, the FBI doesn't use psychics. If we did, we'd have to follow up every crackpot who showed up with a map and a dowsing stick, and we'd be digging up half of Anne Arundel County."

At the mention of digging, Emily gasped.

From the overstuffed armchair nearest the fireplace Montana Martin said, "Timmy's not dead, Mrs. Shemansky. I feel that quite strongly. In my vision, he's on or near the water."

The city of Annapolis is on a peninsula, virtually surrounded by water, so that wasn't a particularly startling revelation.

"And I have an equally strong impression that the person or persons who are holding your son are Asian.

"Asian?" Emily, who had been sitting in the chair next to Montana Martin leapt up and grabbed both the psychic's arms. "Cambodia is in Asia. So is Thailand. Timmy's been stolen for the child porn trade! He's going to be raised as a sex slave!"

Dante dragged his wife away from the clearly flustered psychic and made her sit down on the sofa, where she continued to sob.

"That is highly unlikely, Mrs. Shemansky," Agent Crisp said. "Sadly, there is a surplus of desperately poor children in Southeast Asia for perverts to prey upon. There'd be no need to import them. Besides, we have all the airports and ports covered. If anyone tried to take your son abroad, they'd have to have a passport."

Beside me, Georgina muttered, "Passports can be faked."

"Please," Montana interrupted, raising a hand. "Let me clarify. There's nothing tropical about my visions, so if I'm right, it can't be southeast Asia." She leaned forward, resting her hands flat, fingers splayed on top of her knees. "Japanese, or Korean," she said, switching latitudes more than forty degrees northward. "Or Chinese." Her eyelids fluttered. "Yes, definitely Chinese."

"What bullshit," Georgina huffed.

"Look," Montana interrupted. "My visions are simply that. Visions. I'm the first to admit that sometimes I get it wrong. Or, I might misinterpret what I'm seeing." She covered her eyes with her hands for a moment, then folded them in her lap. "Once I saw a child in a jungle, but it turned out he'd wandered into a nursery hothouse and had fallen asleep under a tray of orchids." She shrugged. "I have a strong feeling your son is alive, though. I hoped that would be a comfort to you."

"It is," Emily sniffed.

"Do you have an object that belonged to Timmy that I might hold, to see if I can pick up any more impressions?"

"Just a minute." Dante dashed down the hallway, returning in less than a minute with a stuffed monkey.

"The police have taken everything else, I'm afraid." He held the monkey out, its tail dangling.

Montana Martin took the monkey in both hands and closed her eyes.

No one breathed, not even Amanda Crisp.

After several minutes Montana shook her head. "Nothing. I'm sorry. Are you sure this is Timmy's toy?" She handed the monkey back to Dante, where it hung dejectedly from his fingers.

"Maybe it's been compromised," Dante suggested. "Our dog chewed on its tail."

"Possibly." Montana managed a weak smile.

"Well, thank you for coming," Emily said.

Montana stood up, smoothing her skirt. "May I call you if something comes up?"

"Of course," Emily said.

I walked Montana to the door. "I certainly trust you haven't given my daughter false hope," I warned the psychic as I twisted the dead bolt that would unlock the front door.

Montana reached into her handbag and handed me her business card. "Timmy's alive. I'm sure of it."

Fingering the card, I stared into her sincere, unblinking eyes, and found myself almost believing her. "Good-bye," I said.

Montana placed a black-booted foot onto the stoop, and the reporters surged forward. She turned back around, as if she'd rather face me than the unruly mob. "Hannah? It is Hannah, isn't it? Your mother says to tell your father that she wants you to have the emerald ring."

"What? How did you . . . ?" Only my mother and I had known how much I'd coveted that ring.

Montana smiled enigmatically before being swallowed up by the sea of reporters.

As I closed the door behind her, I heard Georgina say, "We'd be better off getting a Ouija board."

"How could Montana Martin possibly know about Mom's ring?" I asked Paul later that night as I lay in bed, my head resting comfortably on his chest.

Paul aimed the remote at the television and shut it off. "Maybe she knew your mother."

"That's possible, I suppose."

"Otherwise, it was just a lucky guess, Hannah."

"But Mom's ring *is* an emerald," I insisted.

"As I said before, a lucky guess. If she'd said 'sapphire,' you would have gone, 'Oh, yeah, sure,' and promptly forgotten about it. But since she guessed correctly, the woman's got you believing she's Karnack the Magnificent or something."

" 'There are more things in heaven and earth, Horatio, than are dreamt of in your philosophy,' " I quoted.

Paul dropped the remote to the carpet, turned and buried his lips in my hair. "Hannah?"

"Ummm?"

"Do shut up."

For that small moment in time my whole world consisted of that room, that queen-size bed, that incredible man, his arms wrapped protectively around me. Warm and secure, I wanted desperately to believe that nothing bad could ever happen to me or to anyone I loved.

"You want me to stop babbling?" I whispered.

"Uh huh."

"And you'll make it worth my while?"

"I promise."

And he did.

CHAPTER 12

I arrived at Emily and Dante's house at nine the following morning to find Georgina gone and Erika in charge of the kitchen, making a fresh pot of coffee.

I was relieved to see that Emily was up, dressed in a clean T-shirt and blue jeans. She'd even taken the time to wash her hair. While it dried, she wore it in a loose ponytail that hung down her back, leaking water in a damp semicircle around the collar of her shirt. She sat at a square table in the breakfast alcove and, with surprising energy, was tapping something into the family computer

Erika stood near the sink, grinding coffee beans.

" 'Morning." I called out, depositing a box of doughnuts from Carlson's Bakery on the counter. "Any news?"

Special Agent Crisp appeared in the doorway from the dining room, yawning and stretching. "I'm afraid not."

Emily lifted her hands from the keyboard and rested them in her lap, giving me her full attention for the first time in several days. "It's been quiet so far, Mom, but everytime the phone rings, I practically have a heart attack."

"Where is everyone?" I asked, looking around.

Erika twisted the tap and started to fill the coffeepot with water. "Connie sacked out in the guest room about five this morning. Dante's gone to the spa to meet with somebody-or-other. I took the call." She wrinkled her brow thoughtfully. "A Mrs. Strothers, I think."

Hoo-boy. I wondered what was so important that Phyllis felt it necessary to pull Dante away from his family at such a critical time. It could have been *good* news, I supposed, like she was reaching into the commodious Strothers Family pockets to post a generous reward for Timmy's safe return, but I wasn't placing any bets on it.

"Dad and Ruth went out to Kinkos to get posters duplicated," Emily told me. "Then they'll start distributing them. Connie made up a list."

"Posters?"

Emily pushed her chair back, rose, and stood behind it, optimism lighting her face. "Erika's incredible. She put us in touch with BeyondMissing.com. They have online software that makes it easy to create a missing child poster and print it out. Come see what we've done."

Erika smiled modestly. "BeyondMissing was founded by the father of Polly Klaas, and partially funded by DOJ. They're only one of more than a dozen organizations that do an amazing job of getting the word out about lost children."

I stayed anchored to my spot by the refrigerator, not the least bit interested in seeing the poster Emily had made. Just imagining Timmy's cherubic face smiling out at me from a missing child poster in the post office or from the side of a milk carton made me hyperventilate. *Get a grip, Hannah!* If Paul and Ruth were out canvassing the town, I knew it wouldn't be long before

Timmy would be staring out at me from the bulletin boards of every fast food restaurant, gas station, and shopping mall in the state of Maryland.

Agent Crisp lifted the top of the Carlson's box and considered the options before selecting a chocolate-covered doughnut for herself. "We put in a request to the National Center for Missing and Exploited Children, too. NCMEC faxed Timmy's picture and vital statistics to their network of more than 26,000 law enforcement agencies, FBI field offices, state missing children's clearinghouses, the Border Patrol, and med—" She stopped in mid-sentence and took a bite of her doughnut, then chewed thoughtfully.

I knew what she'd been about to say: medical examiners. I stole a glance at Emily to see if she'd noticed, but she'd resumed work on the computer, seemingly oblivious.

I wondered how long it would be before Crisp began asking Emily for DNA samples. *Medical examiners.*

Suddenly, I needed something stronger than coffee.

"NCMEC's already contacted *America's Most Wanted*," Agent Crisp added. "Are you familiar with the program?"

"Yes," I said. "It's hosted by John Walsh, Adam Walsh's father." I filled a glass with cold water from the tap in the refrigerator door and took a stabilizing sip. Adam Walsh. Polly Klaas. Murdered children with foundations named after them. I shivered.

Crisp licked the chocolate off her fingers. "They'll be running a public service announcement about Timmy on their program this Saturday night. Fox network, at nine."

"You've mentioned NCMEC several times, Agent Crisp. What's NCMEC?" I asked.

"Timmy's picture is already up on the NCMEC website," Erika cut in.

"And we've got it up on FBI dot gov, too," Agent Crisp was quick to add, with a sideways glance at me.

In the next few minutes I learned that the National Center for Missing and Exploited Children had a network so extensive that less than forty-eight hours after his disappearance, Timmy's picture was already appearing on the websites of Nation's Missing Children Organization, Child Quest International, Laura Recovery Center, the Jimmy Ryce Center for Victims of Predatory Abduction, the Maryland Center for Missing Children, and similar organizations throughout the United States and abroad. His face and vital statistics would pop up on tens of thousands of computer screens, courtesy of websites that linked to BeyondMissing's banner alerts, which rotated from missing child to missing child every ten seconds. It seemed to me that the FBI was on top of things, and I wondered how Crisp felt about Erika, who wasn't even a family member, now that she'd entered the picture, seemingly intent on treading all over Crisp's highly polished government shoes.

"Don't you have to work today, Erika?" I asked.

"I requested the rest of the week off." Using a paper towel, Erika scrubbed vigorously at the countertop surrounding the coffeepot. "Emily told me you could use an extra pair of hands." She shrugged. "My firm is used to my going off pro bono like this."

Connie chose that moment to stagger in, kneading her tired eyes with her fingers. "I smelled coffee," she said. "Nature's alarm clock." She poured herself a mug, selected a cinnamon doughnut, then wandered over to the refrigerator, rummaged in it until she found the orange juice. "Anybody?"

"Sure," said Emily.

Connie poured her niece a glass, and set it on the table next to the keyboard. I watched as Emily slipped her fingers into the pocket of her jeans and pulled out a blister pack containing several pills. She popped a tablet out of the pack and into her mouth, chewed it, then washed it down with a gulp of orange juice.

"What's that you're taking, Em?" I asked.

"Can't remember. Rema-something."

Connie gave me a look. "One of her friends brought it over. Judy somebody-or-other."

"Is it a prescription?"

Emily clicked the mouse, and pages began to spew out of the printer. "I guess so."

Sometimes my daughter hadn't the sense God gave a goose. This was the same good sense that inspired her to drop out of school to follow the rock band, Phish, for several months out of her young life. I wondered if Emily's lackadaisical attitude toward prescription medications dated back to that troubled time when everything was relentlessly share-and-share-alike.

I played the mother card, although I hated myself for it. "Emily, do you think it's wise to be taking drugs that are prescribed for somebody else?"

Emily rolled her eyes. "It didn't kill Judy, so it's certainly not going to kill me."

Before I could counter with words I might be sorry for later, Connie stepped in to defuse the situation. "Amanda? Anything happen while I was sleeping?"

Amanda. Connie and Agent Crisp were on a first name basis. They must have bonded over the long night they had just spent together.

"I'm afraid not. We've been working on Timmy's poster." Agent Crisp snatched one of the pages out of the printer tray and passed it to Connie, who happened to be standing next to me. Under the circumstances, I couldn't avoid looking at it.

MISSING CHILD ALERT
Timothy Gordon Shemanski
Last seen . . .

I blinked rapidly, fighting back tears, skimming to the bottom of the poster:

2.5 feet tall
30 pounds
Red hair, green eyes

They'd used the snapshot that I kept in my wallet, and added a second one of Timmy in three-quarter profile, cuddling Lamby under his dimpled chin.

"Excuse me." Hand pressed to my mouth, I fled the room. I made it to the bathroom just in time.

When the tapping began, I ignored it. I was sitting on the chenille toilet lid cover, using both hands to press a cold, wet washcloth over my face.

"Hannah?" The tapping turned to knocking. "Are you all right in there?"

"I'll be out in a minute, Connie."

I hung the washcloth on the towel rack to dry, and examined my face in the mirror. I'd aged ten years in a few short days. I needed a haircut, badly. My tongue tasted like I'd been licking dirt off the sidewalk.

I slid the door to the medicine cabinet to one side, hoping to find some mouthwash to rinse the taste of bile out of my mouth. I rummaged unsuccessfully through the bottles—rubbing alcohol, nail polish remover, cough syrup (expired)—then turned my attention to the plastic bins Emily used to organize her odds and ends. Plastic razors, sample packets of shampoo, cotton balls, a comb with the American Airlines logo AA stamped on it, and—ah-ha!—a similarly marked cellophane packet containing a toothbrush and a miniature tube of toothpaste.

As I was sliding the door shut, I noticed another container on the top shelf filled with random packets of pills—pills in blister packs, pills in foil, pills and capsules sorted by color into mini-plastic Ziploc bags. Curious, I pulled the container down and dumped it out on the Formica counter. Among the cold tablets and remedies for diarrhea and acid indigestion, I counted four pink pills marked Paxil 20 and six yellow pills marked Amitrip 25.

Jeeze Lahweeze!

I pawed through the pile, sorting as I went. Valium, Percocet, Oxycodone, Efexor, Zoloft, Wellbutrin. Emily was stockpiling painkillers and antidepressants. That plus the "Rema-something" she'd just swallowed in the kitchen made six. I wondered if her doctor knew. I wondered if Dante knew.

Ten years ago I would have had a knockdown-drag-out confrontation with my daughter, then tossed the pills one by one down the garbage disposal.

Now? I wanted to bring it up with her, but Emily was no doubt too stressed for anything I could say to register. Knowing how she would feel about my snooping around in her medicine cabinet, I returned the pills to the container and put it back where I'd found it. Eventually I'd end up speaking to Dante about them, especially in light of Emily's temper tantrums on Monday night. Overwrought and over-medicated, a volatile combination.

I ran the airline comb through my hair, brushed my teeth, and returned to the kitchen, where I found everyone except Emily talking into their cell phones. I poured myself a cup of coffee, trying to pick up the gist of the three one-sided conversations going on around me.

Amanda Crisp was giving directions to someone in Quantico who was going to speak at the press conference at two if he could navigate his way around the ongoing construction on I-95 North.

Connie was issuing instructions to an associate at Kinkos about making "Timmy" buttons. From the deliberate way she spoke, I gathered that English was a second language for the hapless associate. Either that or Kinkos was hiring six-year-olds these days.

Meanwhile, Erika stood at the window, staring into the backyard, cell phone pressed to her right ear, hand covering her left, going—*um, ah, no way, my God, you're shitting me, right?*—until I was wild to know what the party on the other end of her cell phone was telling her. Erika had just exploded with a particularly vigorous *Oh my God!* when my own cell phone burst into the opening bars of Mozart's Symphony No.40.

That would be Paul.

I took the call in the living room. "What's up?"

"Just checking in, sweetheart. I'm with Ruth."

"Where?"

"At Safeway, out near Best Buy. We've just finished postering the mall. Dennis is doing south county, and I was thinking if you'd meet us here and pick up some posters, maybe you and Ruth could take care of the grocery stores in Crofton so I can get back to the house in time for the press conference."

The posters. I swallowed hard. How could I not agree to hang up posters, plaster the whole world with posters if it came to that, for Timmy's sake?

I must have been quiet for a long time because I heard Paul say, "Hannah? You there?"

"Yes, I'm here."

"Good. We'll be waiting in Safeway at the Starbucks counter. I'll order you a mocha frappaccino for the road," Paul said, not doubting for a moment that my answer would be yes.

In the time it took me to finish my conversation with Paul, press the End button, and rejoin the other women in the kitchen, Agent Crisp had pulled up a chair and was sitting next to Emily at the computer. Connie stood just behind, sipping from a bottle of springwater. Erika still stood at the window, cell phone glued to her ear.

Agent Crisp glanced up as I entered the room. "Come, take a look at this."

I'd made it halfway across the kitchen when whatever curiosity I might have had about what Amanda Crisp was looking at was driven straight out of my head by the shrieks of Ms. Erika Rose, Attorney-at-Law. "Why are you just now telling me this, Andrew?"

Four heads swiveled Erika's way.

"What do you mean you had to keep it under wraps?"

Connie poked my arm and mouthed, *What?*

I shrugged.

"Ohmahgawd!" said Erika Rose. "Oh. My. God."

Erika must have sensed four pairs of eyes staring at her, boring into her back, because she turned around about then, wide-eyed, and flapped her free hand in our direction. "That is so fanfuckingtastic!" she said into the phone. "I am so psyched." And then, "Yeah, yeah. I got it."

"What?" I said aloud.

"Yeah, what? What?" echoed Connie.

Erika held up her hand, palm out, signaling patience. I didn't know about the others, but the suspense was killing me. There could have been a breakthrough in the search for Timmy, George Bush could have resigned his presidency, or maybe one of her girlfriends had just gotten engaged. It was impossible to tell.

"Okay," Erika said, wrapping up the conversation at last. "I'll be right over."

With her thumb, Erika pressed down on the End button of her cell phone, a self-satisfied grin spreading across her face. She puffed air out through her mouth. "Sorry, girls, but I have to go."

Emily leapt to her feet. "Is it Timmy?"

"No, sorry, Em. I would have told you if it were Timmy, you know that."

"Then, *what*?" I repeated.

Erika scanned the room until she located her handbag in the corner where she'd tossed it, shouldered the bag, tucked her cell phone into an outside pocket and headed for the kitchen door. "Well, ladies. Something I've been working on for quite some time is about to hit the fan big-time, but in a very good way." She disappeared into the hallway.

We stood there like statues, our mouths slack, staring at the empty space where Erika's back had just been. "Does that mean we've just got one less volunteer?" I asked of no one in particular.

Suddenly, Erika's face reappeared around the door frame. "You can't get rid of me that easily, Hannah Ives." Her teeth flashed white in the dim light. "Watch *Cross Current* tonight. NBC. Ten o'clock. You will not be sorry."

CHAPTER 13

In the bleak reality of day after endless day, at least Erika's breezy announcement gave me something to look forward to. *Cross Current* had been a highly hyped addition to NBC's fall lineup, successfully challenging CBS's popular prime-time news program, *60 Minutes*, in the television ratings wars. I couldn't imagine what connection Erika Rose might have to the show, but it had to be something controversial. If *Cross Current's* host, Mitch Harmon, ever showed up on your doorstep, it would be prudent to keep your mouth shut and duck out the back way, speed dialing your attorney as you went.

My sister Ruth had insisted on staying with me for the remainder of the day, lending both physical and moral support as we plastered public buildings and business establishments in Crofton with Timmy's poster, with the full cooperation of the various merchants. With her help, we finished in time for me to hustle back to Annapolis to pick up Chloe and Jake from school.

That evening, because they taunted me with it, I knew that Connie and Dennis were sharing a hot King Ranch chicken casserole with Emily and Dante, one of a half-dozen casseroles now overflowing Emily's freezer courtesy of the ladies of St. Catherine's Episcopal Church. Meanwhile, at our house, Ruth helped me fix dinner, or at least what passed for dinner those days: pizza. I dumped the ingredients for pizza dough into the bread machine, punched a button and let it do its thing, while Ruth kept her mind off things by chopping up assorted toppings.

After dinner, Ruth supervised bathtime upstairs, then picked up reading where I'd left off in the first Harry Potter. We'd been reading *Sorcerer's Stone* to the kids for what seemed like ages—Emily thought that *Goblet of Fire* was too violent. Downstairs, Paul helped clean up the kitchen, debriefing me on the press conference Ruth and I had missed that afternoon.

"I wish there were more to tell, Hannah, but at least there's no really bad news. Ron Powers reported that the Anne Arundel County police were still reviewing the shopping center videotapes." He handed me a dirty plate. "They're pretty bad quality, apparently, having been erased and taped over many times. Then the FBI profiler from Quantico made a statement suggesting that Timmy's kidnapper may have no intention of returning him to us."

"Oh, no," I moaned, feeling the pizza turn over in my stomach. "Poor Emily. That news must have really stung."

Paul grunted and handed me another plate. "Very disturbing. According to the profiler, when the victim is an infant, and the infant is abducted by a nonfamily member from a hospital or other location, not from a home, the abductor's motive often is to raise the child as her own. There have been cases of women who faked a pregnancy, then stole a child in an attempt to strengthen a crumbling relationship with a significant other. And other women who have miscarried, then snatched a baby to fill the void of darkness and despair brought on by the death of that child."

I retrieved the box of dishwasher soap from under the sink, poured some into the soap cup, twiddled with the dials, and slammed the door shut over the dirty dishes. "Damn! If that's the case, how will we ever find him? Or her." I'd been imagining the kidnapper as a man for so long that switching to the image of a woman was a major paradigm shift.

"Agent Crisp told the reporters that the FBI is checking hospital records," Paul continued. "They're trying to identify women who have lost children recently. At the press conference, Crisp urged the public to report anyone who has turned up unexpectedly with a baby, particularly if they haven't appeared to have been pregnant."

I grabbed a broom and started attacking the bits of cheese and vegetable scattered over the tiles. "It seems like such a long shot."

Paul smiled grimly. "I agree. But the other bit of news is more positive. According to Dante, Phyllis Strother is starting a reward fund for Timmy's safe return, and has contributed ten thousand dollars to kick it off."

I dumped the contents of the dustpan into the trash can. "Paul, that's wonderful! I take back every snide remark I ever made about the woman."

"The bad news is that the cops are dead set against it, the FBI included. Ron Powers in particular is concerned that offering a reward will result in a flood of false leads that will take valuable time away from the search for Timmy."

I began to work on the area nearest the stove. "But,

Paul, only one tip needs to pan out! Just one! If a reward helps motivate somebody to turn in the kidnapper, then I'm all for cleaning out our savings account to do it."

"I agree, and that's what I told Agent Crisp, especially since Emily and Dante are so keen on doing it." Paul gently removed the broom from my hands. "Sit down, Hannah. You're sweeping the pattern clean off the linoleum."

"We don't have linoleum."

"Well, sit down, anyway. Have some wine. Chill."

I plopped down in a chair, folded my hands primly on the table in front of me, and asked, "How does putting together a reward work, exactly? We can't set a table up in front of the Safeway and solicit donations, can we?"

"We've asked Jim Cheevers to help us sort that out. We need to make sure the terms of the reward are clear, otherwise we could get sued. It's happened. Jim recommends setting up a separate bank account for the donations, which somebody outside the family will control, of course."

"Do you think Hutch will be willing to do that? Ruth mentioned that he'd asked if there was anything he could do to help."

"Did someone mention my fiancé?" Ruth asked, wandering into the kitchen and waggling her magnificent 1890s-style engagement ring in my direction for what seemed like the umpteenth time.

Without asking, Paul refilled Ruth's wineglass and handed it to her. "We were wondering if Hutch might be interested in managing the reward fund for Timmy."

"I'll ask, but I'm sure he'll say yes. Should I call him now?"

Paul nodded. "If he's willing, please tell him that Cheevers will get in touch with him."

"So many people have expressed concern over Timmy, Hannah. I know they'll be willing to contribute," Ruth said, digging in her purse for her phone. "That reward fund will go sky high!"

Paul set his wineglass down on the kitchen table. "That may be true, but Agent Crisp advises that we settle on an amount for the reward in advance and keep it there. Otherwise, we might have tipsters waiting around for a more lucrative offer before calling in."

I gaped at my husband. "They'd *do* that? How appalling."

Cell phone attached to her ear, Ruth disappeared out the kitchen door, slipping into the backyard and the cool of the spring evening. Paul barely had time to refill our wineglasses before she was back, smiling with satisfaction. "Well, that's settled. Hutch will manage the reward fund."

"That means a lot, Ruth. Thank you."

Ruth joined us at the table. "I need to tell you something, Hannah. Upstairs just now? Jake asked me about the search for Timmy, and I didn't know quite what to say. So I simply told him that the police were looking everywhere for Timmy and that we hoped his baby brother would be home soon."

I felt my eyes fill with tears. "What else *can* we say? You did great, Ruth."

We sat quietly with our thoughts, sipping our wine. After a few minutes I rose and set my empty glass in the sink. "I'd better go upstairs and tuck them in." On my way out of the room I stopped behind Ruth's chair, stooped, and gave her a hug. "I can't tell you how much I appreciate your help, Ruth."

Upstairs, I found Jake already asleep, thumb in

mouth, a habit I hoped he'd outgrow one day. On the floor next to his bed lay his blanket, all in a heap.

In the next bed, Chloe had pulled her covers up to her chin, and she appeared to be sleeping. But when I drew closer, I noticed her eyelids quivering. The little scamp was faking it.

I picked up Jake's blanket and covered him with it. "Oh dear," I muttered as I tucked the blanket around Jake's solid, future soccer-player body. "Chloe's already asleep so I can't tell her good-night."

Chloe's eyelids flew open. "I'm not sleeping, Grandma!"

"So you aren't."

"Did I fool you, Grandma?"

"Utterly and completely."

"What's utterly mean?"

"It means completely."

Chloe's brow wrinkled. "So, I fooled you completely and completely. That's silly."

"I guess you're right, Chloe. You're too smart for me!"

Under the blanket, Chloe squirmed. "Will the bad man who took Timmy away take me away, too?"

I smoothed back her hair. "Oh, no, sweetheart. We will watch you every minute. He won't get you."

"Will the bad man steal Jake?"

"No, he won't."

Chloe seemed to be considering what I had said, then surprised me by asking, "Can I live with you forever, Grandma?"

"Don't you think your mommy and daddy will miss you?"

"Mommy's sad all the time."

"We're all sad, Chloe."

"That lady was sad, too."

The hair stood up on my arms. "What lady?"

"The lady at the ice cream store. She said I had pretty hair. She said she used to have a little girl like me, then she got sad."

"Did the lady work at the store?" I asked, struggling to control the quaver in my voice.

"Nuh-uh."

"What did the lady look like?" I asked, all the while thinking, *This is ridiculous. Lots of people stop to talk to children in stores.* I'd been known to make coochie-coochie-coo noises to children in shopping carts myself from time to time. Nothing unusual about that. But nothing about our present circumstances was the least bit usual, so I decided to press Chloe for information about this mysterious lady. "Do you remember what the lady looked like, Chloe?"

Chloe turned onto her right side, hugging her doll. "Like a lady."

"Was she an old lady or a young lady?"

"She was real old, like Mommy."

I suppressed a smile, hesitating to think what age bracket that must put *me* in, and moved on. "What color hair did the lady have?"

"Brown."

"What color were her eyes?"

"Dunno. She had sunglasses on."

"Was she fat, or was she skinny?"

"Skinny, like you, Grandma."

The little scamp got points for that, at least!

"Who else was with you in the ice cream store, Chloe?"

"It was Ben and Jerry's," Chloe said. "I got chocolate with sprinkles."

"Yum yum," I said. "Were Timmy and Jake with you at Ben and Jerry's, Chloe?"

"Uh-huh. And Daddy."

"Did your daddy talk to the lady, too?"

Chloe's head wagged vigorously from side to side on her pillow. "When Daddy brought me my ice cream, the lady went away."

"I see." I tucked an errant strand of hair behind her ear. "Thank you for telling me about the sad lady."

Chloe hugged her doll tightly under her chin. "Missy is sad, too."

I kissed my granddaughter on the forehead. "Good night, Chloe."

Chloe thrust her doll out. "Missy wants a kiss, too."

I planted a kiss on Missy's porcelain cheek. "Good night to you, too, Missy. See you in the morning."

I was halfway to the door when Chloe piped up again. "Grandma!"

"What, sweetie?"

"You forgot our prayers!"

In the subdued light from the bedside lamp, I hoped Chloe wouldn't notice me flushed with embarrassment. "Silly me."

I tiptoed past Jake and sat on the edge of Chloe's bed, resting my hand on the quilt where it covered my granddaughter's knees. "Let me hear your prayers, then, Chloe."

Chloe squeezed her eyelids shut, laced her fingers together, tucked her hands under her chin and began to pray.

"Jesus, tender shepherd, hear me,
bless thy little lamb tonight;
through the darkness, be thou near me,

keep me safe till morning light.
And God bless Mommy, and Daddy, and Jake, and Timmy, and Grandma, and Grandpa, and Coco."

Chloe took a deep breath, then squeezed her eyelids even more tightly together. "And tell Timmy I'm not really mad at him for chewing the fingers off my Barbie. Amen."

"Well done, Chloe," I said, and hurried into the hallway so she wouldn't see me cry.

When I got myself together, I left the children's door ajar, made sure the antique Mary Had a Little Lamb nightlight was burning on the table in the hallway, then wandered downstairs, feeling increasingly uncomfortable. The woman who spoke to Chloe at Ben and Jerry's could mean nothing. Or it could mean everything.

I rejoined Paul and Ruth in the kitchen and told them about my conversation with Chloe. "I think I should call Agent Crisp about this woman, don't you? Especially in light of what the profiler said at the press conference this afternoon."

"Absolutely," Paul agreed.

"Do you think Crisp will want to interview Chloe?"

Paul nodded. "If she doesn't, she's not worth what they're paying her."

"I wonder if Chloe will be able to tell Amanda Crisp anything she hasn't told me?"

Paul smiled. "The FBI has people who are experts at interviewing children, drawing information out of them. At least they always seem to do so on *Law and Order.*"

Ruth chimed in. "I'd mention it to Emily and Dante first, though. I'm assuming the FBI needs the parents' permission when they interview a child."

"Right," I said. "And there's always the chance that

Dante himself noticed something unusual about this woman. He might not have been so blind as Chloe thinks."

Once again I felt cold fingers of doubt creep along my spine. What if Dante had known the woman in the ice cream shop? What if he were in cohoots with her? I shivered and checked the clock. It was almost ten o'clock, time for *Cross Current* to begin. "Should I call now or wait until morning? I don't want to wake anybody up."

Paul scowled. "The FBI is working Timmy's case 24/7. Why would you consider waiting even for a single minute?"

Paul was right, of course, and I was an idiot. While he and Ruth migrated to the living room, I used the telephone in the kitchen to contact Amanda Crisp on her cell phone and report directly to her what my granddaughter had told me. I detected a reassuring note of optimism in Crisp's voice when she said that, indeed, the FBI had a child abuse unit specially trained to work with children, and she would encourage Dante and Emily to arrange for an appointment for them to talk with Chloe.

When I got back to the living room, Paul was aiming the remote at the cable box, scrolling down to Channel 4.

Aside from Erika's interest in the program, we still hadn't the slightest clue what the show was about. We'd kept the television turned off until the kids went to bed, so if NBC had been running any trailers about *Cross Current* that night, we'd missed them. Earlier, I'd checked the TV listing in the newspaper, but it provided no hints whatsoever to what person or institution Mitch Harmon would be skewering that evening.

Our wineglasses had miraculously refilled themselves, however, so we were prepared for anything.

Paul patted the spot next to him on the sofa. I sat

there, curled my feet up under me, and endured the final five minutes of some ridiculous reality show before the *Cross Current* theme music began.

"Good Evening. This is Cross Current, *and I'm Mitch Harmon. Several months ago we reported to you that the Internet has opened doors for pedophiles and child predators to enter, uninvited, into the privacy of our homes. Not only are children being lured into traveling to meet a person in the physical world whom they've met online, but pedophiles are traveling to our children! And it's happening worldwide."*

Ruth groaned. "Pedophiles! Erika thinks this is the kind of thing we need to watch right now?"

"She's a children's rights advocate, Ruth. She implied that she has some sort of connection with the show." I turned to Paul. "Maybe she's on it!"

"Shhhh," Paul ordered. "Just watch!"

I returned my attention to Mitch Harmon, as ordered. The reporter had a square face, handsome in a rugged sort of way, and a shock of wavy brown hair. At that moment his normally smooth thirty-something brow was deeply creased. Mitch and his brow disappeared, to be replaced by a slide show of men, all fairly normal-looking. The guy who changes the oil in your car. The teen who cuts your grass. The manager at the bank. Your next door neighbor.

In voice-over, Mitch continued, "*So many children are at risk, that we decided to go undercover, filling an upscale home in a Maryland suburb with hidden cameras. Soon, a long line of visitors came knocking, expecting to find a youngster they'd been chatting with on the Internet home alone. Instead, they found* Cross Current.

"To demonstrate the disturbing reality of what goes on in some chat rooms, we enlisted the help of volun-

teers from a vigilante organization called Predator-Beware. Volunteers of this controversial group are experts at pretending to be children online in order to catch and expose potential predators. One of these vigilantes is Debra Darden."

A new face filled the screen. Debra Darden looked to be about forty, with close-set brown eyes and a cap of blunt-cut gray hair.

"Debra, how do you, as a PredatorBeware operative, go about catching sexual predators?"

"Well, Mitch," Debra explained to the viewing audience, *"it's ridiculously simple. First we go into chat rooms, usually through AOL or Yahoo, and set up a profile of a twelve-, thirteen-, or fourteen-year-old . . . a profile that often includes a photo of a child who is quite obviously underage. Then we just sit and wait to be contacted by an adult."*

Somewhere off-camera another voice spoke low, as if reporting on a golf putt. *"Tony thinks he's coming to the house of a twelve-year-old boy whose parents have left him alone for the weekend. Tony has brought along a six pack of beer."*

We watched transfixed as a man who must have been Tony entered the kitchen wearing nothing but his smile and the six pack. Electronic fuzzing covered his naughty bits.

Ruth, who had been leaning toward the television screen, flopped back in her chair, covered her mouth with both hands. "Excuse me while I barf."

When confronted by the *Cross Current* team—who thoughtfully tossed him a dish towel—Tony claimed he simply felt sorry for the boy and he brought the beer along to go with the pizza he planned to order. He'd also brought along some DVDs.

On the hidden tape, Mitch looked visibly pained. *"And just where are you keeping those DVDs, sir?"*

Suddenly, Mitch was back in real time, still looking pained. *"Law enforcement officials estimate that fifty thousand predators are online at any given moment, and the number of reports of children being solicited for sex is growing."*

"Hello? Knock knock?"

I squinted at the screen, trying to make out the face of another man looking around, shifting uncomfortably from foot to foot at the back door of the decoy house. He wore a track suit and a ball cap, its bill slightly askew.

"Roger thinks he's coming to a house to meet a thirteen-year-old girl named Cyndi, apparently for sex."

Roger? Not many men named Roger these days. The only Roger I knew was Roger Haberman.

I watched in morbid fascination as the man in the ball cap entered the kitchen.

A youngish voice off camera, presumably the decoy, chirped, *"I've spilled Coke on my jeans. I'll be down in a minute. There's some chips if you want them."*

The man called Roger wandered around the kitchen for a minute or two, picked up the bag of chips and read the label, but didn't eat anything. Perhaps the percentages on the nutritional panel had alarmed him. Roger put the bag down, then looked straight up into one of the hidden cameras.

I grabbed Paul's arm. "Oh my God, it *is* Roger Haberman!"

Paul, who had charge of the remote, punched the volume up just as the real-time Mitch launched into: *"Roger thinks the girl in this house is a thirteen-year-old virgin home alone and willing to perform oral sex.*

But like many of the men you'll meet tonight, he's in for a big surprise when I walk out. Some think I'm the child's father, others believe I'm with the police. One thing's certain: none of them knows our hidden cameras are recording their every move and they'll be appearing on Cross Current."

Back in the kitchen, Roger was stammering to Mitch and the hidden camera, *"I've never done anything like this before."*

"And yet," real-time Mitch said, *"we learned that while Roger Haberman was living in California, he was twice convicted of a second degree sexual offense and served a year in jail."*

I felt like I'd been kicked in the stomach. Roger? *Eva's Roger* was a convicted sex offender? No wonder Erika had been so secretive about the television program. Erika served on the vestry at St. Cat's. But none of that explained how she knew about the program and what her connection with it was.

Mitch shook his head into the camera. *"You'll hear more from Roger a little bit later. First, there are more men headed to our house. Meet VAguy 23458. In his online chat with Debra he said, 'There's nothing in the world quite like a teenage body.' He's twenty-eight, and thinks he's talking to a fourteen-year-old."*

Paul hit the mute. "This is simply dreadful. Does Eva know, I wonder?"

"She has to know, Paul. She's been married to the man for over twenty years."

"I mean, does she know about this program?"

"Surely Roger told her about the broadcast, and if he was stupid enough not to, I imagine she'll know shortly. Her phone will be ringing off the hook."

Ruth, a loyal parishioner of First Presbyterian,

didn't know Eva Haberman. "This could ruin her marriage."

"Marriage? Ruth, she's a priest. This could ruin her life!"

"Ladies! The show's on."

Mitch was on camera again, talking with Roger. *"This is being taped for the record, you know, and for broadcast on* Cross Current *on NBC."*

Now that he knew the cameras were there, Roger tugged on the bill of his ballcap and turned his face away. *"Oh, no, guy. No."*

"But if there's anything else you want to say?"

Roger dipped his head. *"Nothing."*

We sat in numb silence for the rest of the hour, watching Mitch and his crew nab a rabbi, a soccer coach, a pediatrician, a school bus driver, and a guy who worked at the airport for TSA.

"So what happens now?" Mitch was wrapping it up. *"As they always do with law enforcement, the volunteers from PredatorBeware have turned over all of their online evidence, from the pornographic photos to transcripts of the online chats, to the Child Sex Crimes unit at the Montgomery County Police Department, which is actively looking at some of these cases. PredatorBeware has also posted the men's pictures and entire chat logs, including their phone numbers, on their website, PredatorBeware.com."*

Jeeze Laweese! Would I have the stomach to visit their website and read the details of Roger's chat with Cyndi? Of course I would, but I'd hate myself for it.

When the show was over and Ruth had returned to the home she shared with Hutch a few blocks away on Conduit Street, I rummaged in the kitchen cabinet behind the spices, where I'd kept my prescription medications since the grandkids came into our lives. I found one bright yellow sleeping capsule left over from my postreconstructive surgery. It had expired two years ago. I washed it down with a slug of club soda. It was the only way I could think of to get some sleep.

CHAPTER 14

The Feds moved fast, you had to give them that. At seven the following morning Dante telephoned us to report that the children wouldn't be going to school that day. He was driving them to the FBI office up in Baltimore to be formally interviewed. Although it would have been hard to refuse the FBI, I was relieved Dante hadn't dragged his feet on the matter. I took that as sign he had nothing to hide.

Our son-in-law arrived looking fashionably casual in clean chinos, a blue open-collared shirt, and loafer-style leather boat shoes. In response to my question about the woman at Ben and Jerry's, Dante replied, "I told Agent Crisp that I didn't notice anyone speaking to the kids, but I had my back to them while I ordered. It was kinda complicated. Chloe's very picky about her sprinkles."

"Tell me about it," I said, remembering that the brown sprinkles couldn't touch the red and white sprinkles, or we'd have to scrape them all off and start all over again.

"But if there's the slightest chance this woman was stalking us . . ." Dante's voice trailed off.

"Have they interviewed your neighbors?" I asked. "If

she were stalking the kids, maybe someone saw her hanging around the neighborhood."

Dante took a deep breath, let it out. "Agent Brown was talking to the neighbors yesterday, but nobody reported seeing anything unusual, I'm afraid."

"Any strange cars?"

"Nope."

I touched his cheek. "You look so tired, Dante."

"I was up half the night listening to Emily rave on about Roger Haberman."

"I tossed and turned, too. What a total shock. Did Erika tell you what her connection with the show was?"

"Erika's already at the house, but I didn't have time to ask. She and Emily have their heads together in the kitchen, plotting something." He sighed and leaned back against the door frame. "Frankly, if it will keep Emily occupied and distract her from her grief over Timmy, even for a moment, I'll be thankful."

"Still no ransom demand?"

"No. And this late in the game, the police doubt that there will be. And that means they'll be closing up shop at our place within a day or two."

Closing up shop. That was a blow. But then, we could hardly expect the FBI to stay at the house forever.

I steered the conversation toward less land-mine-strewn territory. "The kids have had some Froot Loops, and Chloe is helping Jake get dressed. Would you like some coffee while I go up and check on them?"

"Please."

"You know where everything is."

"Sure."

I had been thinking it was time to send the children home to their parents, particularly with the FBI presence no longer dominating the scene. But as I watched

Dante carry his burdens down the hallway, practically dragging himself into the kitchen, I knew I couldn't do it. Chloe and Jake would be our houseguests for the foreseeable future.

After Dante drove off with the children, I hightailed it over to Emily's, praying that Erika would still be there. I was dying to talk to her about *Cross Current* the previous evening.

Dante was right. While Agent Crisp and Ron Powers conferred at the large oak table in the dining room, Emily and Erika huddled in the kitchen, hunched over the computer monitor. They glanced up briefly at my *hi-how-are-ya*, but otherwise barely acknowledged my arrival.

"Put in 21401," Emily instructed Erika, who was driving the keyboard.

"Ten predators in that zip code," Erika said as she worked the mouse, "but Roger Haberman isn't one of them."

Still dressed in her pink terry-cloth Paradiso bathrobe, Emily leaned forward. "Try 21403."

Erika tapped away, then fell back in her chair. "He's not there, either."

Erika looked up at me as if noticing me for the first time. "Will you please explain to me, Hannah, why Roger Haberman isn't registered in the Maryland Sex Offenders Registry as required by Maryland law?"

"You're asking *me*?"

"What slime!" Emily made a face. "And to think I actually attended church with that man! He served me punch at the Christmas party! I shook his hand at the Paradiso party! Gross!"

"I wonder what's going to happen to Roger now that he's been outed?"

Emily stood up, tightened the belt of her bathrobe around her waist, and smiled with satisfaction. "PredatorBeware has turned over the transcripts of their conversation with him to the Maryland authorities. Hopefully they'll arrest him, and lock him away so he can't traumatize any more children."

"Mitch Harmon only touched on this in last night's special, Erika, but how on earth does PredatorBeware avoid being accused of entrapment by these guys once their cases go to trial?"

"The creeps hang themselves, Hannah. Do you have a minute?"

"Of course."

"Let me show you our website."

"Our?"

"I like to keep a low profile, but yes, I've been working with PredatorBeware for several years."

Erika typed in a URL, jabbed the Enter key with her forefinger, and waited for the screen to refresh. "This is the PredatorBeware Web page, and these are some of our latest busts," she explained, moving her cursor over several green tabs. Each had been labeled with a Yahoo or AOL screen name. Erika moved the cursor over the screen name of one of the latest busts—MDGUY4U—and clicked the link. Several options came up, along with—already!—a link to the *Cross Current* television show. Erika moved the cursor again, clicked, and I watched in wide-eyed wonder as Roger's picture materialized on the screen.

"Wait! I recognize that photograph. It's from the St. Catherine's membership directory!"

Erika grimaced. "He e-mailed that photo to thirteen-year-old Cyndi," she said. "But wait, that's not all."

Erika clicked on another link. "This is what Roger sent to Cyndi via his webcam."

I held my breath while Erika scrolled through a slide show starring Roger Haberman, tilted, slightly out of focus images all obviously captured by his webcam. Roger lounging on a sofa, grinning sappily. Roger bare-chested. Roger with his fly undone.

"Eeeek!"

Erika's forefinger hovered over the mouse. "Shall I go on?"

"God, no. I've seen more of Roger Haberman in the last few seconds than I ever want to see."

Emily raked her fingers through her long blond hair, working out the nighttime tangles. "What I want to know, Mother, is what makes guys think that looking at a photo of his, um, equipment, is going to turn a woman on?"

"It sure doesn't work for me," I told my daughter.

"Not to mention that it's totally against the law," Erika reminded us. "In almost every state it's generally a crime to send children obscene material, even if it turns out the recipient is an adult posing as a child."

"Sounds like Roger's toast," I said.

"Totally. For that alone. Now, let's take a look at some of Roger's chat with little thirteen-year-old Cyndi."

MDGUY4U: when is ur mom not there?

CYNDI_WITH_NO_FELLA: when shes at work r with her bf r out at the jim

MDGUY4U: so ur home alone?

CYNDI_WITH_NO_FELLA: yeppers

MDGUY4U: Mind if I call?

CYNDI_WITH_NO_FELLA: monday is my day off frm skool

MDGUY4U: Lucky u

CYNDI_WITH_NO_FELLA: for teachers meeting r sumthin

MDGUY4U: Kewl

CYNDI_WITH_NO_FELLA: lemme go see if moms got her stoopid skedule on da fridge

MDGUY4U: ok

CYNDI_WITH_NO_FELLA: shes off dis weekend

MDGUY4U: Kewl

MDGUY4U: wat u wanna do?

CYNDI_WITH_NO_FELLA: LOL I DONT CARE

MDGUY4U: DO U WANT ME TO SUCK ON UR TITTIES ?

Feeling ill, I scanned down the chat, all the way near the end where MDGUY4U had arranged to meet CYNDI_WITH_NO_FELLA and her titties at her home in Rockville, Maryland, which turned out to be the sting house where he would later get busted.

"Enough!" I cried.

But Erika chugged on. "And down here we have . . ." She worked the mouse, scrolling quickly to the end of the chat. "See here?"

CYNDI_WITH_NO_FELLA: whats ur number?

MDGUY4U: I cn get in trouble just talking to you. lol

CYNDI_WITH_NO_FELLA: lol. No 1 will ever no, silly.

MDGUY4U: ok

"The bastard knows she's underage." Erika snorted. "But watch how fast he sends Cyndi his phone number anyway."

While I stared in disbelief—this was my pastor's husband talking dirty here—Erika highlighted the phone number. "That's Roger's actual cell phone number. And that's my job."

"What do you mean?"

"I'm the verifier. I call the guy up, pretend to be Cyndi, and verify that he's for real." Her voice slid up an octave; she sounded no more than twelve or thirteen. "Oh, snap! Dad just walked in. He's so bunk."

Emily smiled. "Erika's got the lingo down pat."

"How do you sleep at night, Erika," I asked, "knowing all these perverts are out there lurking on the Internet?"

"I sleep because for every perve we catch, there are ten, maybe twenty, little girls and boys who won't be abused.

"Listen to this." Erika clicked around, then read an excerpt from another long, dirty chat.

" 'If you are interested, I could show you a few tricks.' And the child replies, 'What kind of tricks?' Then he IMs back, 'Let's put it this way. I am a little older and more experienced than you. I have been married and have tried many different things and can probably show you things that your boyfriend never even thought about.'

"It goes on and on," Erika said.

"Sick."

"What happens now, Erika?"

"My best guess is that the police will eventually come calling on old Roger and he'll be heading for the slammer."

But it wasn't Roger I was feeling sorry for, it was his wife, Eva.

My heart ached for my friend. I prayed she hadn't seen the broadcast—that would have been too cruel. "Poor Eva."

"What do you mean, 'Poor Eva'? She had to have known about this."

"Not necessarily."

"But she certainly knows now. And I, Erika Rose," she said with a flourish, "took the liberty of notifying the congregation via the St. Catherine's e-mail list."

"My God, Erika!" Even for a lawyer, the woman had chutzpah. "Isn't that list supposed to be used for church business only? No one wants to be swamped with used car notices and the latest religious jokes making the rounds on the Internet."

"Chill, Mom. I told her to do it."

"You?"

"I can't think of anything more relevant to the business of the church than to inform its congregation that their pastor is harboring a pedophile."

Erika demonstrated how easily we could e-mail anyone a link to Roger Haberman's special Predator-Beware Web page featuring his picture, his cell phone number, and the full text of his revolting chat room sessions with Cyndi, page after page of it. "We sent it to his boss on Monday, asking if this was the kind of guy they wanted working around the kids enrolled in the sailing program."

Cassandra Matthews would have found out about the *Cross Current* program soon enough anyway, but even so, I thought that Erika's actions were a bit over the top. Roger was guilty as hell, of coursc, and he'd brought it all upon himself, but with everyone ganging up on him, I worried about the guy. "He'll have some excuse to explain away his behavior," I suggested.

"They all do," Erika said. "You heard it on the show last night, didn't you? Same old thing. I've never done this before. I knew she wasn't twelve, I was just playing along. I'm here because I thought the house was for sale. How lame is that?"

"I'm a bit uncomfortable with it, to tell you the truth. At the end of the day, your group is just a bunch of vigilantes. It's the twenty-first-century version of tar, feathers, and running a guy out of town on a rail. Almost makes me feel sorry for some of them."

"Look, we're not totally devoid of compassion. We offer pedophiles the opportunity to post rebuttals, for example, and we'll actually remove them from the website if they can prove they're getting help. But, trust me, Hannah. These guys are dyed in the wool perverts. Do you want to see how ridiculously easy it is?"

"Convince me."

Erika relinquished her chair and motioned me over to the keyboard. "Have you ever signed up for an account on Yahoo?"

"Sure."

"Okay, then. Log on to Yahoo dot com and set up a new user ID."

While Erika and Emily watched, I tried half a dozen combinations before I came up with a screen name that hadn't already been used: Krazy_4_Katz.

"Now, go ahead and set up a profile."

With Erika coaching me, I filled in the blanks for Candy Williams. When I came to the section for date of birth, I closed my eyes and started counting backward, trying to come up with a date that would make Candy turn thirteen on her next birthday.

When I started to fill in the age blanks, Erika raised a cautionary hand. "Don't do that. If Yahoo thinks you're under eighteen, they won't let you into the chat room. Either lie or leave it blank."

"But how will the guy know that I'm only thirteen?"

"When the time comes, you'll tell him." She flapped

a hand. "Now, go on. Try out your ID in a chat room."

Erika showed me how to find the chat rooms, and suggested that I join one of the regional chats. There were chat rooms for every major metropolitan area. Washington, D.C., had five. I clicked my mouse and, simple as that, I was in.

"What now?"

"Now you wait."

I watched, alternately amazed and disgusted, by the amount of traffic scrolling by me in the room. People joined the chat, stayed for a while, and left. One strange, misspelled message repeated itself so many times that I was certain it was being generated by a robot. Hands off the keyboard, folded in my lap, I ignored them all.

"Some of these guys are just goofing off," Erika commented. "Others are probably kids pretending to be horny, thirty-five-year-old guys, but way too many are exactly who they say they are, and they'll end up arranging to meet the child."

After only two minutes a box popped up on my screen titled PM. DonnieWants2Screw had dropped in to say "Hi."

"It says PM. What does that mean, Erika?"

"Private message. That's where they'll try to lure you in."

"Do I want to talk to someone named DonnieWants2Screw? I don't think so."

"That's okay. Just wait."

After a few *Hello U Theres*, DonnieWants2Screw gave up and Randy_in_Rockville29 stopped by, desperate to talk to Candy, too. "What should I say?"

Erika shrugged, so I typed *Hi.*

A/s/l, Randy replied.

From reading the previous chats, I knew what that meant. Age, sex, location. I typed in *13/F/Rockville*, lying to Randy about everything except my sex.

Randy was twenty-nine, male, and lived in Rockville, if he weren't lying, too. *Got breasts?* He wanted to know.

A/s/l were the last keystrokes I ever sent in Randy's direction, but my dance card was far from empty. In just five minutes more than ten guys had PM'd Candy. I played along with one guy for a while, abbreviating willy-nilly and using words I had learned such as *kewl* and *lol*. When he started to get personal, though, asking whether I shaved "down there," I groaned and turned to Erika. "What do I say now?"

"Type POS," she said. "Parent Over Shoulder."

"Jeeze," I said, typing. I remembered that I'd first heard the term POS from Chloe, and she'd gotten it from her friend Sammy. I hoped it was innocent Internet slang passed down to an unsuspecting Sammy by an older sibling, but at least Chloe wouldn't be visiting with Sammy and playing on any questionable websites while she stayed with us.

"I wouldn't recommend pursuing that chat," Erika said, "but I guarantee you that if one of our volunteers got a hold of that guy, he would be arranging to meet Candy in a few days' time."

I logged out of Yahoo feeling dirty, like I needed to run the keyboard through the dishwasher set on scald.

"I don't imagine I'll be able to face Roger, but I will talk to Eva about him."

"Mother! How can you even go back to that church?" Emily's breath was hot against my cheek.

"Eva's my friend. I can't tell you how helpful she's been to me since Timmy disappeared."

Emily ignored me. "Erika, tell me how I can help with PredatorBeware. Do you think I could learn to be a decoy?"

"Emily!" I couldn't believe my daughter had volunteered for stressful work like that.

The look Emily sent me was pleading. "But what else can I do? Nothing is happening, and now the FBI thinks that the person who took Timmy did it because they wanted to keep him! There's no ransom demand. The tip calls are going to 1-800-TheMissing, and our phone just sits there, mocking me! I have to do something, and helping to get a pedophile off the street is a very good start."

I found myself agreeing. Eva was my friend, but I owed Roger nothing. I thought about watching *Cross Current*, and about what I'd just seen, and felt I needed to do a bit of outing myself. "I don't think there's any connection, but Roger was in the parking lot at Paradiso on the day Timmy disappeared. He'd come to apply for a job."

"Mother! Roger could have taken Timmy!"

"He didn't have Timmy when I saw him, Emily, and that was *after* we sounded the alarm."

"Timmy could have been drugged, and hidden in Haberman's trunk!"

"Emily, think! He'd have to get by the police roadblock."

"Maybe he had an accomplice, then," Emily continued. Lord, my daughter was hard to turn.

"Let me weigh in here," said Erika. "We know Roger is involved with children for sex. It doesn't take much stretching of the imagination to . . ." She paused, as if weighing what to tell me and what not. "Oh, hell. For all we know, Roger's been flying back and forth to Bangkok for years, paying to have sex with children. Maybe he can no longer afford the airfare."

I nearly gagged. "I really don't think so. Roger seems to like his victims young, but he also likes them female, and hovering on the cusp of puberty."

"Some people think you can cure a pedophile. I don't. They almost always reoffend, we know that, so whether Roger took Timmy or not, he needs to be off the streets, cooling his heels behind bars."

Emily set her lips in a firm line. "We'll organize pickets, won't we, Erika."

Erika nodded. "Damn straight."

Whatever Roger had done, I thought, Eva didn't deserve to be punished. She'd taken St. Cat's from a tiny congregation of one hundred communicants to upward of five hundred. We had a strong young program, a single parents' group, and one for swinging—well, maybe not so swinging—seniors. We supported a missionary couple in Guatemala.

I dug Eva's card out of my purse and punched her private number into my cell. I had to warn her that the pickets were coming.

CHAPTER 15

Why I felt like I had to ride off like Paul Revere, carrying the warning to Pastor Eva that the pickets were coming, the pickets were coming, I couldn't say. Perhaps it was the calm warmth of her voice when she picked up after the first ring, recognizing my number from caller ID. "Hello, Hannah. Please tell me you're calling with good news about Timmy." Typical Eva. When her own world must be falling apart, her first thought was for others. Either that or she hadn't a clue about Roger, which I found almost impossible to believe.

"No word about Timmy, I'm afraid. But I'd like to talk to you, if it's convenient."

"Of course. When would be good for you?"

"Are you busy right now?"

"I'll always have time for you, Hannah. You've caught me at the grocery store, but I'm heading for the checkout counter as we speak. Can you meet me at my office in about thirty minutes? I'll need to go home and put my groceries away first, so if I'm a bit late, just wait."

I thought about what I'd overheard of Erika's elaborate plans to plaster the West Annapolis neighborhood with flyers warning the residents about Roger, the pedophile in their midst, and about her decision to target St. Catherine's with her picket lines because of the church's "symbolic value." So, just in case she had already been able to muster her troops, I said, "Do you think we could meet at the parsonage instead?"

If Eva thought this was a strange request, she didn't say so. "Of course. I'll put the kettle on."

I left my daughter's home and drove straight out of Hillsmere, across Forest Drive and down Bay Ridge, feeling that my luck must be changing for the better because for once in my life I made all the lights. But my winning streak ran out at the foot of Sixth and Severn when the keeper of the drawbridge that joins the suburb of Eastport to Annapolis proper raised the span to allow a procession of sailboats to pass through to the bay from the inner reaches of Spa Creek. Stuck in traffic near Eastport Elementary, drumming my fingers on the steering wheel, grumbling to myself, I knew there was no good way to open up the subject of Roger with Eva, so I'd just have to wing it.

At the home she shared with Roger on Monterey Street, Eva was waiting for me. She escorted me immediately from the front door to her kitchen.

"Have a seat," she said, pointing to a white-painted table with matching chairs covered in a cheerful blue and yellow floral chintz. "I've got Earl Grey and lemon ginger," she said. "What'll it be?"

"Lemon ginger will be fine, Eva."

I watched silently while she poured hot water over the bag in my cup, then still at a loss for words, I decided to wade right in. "Eva, I watched *Cross Current* last night."

Eva's cheerful facade crumbled. Still holding the kettle, she said, "Yes. I suppose everyone did."

"Well, maybe not everyone, but I'm sure the word will be getting around."

Her face darkened. "And if anyone just happened to miss tuning in, they'll soon be able to pick up the program in streaming video off the NBC website."

I stared at her stupidly.

"I don't mean to minimize Roger's role in all this—his actions are reprehensible—but the way NBC went about it . . ." She swallowed hard. "The whole sordid mess makes me physically ill."

Seeing Roger's face turn up on my television screen had made me feel ill, too. If it had been *my* husband, I would probably still have been in seclusion, rather than toughing it out and facing it head-on, and talking to someone like me. "Did you watch the show, Eva?"

"No. I had been called out to the hospital, thank God, and I mean that 'thank God' quite literally, Hannah. Apparently I'm one of the last to know about that blasted PredatorBeware website, too." Eva shoved her mug aside as if she'd lost interest in it, and everything else.

"Roger didn't warn you?"

She smiled grimly. "Not until the e-mails started coming. Roger knew he'd been entrapped by PredatorBeware, of course, and he knew he'd been caught on tape by the *Cross Current* sting operation, but so were a lot of other men." She rested her forearms on the table and leaned toward me. "Roger was in denial, I think, crossing his fingers that his segment would be cut from the show."

"But even so," I said, "his photograph and the transcript of that chat he had with Cyndi would still be posted on the PredatorBeware website."

"Yes. And that's how I first heard about it, when someone sent me an e-mail helpfully informing me of the website, and providing me with the URL." She bit her lip. "I forced myself to read the transcript of Roger's conversation with Cyndi, then I threw up. It's still hard for me to believe that those salacious words came out of the mouth of the man I love." Eva suddenly remembered her tea, picking up the cup in both hands and taking a sip. "Roger lost his job, you know."

"No, I didn't."

Eva bowed her head and seemed to be examining the contents of her cup. "Cassandra Matthews got an e-mail, too. She fired Roger on Monday afternoon. He didn't tell *me* about it, of course."

Remembering Eva's friendship with Cassandra, I said, "I'm surprised Cassandra didn't tell you herself."

Eva shrugged. "I can't explain that. Perhaps she thought I was involved somehow."

"As if."

Eva grimaced.

Monday afternoon. So when I ran into Roger hanging about in the parking lot at Paradiso on Monday morning, he hadn't been unemployed, desperate, seizing on a spur-of-the-moment opportunity to kidnap a child. Somehow, I found that bit of information reassuring.

"Where is Roger now?" I asked.

"I don't know. He left home yesterday morning, after I pleaded with him to get help. Demanded, would be a better word. He's probably holed up at a motel somewhere."

"They said on the show that Roger had done time in prison. Is that true?"

She nodded. "That's where we met, actually. I was doing an internship as a prison chaplain. Roger was intelligent and so sweet that, frankly, I thought the charges against him had been exaggerated. He'd been through months of court-ordered therapy by then, and he eventually served his time. I thought he was well past his addiction, but even so, we dated for three years after his release. I wanted to be sure."

"And were you? Sure, I mean."

"Hannah, Roger and I have been married for more than twenty years." She buried her face in her hands and continued to speak to me through a gap in her fingers. "This has been a horrible shock."

"Did the bishop know about Roger's record?"

Eva laid her hands flat on the table. "When I got the call to St Catherine's, I consulted with the bishop about Roger, of course. Even though *no one* thought that Roger was likely to reoffend, especially after nearly two decades, they made it a condition of my taking the job that Roger not be involved in any activities involving children."

St. Cat's volunteers, I knew, had recently gone through a training program called Safeguarding God's Children, which mandated that all children's groups be supervised by two people—one male and one female—who were not related to one another.

"Yeah. I noticed except for special occasions, Roger pretty much stayed away from St. Cat's. Paul and I thought he was attending another church."

"He was. Roger's a Methodist."

"Have you talked to Bishop Williams?" I asked. Even thought the Right Reverend Ronald Francis Williams had only recently been installed as Bishop of Maryland, he would be Eva's spiritual advisor, the pastor's pastor, so to speak.

Eva nodded. "Ron's been incredibly supportive, Hannah. He's already issued a statement to the meda. I'm 'understanding, compassionate, and one of the most effective pastors he's ever worked with.' " Her face flushed. "But I doubt all those ten-dollar adjectives will do anything to head off the members of my flock who are clogging up cyberspace with demands for my immediate resignation."

I'd been cradling my mug in my hands, sipping tea from time to time, but I put it down on the table. "Eva, I'm so sorry. It's got to be devastating, both to you and to Roger. What made him backslide, do you think, especially after all these years?"

Eva didn't hesitate a second before answering. "It's that goddamn Internet. The Internet makes it far too easy for someone as vulnerable as Roger. Think about it! Before the Internet, Roger would have had to make a conscious decision to drive out to a Wal-Mart, wait around for a young girl to show up, make sure there were no surveillance cameras focusing in on him, before unzipping his pants and exposing himself." She sighed. "Now Roger has a computer. He's got a webcam. The chat rooms were beckoning. He could hide out on the other side of a computer screen behind an alias. Nothing happens face-to-face. No one gets hurt. It was seductive, and in the end, irresistible."

"What's Roger going to do now?"

Eva's eyes glistened with tears. "I don't know. He's a sick man, Hannah. That's crystal clear to me now. But I'm afraid the police won't be interested in getting Roger the help he needs. They'll throw the book at him instead."

I wracked my brain, searching for words of comfort, but based on what I knew about the Montgomery County police, Roger was in deep, deep trouble, and would more than likely do time in jail. No way to sugar coat that. "I'm afraid you're right, Eva."

Eva stared at me for a few seconds, then laid her head on her arms and began to sob.

I'd gotten up from the table to get her a tissue when the doorbell rang. *My gosh, Erika works fast!*

"Don't answer it, Eva." I handed her the tissue, and while she wiped her eyes, I heaped bad news upon bad news, explaining to Eva what I knew about Erika Rose and her group of vigilantes, their numbers so recently swelled by one with the addition of my own daughter. "Let's ignore them and have some more tea."

I reached for the kettle and covered my limp tea bag with hot water. We discussed what might be the best course of action for Roger, and I asked her if he had an attorney. "He's already called Dean James," she said.

I'd heard good things about Dean James. "Whenever a midshipman gets in trouble, James is a top choice. Roger's in good hands." I told Eva what I'd heard about one of James's cases, where a midshipman had been kicked out of the Academy because of his addiction to Internet porn. James had negotiated a medical discharge for the mid, rather than a disciplinary one. This was an important distinction because it meant that the mid, who was a first classman, wouldn't be asked to reimburse the Navy for the money they'd spent on educating him for four years: a cool $100,000 by their calculations.

Whoever was ringing the doorbell refused to give up. By the time I'd dunked my tea bag up and down a few more times, the ringing had stopped and the knocking began.

Half rising from her chair, Eva pressed her palms to her ears. "That pounding's driving me nuts, Hannah. It's impossible to ignore."

"Let me go," I said.

The knocking seemed to intensify as I hustled through Eva's tidy dining room, comfortable living room, and into the entrance hall. When I opened the door, I staggered back into the hallway in my attempt to avoid the microphone being thrust into my face. The microphone was at the end of the arm of a woman I recognized as an investigative reporter from WBJC-TV in Baltimore.

"If you're looking for Roger Haberman," I told the microphone, "he's not here. Reverend Haberman doesn't know where he is. If you have any questions, please refer them to Mr. Haberman's lawyer, Mr. Dean James. Thank you."

I shoved the door, and almost got it closed before the reporter shouted, "And who are you?"

"Nobody," I replied, relieved that I'd kept such a low profile during the press conferences involving Timmy's disappearance that I hadn't been recognized. "Just a friend of the reverend."

I'd pushed the door another millimeter toward the closed position when another reporter piped up, "Mrs. Ives! Mrs. Ives!"

Damn. I'd been busted.

"Mrs. Ives," the reporter continued while my eyes shot shrapnel her way. "Doesn't it concern you that Roger Haberman, a convicted pedophile and repeat offender, was seen in the vicinity of Spa Paradiso on the day your grandson was abducted?"

I wanted to punch the woman out, but I took two deep breaths, dug my fingernails into my palms and asked, "And you are?"

"Michele Pickett, one *l*, from the *Sun*."

"Ms. Pickett . . ." I paused, as if committing her

name to memory, with or without the extra *l.* "May I suggest that you ask the police about that."

This time I managed to shove the door shut and lock it behind me.

I returned to the kitchen, where my tea had grown cold. "It's the press," I reported to my friend. "I think we better start planning escape routes."

"You're serious, aren't you, Hannah?"

"Very."

As if to punctuate my remarks, the pounding began again, even louder, if that was possible. Fearing for the paint on Eva's front door, I headed back to the entrance hall, unlocked the door, threw it wide and opened my mouth to give the pesky reporters a sizable piece of my mind.

But it wasn't a reporter standing there. The reporters had retreated to a pair of noisy, raggedy lines on both sides of the sidewalk. What greeted me now were two men in suits who might as well have had "cop" written all over their chests in bright, flashing neon letters. Behind the cops stood another man dressed in slacks and a windbreaker, carrying a tool kit.

"Mrs. Haberman?" the tall cop asked.

"No."

"Is she here?"

"Who shall I say is calling?"

"I'm Officer Peter Cook with the Anne Arundel County police." He produced a badge and showed it to me. "We have a search warrant."

I waited until the two other officers had shown me their badges, too, then said, "I guess you'd better come in, then. Please wait here in the living room while I get Reverend Haberman."

I had more experiences with search warrants than I cared to admit, or remember. When the FBI came to arrest me for murder, they'd torn my house apart looking for evidence, going so far as to empty my flour canister and dump out my silverware drawer, although it's fair to say that they put everything back together afterward.

When I got back to the kitchen, Eva was standing next to the pantry door, using a kitchen knife to pry the top off a box of shortbread cookies.

"It's the police this time, and they've come with a search warrant," I told my friend.

She laid the box of cookies down on a nearby counter and glanced about the kitchen, waving the knife, eyes wide. "What should I do?"

"There's really nothing you can do about it, Eva. It's like emergency dental work. You just sit back and let it happen."

She drooped. "They'll be after his computer, I suppose."

"Right."

"And books, and magazines. Notebooks?"

"Uh-huh."

"And weapons?" The furrow deepened between her eyes.

"What do you mean, weapons?"

"I've got to tell somebody. Roger kept a gun in his bedside table. Now it's gone."

CHAPTER 16

My daughter screwed up her eyes. "How can you even *think* about going back to work?"

Dante captured both of Emily's hands in his and drew them to his chest. "I *have* to go back, Em, otherwise there won't be any money to pay the mortgage, or put food on the table. The ladies from St. Catherine's aren't going to cook for us in perpetuity, you know."

Emily jerked her hands away. "You should be ashamed of yourself for deserting Timmy."

"I'm not deserting our son, Emily. I'm doing what has to be done to maintain the health of my family including my other two children, and if that means returning to work, so be it. All of our money is tied up in Paradiso, you know that. If Paradiso fails, we're doomed."

"He's going back to work," Emily said to me, ignoring her husband, using the same petulant tone of voice she'd often used with me at the dinner table after an argument with her father: "Please ask your husband to pass the potatoes."

Dante turned to me, a can't-live-with-her-can't-live-without-her look on his face. "Phyllis says some of our investors have threatened to pull out if we don't open by Monday."

"I can't go back to that day care center," Emily pouted.

"You don't have to, Em. For the time being I can move Alison over to Puddle Ducks—if you approve, of course. She's actually a certified teacher."

"You don't understand what I'm saying, Dante. I can't *ever* go back to it."

A slight twitch along the jaw, a barely detectable narrowing of the eyes, were the only clues that this news bothered Dante. "Emily. I've told you all along. It's okay for you to stay at home with the children. You don't have to work your tail off at the spa."

Emily began to weep quietly. "But I *so* wanted Paradiso to be a success." She turned her devastated face to me. "It's been our dream for so long. We're so, so close, and now it's all falling apart."

I was worried, too. Now that Dante's grandiose plans for Paradiso seemed to be unraveling, so was his marriage.

I grabbed my daughter's hand and squeezed it tightly, surprising myself by saying, "Dante's right, Emily. He's the driving force behind the spa. You say you want it to succeed, right?"

Emily sucked in her lips and nodded.

"Then he's *got* to get back to it."

Up until then Connie had been sitting quietly in the corner of Emily's living room. Suddenly she spoke up, putting into motion a carefully orchestrated plan to get Emily out of the house and off Erika's picket lines. "Anybody up for a movie? *Do or Die* is playing at the mall. It got good reviews."

Emily rolled her eyes at her aunt, but at least she had stopped crying. "I don't feel like going to the movies."

"Yes, you do," I said. "It's all set. Dennis and Connie are taking Chloe and Jake to Chuck E. Cheese's, and you, your father, and I are going to the mall. We're having dinner at the food court, we're going to sneak home-popped corn past the ticket taker, and we're going to enjoy ourselves for a couple of hours."

I was enormously grateful that Connie had volunteered for the Chuck E. Cheese's expedition. Her stomach was far more galvanized than mine.

Reluctantly, Emily agreed to see the new thriller. She left the room to freshen up, and I was pleasantly surprised when she reappeared ten minutes later wearing a flowered sundress and sandals, her face glowing with the first touches of makeup I'd seen on her for days.

On the way to the mall, with Paul driving and Emily sitting in the backseat, it felt like old times, except back then we'd have been singing the traditional family round, "It's a Small World," in combination with "Ninety-Nine Bottles of Beer on the Wall," and laughing hysterically about it. There wasn't much to laugh about these days.

Paul parked the car near the Borders end of Annapolis Mall. We followed him in and loitered by the large ticket kiosk near Sears while he bought three tickets for the seven-fifteen showing. Tickets safely tucked into his breast pocket, Paul stood on the elevated deck that surrounded the food court, raised both arms as if he were Moses parting the Red Sea, and said, "Divide, and conquer."

As usual, the food court was a happening sort of place, bustling with men, women, and children, with teens strutting their stuff, showing off for one another and for whoever was on the other end of their cell phones.

I stood in a paralysis of indecision. Salads to the left of me, yogurt to the right. Ichiban, Little Panda, Mickey D's, and a thousand-and-one varieties of fast food in between. Paul headed off with determination for his monthly cholesterol fix at Steak-Escape, while Emily and I trundled off to see what was being offered on the Chinese buffet. Balancing the food on our trays, we headed back to find a table, catching sight of Paul, who nodded at a vacancy near the escalators that carried movie-goers up to the theaters.

We'd taken only a half dozen steps toward our table when Emily's voice rasped in my ear. "Mother. Look!" She gestured with her tray. "See that woman over there?"

"Where?" My eyes ping-ponged over the crowd. There were several women in our immediate area, so it was impossible to tell which woman Emily was referring to.

"That one," she croaked. "The one with the Kiddie Kruzer stroller!"

"Where?" I began, but then I saw what Emily saw. A dark-haired woman about Emily's age, wearing eyeglasses and a yellow beret, pushing a child in one of the bright red, car-shaped strollers that Westfield management loaned out to mall customers.

"My God, that's Timmy!" Emily shouted.

"What?" My head snapped around from the woman and her baby to Emily, who stood next to me clutching her tray so tightly that her knuckles had turned white. On the tray, her spicy tofu quivered on its plate, and the ice in her Coca-Cola actually chattered.

As I watched, Emily relaxed her death grip on the

tray, and it tumbled end over end, splattering food and drink all over the floor and the Nikes of a teen unfortunate enough to have his legs sprawled in the aisle. Shaking off my restraining hand, she rushed forward.

"Paul!" I yelled, scanning the crowd for my husband. I set my tray down in front of a surprised senior and chased after my daughter.

"Timmy! Timmy!" Emily knocked over chairs, her arms flailing against the sea of humanity that seemed somehow to have closed in around us. "Mother, it's Timmy!"

When I caught up with her seconds later, Emily was kneeling in front of the stroller. "Timmy, it's Mommy! Mommy's here."

"Ma'am, ma'am," the child's mother was saying. "I think you've made a mistake."

The baby in the stroller certainly looked like Timmy, could have been his twin, in fact, except that she was wearing pink overalls and a lace-trimmed shirt. Her mother had drawn the little bit of hair that sprouted from her head into a tiny topknot and secured it there with a beribboned barrette.

"This is Jennifer," the little girl's mother said, her voice shaking. "Jenny, can you say hello to the nice lady?" She pulled the stroller toward her protectively.

Emily straightened, her face rigid. "You think a mother doesn't know her own child? This is Timmy. You took him, and he's mine."

The mother, eyes wide and frightened by this nutcase standing in front of her, seemed to be appealing to me for help.

"Emily!" I grabbed my daughter's arm and held her back until Paul reached us.

"What the hell's going on here?"

Emily stood her ground. "This woman has kidnapped Timmy, Daddy. She thinks she can fool me just because she dressed him up in little girl's clothes, but she can't."

In the stroller, Jenny said, "Buh buh buh," waved a nubby rubber rattle in the air, and then began gnawing on it in a way that seemed so familiar that for a few seconds my heart stopped beating altogether.

Could Emily be right?

Paul's arm snaked around his daughter's shoulders, his head bent to touch hers. "Emily, you're upsetting this woman. You're upsetting her child."

Jenny, in point of fact, seemed perfectly oblivious to the chaos going on around her, continuing to chew contentedly on her rattle.

"If you'll excuse me, then," Jenny's mother said, giving the stroller a tentative tug in a backward direction. "I need to be going."

"Not until you give me back Timmy!" Emily surged forward, reaching for the child, but Paul restrained her.

Jenny's mother backed away, dragging the stroller with her. "Don't make me call Security," she snarled.

Paul led Emily to a nearby chair and forced her to sit down on it. She threw her arms across the table, rested her head on them and began to cry, deep wracking sobs that nearly ripped my heart out of my chest.

"Emily." I knelt on the cool tiles next to my daughter's chair. "The woman is getting away. Do you want me to grab the baby?"

Paul's eyebrows shot skyward. "Hannah, are you out of your mind?"

My heart pounding, my breath coming in short gasps as the stroller and the woman in the yellow beret began beating a hasty retreat, I said, "What's the worst that could happen, Paul? The police come. The child is not Timmy. News at eleven: distraught mother of kidnapped child makes terrible mistake. Apologies all around. Everybody goes home."

Emily turned her tearstained face to me, her eyes wide, pupils dilated. No telling what she was high on this time.

"Emily, are you *sure* that's Timmy?"

"I don't knoooooow," Emily howled.

Behind her, her father looked at me pleadingly and mouthed the word *pills*.

I had been fully prepared to snatch the child and damn the consequences, but without Emily to back me up, I felt my resolve waver.

I glanced from my daughter to Jenny's mother, who was negotiating a difficult three-point turn between the closely spaced tables and chairs of the food court. As she pushed off in the direction of Greenleaf Grille, the crowd separating us suddenly seemed to thicken. I looked to my left, where the escalator was disgorging a steady stream of moviegoers into the food court. One of the features, perhaps several of them, had just let out, and Jenny's mother's yellow beret was rapidly disappearing into the boisterous throng.

"Paul?" I whispered. When I had his full attention, I said, "When she calms down, take Emily into Borders or something. I'll meet you there."

Before Paul could reply, I took off, following the woman with the fire-engine-red Kiddie Kruzer that may or may not have contained my grandson as she pushed it up the ramp that led out of the food court. I trailed the yellow beret as it bobbed past CVS, stopped for a few seconds to look into the window of the Disney store, and hurried along to the Gap for Kids.

At Lord and Taylor, I nearly lost it. I stood at the cross aisles, gazing frantically in four directions, before spotting the beret again outside Build-a-Bear. Jenny's mother was kneeling next to the stroller, pointing out to her daughter a stuffed Easter duck perched on a block in the window. She certainly didn't look like a woman with something to hide, but I continued to follow her anyway, as she wandered through the linens department of JCPenney. She ditched the stroller at the door and carried Jenny in her arms into the vast wilderness of the parking lot.

I followed at a discreet distance, weaving and ducking between parked cars, keeping one eye on them all the while I was scrabbling blindly in my purse for a pen and a scrap of paper—any paper—to write on.

Jenny's mother unlocked the door of a white Toyota Corolla, put Jenny into the backseat, fussed for a moment—presumably buckling the child in—then climbed into the car herself and backed out of the parking spot.

As the Toyota approached, I jotted down its license number on the back of a business card some guy named Ed had given me when I considered availing myself of his stump removal service. I stepped aside to let the Toyota pass, staring at the driver's profile, trying to memorize it. But I didn't need to memorize it. Just as she turned the corner, I realized with absolutely certainty that I had seen the woman before. But where?

We took Emily to see a doctor after that.

He talked with her for fifty minutes, and sent her home with a legitimate prescription for something she already had samples of in her medicine cabinet.

I held on to Ed's business card with Jenny's mother's

license number scrawled on the back of it and wondered what to do.

"Leave no tern unstoned," would have been my husband's advice.

My late mother would have said, "Follow your instincts."

Emily, had she been saying anything, rather than sleeping soundly courtesy of the good doctor, would have said, "Go for it, Mom."

So I did what anyone with a police lieutenant for a brother-in-law would have done. I called him, at home this time rather than on his cell, interrupting his dinner, or almost interrupting his dinner, since he mentioned that Connie was still fixing it.

"I have a big favor to ask, Dennis."

"Should I hang up now, or wait to hear what the favor is before hanging up?"

I ignored the jab. "You heard about what happened at the mall last night?"

"My niece practically assaulted some poor woman with a child who looked like Timmy? Connie told me."

"Exactly. But Dennis, here's the thing. As I was looking at that little girl, all *my* bells and whistles were going off. I felt so strongly about it that I nearly snatched the kid. But I decided to follow the woman instead, although taking the time to look at stuffed animals through the window of Build-a-Bear isn't exactly fleeing in panic, I suppose.

"Dennis, I've been thinking about it all night," I rattled on, "and I've almost convinced myself that the child she calls Jenny is actually Timmy. But even if Jenny isn't Timmy, even if I'm dead wrong, it wouldn't hurt to check it out."

"Check what out?" Dennis sounded wary.

"I followed the mother to the parking lot, and I have her license plate number."

"Absolutely not."

"But, Dennis, what harm could it do? Looking up a license plate number would hardly get *you* into trouble."

"Hannah, what you're really asking me for is the name of the owner of that vehicle. And if I give it to you, the next thing I know you'll be knocking on her door, asking questions. Are you just itching to be charged with harassment? Or stalking?"

"I'd happily do hard time for assault and battery if it brought Timmy home."

"Sorry. I just can't do it."

"How about I give you the number anyway?"

"No."

"Please?"

"No."

"It's Maryland plate BBL6K4."

"I'm hanging up now, Hannah."

"Will you put Connie on?" But the line went dead.

I hung up in satisfaction. Knowing Dennis, he would be running that number through the DMV computers before five minutes had elapsed. He'd share what he found with the FBI, too. But just in case he didn't, I telephoned Agent Crisp and left a message on her machine.

Sitting in my own kitchen with the muffled sounds of children's laughter wafting up from the basement playroom where they were playing Chutes and Ladders with their grandfather, I brewed myself a cup of Lady Grey and sat down to think.

Staring into the amber liquid, I ran through my catalog of friends and acquaintances—Naval Academy wives, Go Navy/Beat Cancer team, St. John's College friends, St. Catherine's congregants, fellow survivors. I didn't keep up much with my former colleagues at Whitworth and Sullivan, but I knew that one of them, a research librarian named Sallee Garner, might have some contacts.

Did I have any IOUs I could call in? I nibbled on a biscotti.

Duh! I'd once worked as a data consultant at Victory Mutual, a national insurance firm with its headquarters in Annapolis. Even after I left, its office manager, Donna Hudgins, and I had remained friends.

I located the phone book, looked up Donna's home number, and made the call. "Hey Donna. Long time."

"It sure has been," she replied, her voice serious. "I've been following the story about your grandson's disappearance in the paper. How's everyone holding up?"

"Poorly," I said, truthfully. "My daughter, Emily, was hovering on the brink anyway, but when the FBI said they were pulling out, she took it as a sign they were giving up, and I think that pushed her right on over."

"What do you mean, the FBI is pulling out?"

"Not off the case. They've had a crisis management team at the house for four days, which is one more than is customary, but since there hasn't been a ransom demand, they decided to pack it in. They've taken the team back to the office, where they have the resources to focus all their efforts on locating Timmy, rather than negotiating with his kidnapper."

Then Donna said the magic words. "I wish there was something I could do to help."

"Actually, that's why I'm calling." I told Donna about seeing the woman and the child who looked like Timmy in the mall, and how I was dying to know who the woman was. "My brother-in-law thinks I'm out of my mind," I added.

"Hannah, you are the sanest person I know. Impulsive, maybe. But totally sane."

So, I read Donna the license plate number.

"I don't have direct access to the database myself," she said as she jotted it down, "but I know someone who does. Can I call you right back?"

"Sure."

So I waited. Puttering. Wiping down the kitchen counters with a damp cloth. Organizing the magnets on my refrigerator door by shape and by color.

When the phone rang about ten minutes later, I nearly jumped out of my slipper socks.

"Got a pen?" Donna asked.

"You bet," I said, my heart hammering.

"Okay. Here it is, but you didn't get it from me."

"Get what from you?"

"Funny girl. Anyway, that plate is registered to a Joanna Barnhorst, 303-B Scott Circle. Do you know where that is?"

"Off Bestgate Road?"

"Right. She drives a Toyota Corolla, white in color. Right?"

"Bingo!" I said, enormously relieved that I'd gotten the number right. The car Donna described was a perfect match to the one I'd seen Joanna Barnhorst driving. "Donna, I can't thank you enough."

"Good luck, Hannah. And how about lunch soon?"

After I made a date for lunch in two weeks time and said good-bye to Donna, I sat back in my chair, staring at the name I'd written down: Joanna Barnhorst.

I'd never heard of her.

I tripped downstairs to the computer room and Googled "Joanna Barnhorst." Except for some genealogical data going back to the 1830s, and a girl who was a star lacrosse player for her high school in New Jersey, there was nothing. I considered clicking on a link for one of those fee-based background check services, but what good would information about the woman's credit history do me? It was probably a rip-off anyway.

While I was on the computer, I located the Barnhorst apartment on Mapquest. Joanna Barnhorst's condo was just off Medical Drive, one of a series of condominium developments that had sprung up like weeds along the cut-through from Bestgate to Jennifer Road when the hospital moved from downtown Annapolis to a multi-acre campus that adjoined the mall in Parole. A good move for the hospital, I felt sure, but not for the patient suffering a heart attack if the ambulance got stuck in traffic during the holiday shopping season.

I flopped back in my desk chair. I wanted to run right out to Scott Circle, bang on Barnhorst's door, and demand to see her child. Except it was nearly dark.

First thing in the morning I'd get Paul to run the carpool. Then I'd check this Barnhorst woman out.

CHAPTER 17

Early the next morning, with a cappuccino grande screwed into the cup holder on my console and a bag of doughnuts from Carlson's on the seat beside me, I waited in the parking lot outside of 303-B Scott Circle for Joanna Barnhorst to make an appearance. Her Toyota was parked in a space just outside her building, so unless she'd gone out for a pre-dawn stroll, I knew she had to be at home.

An hour later I was down to half a cup of lukewarm coffee and one doughnut, still staring at her apartment window and seeing nothing but white lace curtains, tightly drawn.

Thirty minutes after that I had an empty paper cup and traces of powdered sugar on my lips.

Feeling a bit reckless, I climbed out of my car and tested the glass door that led to the vestibule of Barnhorst's apartment tower. Naturally, it was locked. Her name, J. Barnhorst, was written on a scrap of paper in a slot on the intercom panel outside the door, next to a big white button. I could press the button, of course, but what would I say if Joanna answered? Candygram? UPS?

I could wait until the next resident came in or out, and slip in after him. Or I could push all the buttons until someone buzzed me in, but people stupid enough to do that only lived on the other side of the television screen, right?

Besides, what would I do once I got into the building? Stand outside Joanna Barnhorst's apartment with my ear cupped to the door, waiting to overhear something incriminating?

I could call her on my cell phone. I had her number—thanks again to Google—but if she had caller ID, "Hannah Ives" would scroll across her display panel clear as day.

Discouraged, I leaned against the aluminum siding and toyed briefly with the idea of pulling the fire alarm. I'd already used my Get Out of Jail Free card on that one, though. Pull that trick again, and the cops would probably swoop down, lock me up, and double the fine, just to teach me a lesson, and I certainly didn't have a spare ten thousand dollars lying about.

I groaned. Manning a stakeout was certainly easier on television. Didn't P.I.'s ever need to eat? Sleep? Go to the bathroom? Elliot and Olivia would have found a parking place right in front of Barnhorst's building, too, rather than at the end of a line of parked cars, next to a tacky ornamental fountain, and so far away from a direct line of sight to her door that I had to sit in the passenger seat in order to keep an eye on her building.

I returned to my car, slid into the seat, readjusted the sideview mirror, and plugged my iPod into the cigarette lighter: "Wake Up Little Susie" segued into "Moi, Je ne regrette rien," followed by "Spem in alium" and "Sheep May Safely Graze." The iTunes party shuffle certainly made for strange bedfellows. I listened to Robin Blaze's exquisite countertenor voice soar through "So

Parted You" with one eye glued to the sideview mirror. Watching. Waiting. Hoping.

Tom Lehrer's gravely voice jolted me awake with "Fight Fiercely Harvard." According to the dashboard clock, I'd been asleep for twenty minutes. Damn! I sat up in panic. What if I'd missed her? But angels must have been watching over me because Barnhorst's car was still in its parking space.

My stomach rumbled, responding to the aroma of fried dumplings wafting over from the Joy Luck carry-out in the strip mall across the street. Joy Luck prepared some of the best Chinese food in the Annapolis area, and they delivered. I gazed wistfully at my cell phone, wondering if they'd deliver hot and sour soup to my car.

I rummaged in my purse, looking for a granola bar, a roll of LifeSavers, a stick of gum, anything to tide me over until dinnertime, if, God forbid, I had to sit in Joanna Barnhorst's stupid parking lot that long, when something red flashed in the mirror. I glanced up from the dark maw of my purse to see Joanna walking toward her car, balancing the baby on her hip.

Today, Jenny was a symphony in pink: pink-checked dress with crimson smocking, pink bonnet, and pink socks, trimmed with white lace. Ugh. No wonder Jenny looked so solemn. All that pink would make even the most girly-girl barf.

I scrunched down in my seat, watching in the mirror, as Joanna Barnhorst crossed behind me to her car. In her free hand, Joanna carried an old-fashioned plastic infant seat, the kind with a handle that doubled as a stand when you wanted to prop your kid up in front of the TV to watch *Sesame Street.* I scowled in disapproval at the molded plastic and cheap metal. Not U.S. DOT-approved, that was for sure. I doubted they even made child seats like that anymore, and wondered if she'd picked it up secondhand at the Salvation Army Store.

I watched as Joanna strapped Jennifer into the infant carrier, positioned it in the backseat, fussed with the seat belt for a bit, then climbed in the car herself and drove away.

I started my car and followed at a prudent distance as Barnhorst turned left on Bestgate Road, left again on Generals Highway, circled the mall, and pulled into the parking lot of Toys 'R' Us. She emerged from the store twenty minutes later pushing one shopping cart containing Jenny, two boxes of disposable diapers, a case of Similac, and a Britax car seat. She dragged a second shopping cart behind her, this one containing a box that identified its contents as a Jeep brand stroller.

For the child's sake, I was happy to see the Britax, arguably the Rolls Royce of infant car seats, but the combination of items in Barnhorst's two carts pegged the meter on my suspicionometer. Surely these were items that the mother of a ten-month-old child should have had all along?

I watched Barnhorst install the Britax in the backseat of her Toyota, a complicated procedure, I knew from experience, that involved the use of seat belts and anchor straps. While she struggled with that, Jenny played happily in the shopping cart, sucking on the ear of a stuffed rabbit.

I held my breath, then let it out slowly.

Lots of children chew on their toys that way, Hannah.

But even in my inexpert opinion, the evidence against Barnhorst was mounting. "Jenny" was the same age as Timmy. She had the same color hair and eyes. But most of all, it was a feeling deep in my gut that if I rushed up to the baby now, "Jenny" would spread out "her" little arms, grin from ear to ear, and shout, "Gramma!"

Dream on, Hannah. Timmy was a brilliant child, but even at ten months his vocabulary was limited to "Dada," "Mama," "light," and "shoe." I'd need more evidence if I wanted to convince anyone other than Emily or myself that this child was actually ours.

While Barnhorst was tangled up in seat belts and anchor straps, I worked my digital camera out of the bottom of my purse and aimed it in her direction. With my thumb, I zoomed in nice and close on the baby's face and took a picture, then turned the lens on Joanna Barnhorst's head as she bent over the backseat. "Turn around, damnit!"

Barnhorst obliged, and I clicked the shutter. "Gotcha!"

She turned, and I snapped another picture, this time in profile. And another.

Barnhorst loaded her remaining purchases into the trunk, strapped Jenny a thousand times more safely into the new car seat, and drove north up Generals Highway. I followed as closely as I dared, loitering two cars behind as she turned into Sam's Club, a discount warehouse store opposite the Annapolis mall.

This time I decided to follow her into the store. I put on my sunglasses and the hat I usually use for gardening—not much in the way of disguise, but under the circumstances, it would have to do. Ahead of me, Barnhorst produced her Sam's Club membership card and flashed it for the guy guarding the door. I lost a few precious minutes scrabbling in my bag for my own membership card, but caught up with the pair of them as she turned right past the jewelry kiosk and chugged into the clothing aisle.

Kids' clothes. I should have guessed. Judging from the number of outfits she was buying, little Jenny might well have been triplets.

I kept a safe distance as Barnhorst pushed her clothing-laden cart down the book aisle. From behind a rack of leather jackets, I watched as she parked Jenny near the best sellers, turned her attention for a while to the latest Nora Roberts, and read the final page of it. She put it down, picked up and also rejected two other best-selling novels, then wandered along the aisle, past the Bibles, past the cookbooks, past the dictionaries, to the section where the children's books were displayed.

While Barnhorst appeared to be examining a pop-up book for minute flaws, I took a big chance. I popped out from behind the jackets, wandered up to the cart as nonchalantly as I could with a heart that was practically hammering out of my chest, and looked into the child's eyes. "Hey there, Timmy," I whispered.

A smile spread over Jenny's face with a wattage so bright it could have lit up the entire city of Annapolis. Her arms and legs quivered with excitement.

I poked her gently in her plump little belly with my index finger. "Who does Grandma love?"

After what happened next, it would take more than a ridiculous pink lace bonnet to fool me. Out of Jenny's mouth rolled Timmy's distinctive bubbling, burbling, gurgling chuckle.

I had nearly forgotten about Joanna Barnhorst when I caught sight of her chugging back up the aisle, a stack of children's books in hand. With the lecture I'd received from Dennis that morning still fresh in my mind,

I quickly abandoned my plan to snatch Timmy from the cart, ducked my head and slipped around the corner into the office supplies aisle, where Barnhorst passed me several minutes later. I followed at a discreet distance—examining computer paper, marker pens, paper shredders, and athletic socks—as Barnhorst swung wide, made a U-turn, and headed for an end-of-aisle pyramid of matching luggage. A few minutes later she trundled back down the aisle toward me dragging two suitcases—one large and one small—and heaved them into the cart.

I slipped away, muttering under my breath. *I hope you don't think you're going anywhere with those suitcases, bitch, because I'm going to get you. Sooner or later, I'm going to get you.*

I followed Barnhorst back to her apartment and waited, seething, until she was safely inside, before calling for reinforcements. My options were limited.

Paul was in charge of running the carpools that day.

Ruth had a shop to run, and as much as I loved my sister, even she would be the first to admit she was a bit of a flake.

My friend Nadine Gray, a.k.a. the retired mystery novelist L. K. Bromley, would have leapt at the chance in a New York minute, but, alas, Naddie was on an extended trip to her sister in Seattle, a visit unexpectedly extended by the sister's emergency appendectomy.

My father was so far away managing an engineering project for a contractor in Saudi Arabia that we'd voted as a family not even to tell him about Timmy, unless we had to.

That left me with Connie.

"Hey," I said, when she answered the telephone. "Are you free right now?"

"I don't like the sound of this."

"You've lived with Dennis so long that you're beginning to sound like him," I teased.

"I'm eating lunch," she said, ignoring the jibe. "Where else would I be at one o'clock in the afternoon?"

I moaned. "Don't mention food. I'm starving, but I can't let this woman out of my sight!"

"What woman?"

I explained about what I'd found out about Joanna Barnhorst, her daughter "Jenny," and about the suitcases. "Seriously, Con, I'm in a real bind. I want to print out the pictures and take them to the spa to see if anyone remembers seeing Barnhorst there on the day Timmy disappeared." I paused for breath. "And I also have to pee."

"In that case," Connie said, "I'll be right over."

"Thanks, babe. I'll relieve you by dinnertime. I promise."

It would take Connie approximately twenty minutes to reach me from the family farm in south county, so I spent the time watching Joanna's apartment as sharp-eyed as an eagle on a rock.

And I swear I didn't blink.

Not even once.

CHAPTER 18

With Connie safely in charge of the Barnhorst watch, I rushed home, hooked my camera up to my computer, and uploaded the photos, examining them one by one as they flashed by in a sinister slide show across my monitor screen.

I selected a full-frontal shot of the child I was sure was Timmy, cropped out the background, blew it up to five-by-seven, and printed it out.

For Barnhorst, I printed both a full face shot and a profile. I toyed with the idea of printing them out on the same piece of paper, like a wanted poster. Even if the Barnhorst woman hadn't stolen Timmy, which I seriously doubted at this point, anyone who'd overdress a child like that or drive around with her in such a flimsy car seat deserved to be on a wanted poster.

After the printer spit out the last copy of Joanna's picture into the paper tray, I tucked the photos into a manila envelope, then telephoned Emily. My youngest sister, Georgina, answered the phone instead.

"Any news, Georgina?"

"I'm afraid not."

"Well, I think I have news for you." I confessed to Georgina what I had been up to that morning.

When I finished, my sister said, "Paul is going to kill you when he finds out about it, you know. And I don't think the cops are going to be too pleased that you're stepping all over their toes."

"Frankly, Georgina, I don't care if the Maryland State Police, the Anne Arundel County Police Department, and the entire Federal Bureau of Investigation tack my picture up on their bulletin boards and hurl darts at it. Not if it brings Timmy home.

"I was hoping to bring the photographs over for Emily to look at," I continued. "Is she up to it, do you think?"

"Oh, she's up to it, all right, Hannah, but she's not here. Emily's gone off with her new best friend, that Erika Rose."

I could picture Georgina's lip curling with distaste.

"They printed up a pile of handbills warning the residents of West Annapolis about Roger Haberman, the pedophile living in their midst. They used one of Roger's self-portraits, too. They downloaded it from the PredatorBeware website." Georgina paused. "At least you can see his face in this one."

On my end of the telephone, I cringed just thinking about it.

"They're putting up posters?" I could understand why Emily would want to do this, but so soon after our effort to put posters all over town asking for the public's help in finding Timmy, this new effort left a bad taste in my mouth.

"You bet. She went off with a fistful of them, a roll of cellophane tape, a box of tacks, and a hammer. I suspect they're plastering West Annapolis. Erika's been whipping her acolytes into a frenzy because the Habermans live just two blocks from West Annapolis Elementary School, you know."

I did know. The school dominated the small residential neighborhood, taking up an entire city block.

"I tried to talk Emily out of it," Georgina continued. "Dennis was here earlier, and he tried to talk some sense into her, too."

I could just picture it. Dennis pacing, wearing a path in Emily's carpet, lecturing his niece and thinking: it's hopeless. Like mother, like daughter.

"Dennis warned Emily that Roger could charge her with harassment," Georgina continued, "but it was no good. Emily's one hundred percent convinced that Roger Haberman had a role in Timmy's disappearance, and she's not going to let it drop."

"Emily can't help it. It's genetic," I said, thinking about what I, her mother, had been up to that morning.

Georgina snorted. "So I've noticed."

After Georgina promised to have Emily call me the minute she got home, I tucked the photographs under my arm and drove out to Paradiso. I planned to show the photos to Dante first, and then to other spa employees, to see if anyone recognized Joanna Barnhorst, or had seen her hanging around the spa.

For Dante's sake, I was glad to see that the Spa Closed notice had been taken down from the gates. Two cars trailed behind me as I drove up the drive, and with the parking lot three-quarters full, the spa appeared to be in full operation.

I found a parking spot under a large tulip poplar and made my way quickly inside. Clients stood two deep at the reception desk where Heather and another girl I didn't recognize signed people in. I waited until Heather returned to the desk after launching a blonde with a generous derriere off on her spa journey, before taking her aside.

"Is Dante in?" I asked.

Heather shook her head. "Not right now. He's off somewhere, meeting with the security people to see if they can't get the system up and running ASAP."

I showed her the photographs of Joanna Barnhorst. "The police are looking for this woman in connection with my grandson's disappearance," I said, stretching the truth just a tad. "Do you recognize her?"

Heather squinted at the picture, wrinkling up her smooth German brow. "Sorry, Hannah. I've never seen this woman before. I'm quite sure of it."

I tried not to let the disappointment show on my face. "Well, thanks, anyway."

The other receptionist didn't recognize Joanna, either.

Alison Dutton was a better bet. I found her in the gift shop, assisting a customer who was trying on a track suit. "Not many women could carry off a shade of yellow like that," she was assuring the woman as I walked in, "but on you, with your coloring, it's perfect!"

Alison turned to me for corroboration. "What do you think, Hannah?"

The track suit was a bilious yellow, reflecting its color onto the woman's face and making her look terminally ill. "I'm stunned," I said, truthfully.

"Well, okay then," the woman chirped. "I'll take it."

After she had made her purchase, leaving with the track suit artfully wrapped in tissue paper, lovingly placed in a signature green spa shopping bag, its handles tied together with curled gold ribbon, I showed Joanna's pictures to Alison. "I don't know her," she said, "but she does look kind of familiar. Maybe she came here for an interview or something?"

"Interview?" I stared past Alison to a stacked display of forest green spa mugs, my brain churning.

Interview.

Had Joanna Barnhorst been the owner of that head that popped around the office door looking for Dante last Monday, the day I was reviewing résumés? I was certain I'd not seen her name among the applications I had examined, but perhaps her application and been among an earlier batch.

If that woman had been Joanna, after I'd informed her that Dante was in the conference room, had she actually been able to see him that day?

And what would compel a woman who had simply come to the spa for a job interview suddenly to decide to snatch Timmy? It wasn't making a whole lot of sense.

Unless. The needle on my suspicionometer was pegging the meter again.

Unless Dante knew more about Timmy's disappearance than he had been prepared to admit.

Suddenly I realized that Alison was talking to me. "Did I say something helpful?"

My mind snapped back. "Thank you, Alison. You may have just made my day."

I had been thinking that if someone, *anyone*, could place Joanna Barnhorst at Spa Paradiso on Monday with some degree of certainty, perhaps the FBI would be willing to move in on her.

Alison smiled. "Anything I can do to help, just ask."

I thanked Alison again, then trotted down to the gym, where I found Norman Salterelli bench pressing two hundred pounds without breaking a sweat. I waited semipatiently while he completed twenty reps, slid off the bench, and began dabbing at his face with the towel he kept perpetually draped around his neck. "Hey, Hannah. Haven't seen you around for a couple of days. No surprise, that. Any news?"

"Nothing good, I'm afraid, but I've got a couple of pictures to show you that might help." I eased them out of the envelope. "I'm wondering if you saw this woman hanging around the spa anywhere."

Norman flicked his towel over a Bowflex machine and let it hang there. "Let me see." He studied the pictures for a long time, looking puzzled, as if they were written in a foreign language. He tapped Joanna Barnhorst's image with a sausage index finger. "Nice looking woman, but no, never seen her."

"Like leaving the spa on the day Timmy disappeared?" I prodded.

"No. I would have remembered *her*."

"Well, thanks, anyway." I flashed him a grateful smile and tried to hide my disappointment.

My next stop was Bellissima, where Wally Jessop was shuttling between one beauty shop customer whose head was encased in an aluminum foil cap, and another, a brunette, who was apparently considering a new hairstyle. After dabbing highlights with a paintbrush at bits of hair sticking out of holes in the older woman's foil cap, Wally turned to the brunette, running his fingers through her hair, playing with it, fluffing it up, teasing at it with his fingers.

Standing behind the woman, Wally bent at the waist, stared at her reflection in the mirror, and spoke directly into her ear. "You have natcherwy curwy hair, Mrs. Bwown, and you should never, never bwow it dwy." Wally turned to shine his pearly whites on me. "I'm twying to talk Mrs. Bwown into a henna winse," he lisped, "and a cut that's short and sassy."

Clearly, I was supposed to agree with him. "You're the expert, Wally," I said, wondering where his French accent had gotten to.

"You think so?" mused the brunette, soon-to-be-redhead, in the chair. She studied her reflection thoughtfully.

While she remained paralyzed with indecision, I pulled out my photos and passed them to Wally.

Holding the photos between an elegant thumb and forefinger, Wally drew me behind the reception desk, looking serious. Once he saw the photos, though, his face lit up. "Sure, I know her," Wally said, abandoning his fashionable lisp. "That's Joanna Kerr. She went to Haverford with us."

"Kerr? Not Barnhorst?"

"If she's Barnhorst now, she could have married, I suppose. It's been eight years since we graduated."

"Have you seen Joanna here at the spa, Wally?"

"No, but I'm not exactly the beating heart of the enterprise, tucked away over here in Bellissima."

Wally raised a just-a-minute finger and excused himself to send the lady wearing the tin hat off to sit under a heat hood. When I had his attention again, I asked, "Can you think of any reason why Joanna would show up here at Paradiso?"

Wally shrugged. "If she came to see anybody, it'd be Dante. Before he met Emily, he and Joanna were an item."

"An item?" I repeated dumbly.

"Yeah, you know, they were going steady," he explained, as if I were a doddering septuagenarian who didn't understand the slang.

"I see." My stomach clenched as it appeared that my suspicions about my son-in-law were about to be confirmed. "Does Emily know Joanna, then?"

Wally looked up from the sales slip he was filling out

with pen in large block letters. "I doubt it. After Dante met Em, he continued dating Joanna for a while, but then he and Em got serious and he broke it off."

"Was Joanna okay with that?"

Wally shrugged. "Who knows. She didn't come gunning for Dante with an AK-47 or anything, so I suppose she was okay with it. She dropped out of school soon afterward anyway, and we lost touch."

I thought about all the other Haverford alums Dante had gathered together to work at his spa. "Does François know her, too?"

"Probably. Why don't you ask him?"

"I will." I touched his arm. "Thanks, Wally."

"Don't mention it."

I started to go, but then turned back to the brunette in the chair. "Ma'am?"

She raised a languid eyebrow. "Yes?"

"About the winse," I said. "Go for it!"

I caught François, the chef, in the postlunch, preteatime lull, piping salmon mousse onto round rice crackers that he had arranged on a platter decorated with fresh pansies. When I walked in, he offered me one—a cracker, not a pansy.

"Thanks!" I snatched it off the platter like a starving orphan and slid it into my mouth whole. "God, that's good," I mumbled around a mouth full of crumbs. "Can I have another one?"

François grinned and proffered the platter. "Sure."

"Wally says you might know this woman," I said, still chewing. "I'm pretty sure she came to the spa last Monday." I waved one of Joanna's photos in his general direction.

François put down the piping cone, wiped his hands on his apron, and took the picture from me. "Joanna Kerr?"

"Apparently."

"We went to Haverford together." He passed the picture back to me. "Word got out among the old 'Fords about the good things Dante was planning to do at Paradiso, and she came to apply for a job."

"What job did she apply for, then?"

François began arranging curls of red pepper on top of each artfully moussed cracker. "You'll have to ask Dante about that. Joanna's recently divorced, moved here from Baltimore. She needs to find work. You know the drill. A degree in philosophy from Haverford. Not exactly your most marketable skill." He grinned.

I knew about marketable skills. My degree was in French literature from Oberlin. I had to earn a master's in library science before I got a job that paid real money.

"But wait a minute," I said. "Wally just told me that Joanna dropped out of school."

François opened the refrigerator and slid the finished platter of crackers onto an empty shelf. "She did, for a semester. She came back and graduated a year later."

"But, what could she do here, François?"

"Don't know what she discussed with Dante, but when she stopped by the kitchen, she told me she'd be willing to do anything. Only opening I had was for a salad person. Would have given it to her, too, but when Emily got wind of it at staff meeting, she had a fit and fell in it."

"Emily knows her, then?"

"Knows *of* her, but I don't think they've ever met." His eyebrows danced mischieviously. "Dante dated them both for a while, but when he got serious about Em, he broke it off with Joanna." He began working on a second platter, this one covered with triangles of what looked like crustless cucumber and cream cheese sandwiches. "Em was at Bryn Mawr and Joanna at Haverford, so unless they had classes together, or got onto the Blue Bus shuttle at the same time, there's no reason they would have run into each other."

"I see," I muttered, thinking that I may have just learned the reason for Friday's argument outside Garnelle's massage room door that resulted in damage to a certain valuable spa lounge chair.

"François, I'm pretty sure I saw Joanna here late Monday morning. When I was in the office, a woman who looked a lot like her stuck her head in and asked for Dante."

"Uh-huh."

"Do you think of any reason why Joanna would have taken Timmy?"

"Joanna?" François snorted. "No way. Unless she's gone fucking nuts."

And that was exactly what I was afraid of.

CHAPTER 19

As I drove away from Paradiso, Georgina reached me on my cell to say that Emily had finished terrorizing West Annapolis and was on her way home. I was heading that direction myself when my cell phone burbled again.

"I need to talk to you, Mrs. Ives." It was Special Agent Amanda Crisp, and she sounded serious.

"Just a minute." I figured she wasn't calling with good news. Rather than have a heart attack and crash my car, I pulled into the Bay Ridge shopping center, parked in front of Giant, and cut my engine. "It's bad news, isn't it?"

"No, sorry. I didn't mean to alarm you. It's just that there's something I'd like to discuss."

"I want to talk to you, too, Agent Crisp," I said, thinking of the envelope of photographs that sat on the car seat next to me. "When and where?"

"I haven't had lunch yet."

"Neither have I. Do you know Grumps?" I suggested, naming a quirky local restaurant in the Hillsmere shopping center nearby.

"I know it well," she said. "We used to stop there for

coffee when we were camping out at your daughter's. I can be there in twenty minutes."

"Can you tell me what this is about?"

"Order me a burger. See you in twenty minutes, Mrs. Ives."

Grumps Café serves the best hamburgers in town. When I arrived there five minutes later, I marched straight up to the counter and ordered two cheeseburgers, ice tea, and chips. The cashier handed me a toy frog with *19* written in marker pen on his shiny rubber chest, and pointed me to a booth.

While I waited for the burgers, or Amanda, whichever came first, I worried. What could Amanda want to see me about? Privately? She'd once called me a loose cannon, and warned me to keep my nose out of FBI business. Perhaps she felt I needed a refresher course.

I studied my surroundings—the purposely (and generously) paint-splattered floors, the walls hung with assorted T-shirts, discarded window frames, Frisbees, surfboards, and various other hand-me-downs from Jimmy Buffett's condominium in Margaritaville. Amanda Crisp had also accused me of nearly blowing a carefully orchestrated, multiagency sting operation, but I pleaded emphatically not guilty to that.

On a shelf over the door, a TV was playing CNN with the sound turned off. I watched the closed captioning, fascinated as typo after typo scrolled by. CNN was reporting on a funeral. Someone was singing "The Impossible Dream," "writing unwritable wrongs" all over the place, and pining about loving "pure and chased" from afar while she was about it. I had to smile.

When an ad came on, I pulled the envelope of photos from my purse and spread its contents out on the table in front of me:

Timmy.

Joanna.

Madam X.

The FBI's Identikit technician had drawn a sketch based on Chloe's description of the woman who'd approached them in Ben and Jerry's. I put the sketch side by side with the photo I'd taken of Joanna Barnhorst. The woman in the sketch wore a hat and sunglasses. It looked like Joanna Barnhorst, I supposed, but it also looked like me, or Connie, or any one of the thousands of female tourists who flock to Annapolis each summer dressed in sunglasses and hats bought at Target.

I stared at the TV, thinking about summer, when Paul had no classes and the hot, lazy days seemed to spread out endlessly before us. Family time, spent relaxing on the farm, or sailing the Chesapeake Bay on Connie's boat, *Sea Song*. Last summer had been Timmy's first, and I prayed it wouldn't be his last.

Suddenly, a familiar face filled the television screen. Bette Keating, the idiot reporter with the helmet of improbable red hair who had been camped out at Emily's, dogging our every move for the past several days. I checked my watch. We weren't due for another press conference until two o'clock. What the heck was going on?

The camera panned back, and I could see that Bette wasn't alone. She was standing on Emily's lawn, damnit, and beside her was Montana Martin, the psychic. And beside Montana—my heart did a quick rat-a-tat-tat in my chest—there stood Dante.

"I feel quite certain that Timmy is alive," Montana informed the television audience. "I have the impression that he's being held on, or near the water, and that there may be some sort of Asian connection."

I smiled grimly. *Asian connection.* Whatever happened to the "Chinese, Japanese, or Korean" she'd shared with the press corps from our doorstep the other day? CNN had obviously vetted Montana's "vision" for political correctness, cleaning it up to avoid offending the opponents of racial profiling.

"Yes, I know it's controversial . . ." Those were my son-in-law's words crawling by on the closed captioning. ". . . but Ms. Martin has an amazing track record—you may remember the Lonnie Edwards case—so we're taking what she tells us quite seriously."

I rolled my eyes. Was this another publicity stunt cooked up by Dante and his Haverford chums? If we looked into a certain Ms. Montana Martin's background, would there be a Haverford connection there, too?

In spite of Montana's recent conversation with my dead mother, the whole psychic business was beginning to creep me out. Then the CNN reporter reminded everyone—with accompanying video clips from the CNN archives—that Scott Peterson had called in a pet psychic to interview the family dog about his wife, Laci's, disappearance. My heart turned to stone. Was Dante up to no good, too?

Montana disappeared and another head filled the screen, Professor Avery K. McMasters, if the label to the right of his head was to be believed. McMasters was a professor at Rice University, an expert in—I squinted, but didn't catch what—and, naming no names, he was clearly taking Montana to task. "Such charlatans can be pretty clever." The professor grinned, Sphinxlike, into the lens. "They hook you, reel you in slowly, until you lay at their feet, flopping and gasping, with an empty bank account to prove it."

I hoped Dante was listening.

With her usual impeccable timing, just as the hamburgers arrived, Agent Crisp slid into the booth across from me. "Thanks for coming."

I tore the top off my packet of chips. "You look tired."

"I am. We're working Timmy's case 24/7. With kids, it's triply hard."

"I have some information for you that may help us both," I said.

"Well, Hannah, that's exactly why I called you. It's this *both* business that's troubling me."

"What do you mean?"

Amanda made no move to touch her food. "Since it's your grandson who's been kidnapped, and you understandably have a deep, personal interest in the progress of this investigation, I was willing to cut you a little slack. But now, I have to tell you, you're getting in the way."

A lump began to form in my throat, and as delicious as it had seemed only seconds ago, I suspected my burger would remain uneaten.

"Do you know how incredibly lucky you are?"

I shook my head, fighting back tears. I refused to cry in front of Amanda Crisp.

"If the child you saw is actually Timmy, after your daughter's outburst in the mall the other night, you're lucky the Barnhorst woman didn't head for the hills with him."

"I didn't think of that," I admitted sheepishly. "Emily was so certain it was Timmy, at least at first. I just couldn't let the woman get away."

"If she suspects that you're tailing her, she may *still* get spooked and run off with him."

Once again Agent Crisp had taken me by surprise.

"Are you following me?"

"Let's just say that I wish you'd leave us alone to do our job. Will you promise me that?"

"Do you know that she bought suitcases at Sam's Club?"

Agent Crisp simply smiled. "Promise me you'll stop following Joanna Barnhorst."

"Okay, I promise."

"Have a chip," she said, sliding her bag across the table.

"Thank you," I said, still feeling a bit miffed, "but I'd rather smoke my own."

After a respectable silence, during which Amanda tucked into her burger and I nibbled on the chips from my bag, I said, "I took some pictures," and slid the envelope of photos across the table.

Amanda laid her hand on the envelope. "Thanks. But that's *it*, right? As of right now, you are off the case."

"Your hamburger's getting cold," I said.

After Amanda left, I stayed in the booth, finishing my ice tea. Then I headed for the colorful restroom where someone had painted enormous bird tracks on the wall. They snaked up and around, before disappearing into a ragged hole in the acoustical tiles. From the opening overhead a demonic Tweetie Bird peered down at me as I sat on the toilet and dialed my sister-in-law's cell. I needed to give Connie a heads-up: watch out for the Feds.

When I made that promise to Agent Crisp, after all, I didn't say anything about Connie.

CHAPTER 20

I certainly didn't set out to wreck my daughter's marriage, but the look of pure loathing she sent Dante's way when the words "Joanna Barnhorst" passed over my lips will be tattooed on my brain forever.

Emily tossed the picture she was holding across the table at her husband. "So this is your former girlfriend," she sneered. "I always wondered what she looked like."

Dante turned the photograph face down without even looking at it. "She means nothing to me, Emily. After seven years of marriage and three beautiful children, surely you know that."

"I once had three children," Emily whispered in a long, long ago and faraway tone of voice, as if she were reading the first line of a Victorian novel.

Across the table from his wife, Dante paled.

"If she means so little to you, *darling, honeylamb, sugarpie*, how come you were so hot to give her a job at Paradiso?"

"Correction. *François* was lobbying to give her a job, not me. He said he felt sorry for her."

"Oh, puh-leeze, give me credit for a little intelligence, will you?"

Dante massaged his temples with his fingers, as if trying to erase the pain. In my opinion, my son-in-law had a lot of explaining to do, but I feared that what Emily was about to say might poison the well forever.

"So, you turned her down," she continued, relentless.

"Right."

"You sent her away."

"Yes."

Dante closed his eyes and rested his head against the back of his chair as the significance of what he'd just said sunk in.

"And she came back that Monday?"

"I don't know, Emily. You may recall that I was tied up with that reporter. If Joanna came back, I certainly didn't see her."

As much as I hated to fan the flames, I felt I had to jump in and set the record straight. "She did come back, Dante. She stuck her head into the office for a second while I was sitting there. She was looking for you."

"My God." Emily practically screamed the words.

"Em—" Dante began, but Emily interrupted him.

"What on earth would make Joanna kidnap Timmy? I have *tons* of ex-boyfriends," she added maliciously, "but as far as I know, none of them ever tried to kidnap my children!"

Dante leaned forward and pressed his hands between his knees, as if trying to control their shaking. "I don't know, Emily. I dated the woman. When I met you, I broke up with her. End of story."

"Apparently not," my daughter said.

Dante turned to me. "Did Joanna say what she wanted?"

"Just that she was looking for you."

Dante exploded. "Jesus Christ! I'll kill her. I swear to God I'm going to kill her. Where did you say she's living?"

"She's got an apartment out on Bestgate Road."

Dante bolted from his chair, and considering the black mood he was in, took Emily surprisingly gently by the arm. "Let's go."

Emily shook his hand away. "You go. I'm going to call the FBI."

"Stay put," I told them. "The FBI is already on it. Agent Crisp told me that when she warned me against stalking Joanna."

"The hell with that! Come on, Emily!"

Emily glanced from me to her husband. I suspected she would have gone off with him, too, but was saved from making any decision by the sound of my cell phone, chirping its buttons off to the tune of "Old McDonald Had a Farm" from my purse, which was sitting on the landing.

"Connie?" By the time I reached the phone and punched the Talk button, I must have sounded breathless.

Connie sounded breathless, too. "Joanna's packed up Timmy and the suitcases, Hannah, and she's on the move. I'm right behind her on Route 50, heading west. Unless I miss my guess, she's heading for New Carrollton."

New Carrollton station, at the intersection of Route 50 and I-495, better known as the Capital Beltway. From there, Joanna Barnhorst could take a train, or bus, or hop on the Metro. My bet was on the train.

Thinking about Amanda Crisp and her FBI team who were supposed to be on the case 24/7, I asked, "Have you seen any Ford Tauruses in the vicinity? Crown Vics?"

"You think I noticed *that*?"

"Right. Silly question. Best to hedge our bets, then. Stick with her," I said, "We're on our way."

Except when the children were in the car, my son-in-law drove like Dale Earnhardt, Junior, and had four points on his license to prove it. In his present state of mind, I had doubts we'd arrive in one piece with Dante at the wheel, so I insisted on driving while my daughter yelled encouragement from the backseat. "Can't you go any faster?"

I pulled into the HOV lane. "If I go any faster, I'll get stopped for speeding, and where would *that* get us?"

From a spot in the console, my cell phone chirped again. "You get it," I told Dante as I overtook and passed a truck on the right.

Dante clapped the phone to his ear. "Yeah?" He listened for a few seconds, then turned to me and said, "It's Connie reporting in. Joanna's in the parking garage at New Carrollton, so it's either the Metro or the train."

"Jeeze." I slammed my foot down on the accelerator. The speedometer shot up to a terrifying eighty. In the backseat, Emily kept muttering faster-faster-faster under her breath, nearly driving me insane. Nevertheless, I made it from the Annapolis city limits to the Capital Beltway in a record fifteen minutes. I shot right off the highway and onto the exit ramp, crossed over the Beltway, ruined my shock absorbers by taking a series of diabolical speed bumps way too fast, pulled past the taxi rank and into the Kiss and Ride.

As we climbed out of the car, Dante still had Connie on the line. "Where's she now?" he hissed into the phone. "There's a train for Florida in ten minutes," he reported while punching the End button with his thumb. "Connie thinks that Barnhorst will be on it. Let's go!"

With Dante in the lead, we charged through the double glass doors and into the train station. Just inside, Dante stopped cold, so abruptly that we piled into him. We were all looking around for Connie.

I spotted her first, over by the automated ticket machines.

"Thank goodness you're here. I thought I'd have to buy a ticket."

Connie pointed to a row of seats near the women's restroom where Joanna Barnhorst sat with Timmy in her arms. The very picture of motherhood, she was rocking him gently.

Dressing Timmy for their journey, she'd abandoned the pink theme. My grandson was dressed in yellow overalls and a white top with a picture of Nemo the clownfish embroidered on it. I recognized it as one of the outfits she'd bought for him at Sam's Club earlier in what was turning out to be the longest day of my life.

While I was mindlessly admiring Tim's new outfit, Emily streaked past me in a fury. She stopped dead in front of Joanna Barnhorst and stood there, solid as a tree and about as movable. "Give me back my child."

Joanna looked up with what could only be described as a demented smile on her face. "She's my child. I told you that before. Don't you listen?"

"I'm telling you one more time. Give me back my baby, or I'm going to take him away from you."

Joanna clasped the sleeping child to her chest, burying his chubby face in her bosom. "No. She's mine."

Dante surged forward. "Joanna, whatever I may have done to you, Timmy doesn't deserve to be taken away from his mother."

Still holding Timmy, Joanna stood up and tried to

sidestep the pair of them. "You should have thought about that a long time ago," she snapped.

"Give Timmy back *now*, Joanna."

"No!"

I didn't expect what happened next. Emily's hand shot out and struck Joanna a stinging blow across the cheek.

"Help!" Joanna screamed. "They're trying to steal my baby!"

In the confusion, Emily snatched Timmy from Joanna's arms and bolted for the door, with Joanna close behind yelling, "Stop! Stop!"

At the door, Emily suddenly whirled. With one hand, she grabbed the bib of Timmy's brand new overalls and ripped them off. Then she tore off his disposable diaper. Holding Timmy aloft, naked except for his t-shirt, waving her child back and forth before the astonished room of waiting passengers like an oscillating fan, she yelled, "What did you say your *daughter's* name was, Joanna?" She lifted Timmy higher, like a trophy, and consulted the crowd. "Does this look like a little girl to *you*?"

"Not with that pecker on him," muttered a drunk who had, until recently, been snoozing on one of the chairs.

Abruptly awakened from a sound sleep, and undoubtedly cold, Timmy began to howl.

"My baby, my baby," Joanna crooned, clawing at her own clothing.

On the arrivals and departures board mounted high on the wall above the glassed-in ticket counters, the letters that spelled out the train schedule clattered into their new positions with a sound like playing cards slapping on bicycle spokes. The Florida train had arrived at the station, the letters announced, but no one made a move to get on board. As Emily crowed and Timmy screamed, the crowd continued to grow, forming a semicircle around them.

Suddenly, someone pushed me forcefully aside.

"What the heck's going on here?" a security guard demanded to know.

Grabbing onto the security guard for support, Joanna sobbed, "They're stealing my baby."

"No we're not," Emily insisted in a perfectly reasonable tone of voice. "Timmy is our child. Dante's and mine."

I pushed forward through the crowd to put in my two cents worth. "Have you heard about the Shemansky kidnapping?" I asked the guard.

"The what?"

"Jesus Christ!" Dante exclaimed. "It's been on TV and in all the papers. After all the publicity, you'd think that a *security guard*," he skewered the guard with his eyes and emphasized each word, "that a security guard at a municipal train station, for Christ's sake, would be up to speed on it."

Dante reached into the back pocket of his jeans, pulled out a square of paper, unfolded it, and shoved the paper—a missing poster for Timmy—under the guard's bulbous and red-veined nose. "*This* child," Dante snarled.

Safe in his mother's arms at last, Timmy had stopped crying and buried his head in the crook of her neck. The guard examined the poster, then looked up, his eyes moving from child to the poster, child to the poster, and back again. "Could be," he said after an eternity had passed.

Dante exploded. "Can't you fucking read, man? Red hair, green eyes, thirty pounds. Get me a goddamn scale and I'll prove it to you!"

Ignoring my son-in-law's tendency toward profanity, the guard handed back the poster. "Look, I ain't no expert at identifying babies. They all look like Elmer Fudd to me."

"If you don't believe my husband," Emily said, "take a look at this." Using the arm that wasn't holding Timmy, she eased her hand into the pocket of her sweater and pulled out a piece of paper that I recognized as a photocopy of Timmy's footprints, the ones they'd taken at the hospital the day he was born.

The guard waved the evidence away. "I ain't no fingerprint expert, either, lady."

Dante had reached the end of his rope. He yanked out his cell phone, and as I watched, he dialed 911.

In the meantime, I was placing a call to Agent Crisp, mentally bracing myself for another stinging lecture. "We've found Timmy," I told her. "We're at New Carrollton station."

"I know," Crisp said. "We're on our way. I've called for backup."

While we were distracted with our respective calls, Joanna tried an end run, facing the guard directly and screaming into his face. "He's mine, I tell you."

The guard's face grew red. "Sit down, lady! I ain't no King Solomon, either. We'll let the police sort this one out." And he made a third call on his Nextel.

"You're not fooling anyone now, Joanna," Dante said gently as Joanna took the guard's advice and sat. "It's all over. You can keep up this charade for an hour, maybe two, but we both know that it's over."

Joanna began to sob.

"DNA tests will prove it, you know that. They'll prove Timmy's ours beyond a shadow of any doubt."

Joanna laced her fingers together and stared at them, tears coursing down her cheeks. "He should have been mine. He should have been mine."

"What the hell's she talking about?" Connie whispered.

"She's just sick and confused," I suggested.

But when Agent Crisp arrived a few minutes later with Agent Brown in tow, Joanna collapsed like a punctured tire. "I'm sorry," she whimpered as she wiped at her streaming nose with the back of her hand. "I don't know why I did it. It's just that when I walked by the nursery and saw that little boy lying there so peacefully, something came over me, and I took him."

Amanda Crisp nodded, and Norm Brown took Joanna's arm. "Joanna Barnhorst, you are under arrest for kidnapping." As he read the unfortunate woman her Miranda rights, Joanna seemed barely to be listening. "Do you understand these rights as I have explained them to you?"

Her cheeks still glistening with tears, Joanna nodded.

The crowd parted to let them pass, and everyone's head turned in her direction as Agent Brown led Joanna away.

I was watching, too, and as the door swooshed shut behind them, I heard one last plaintive cry. "He should have been mine."

"You know Joanna better than anyone else here," I ventured, turning to my son-in-law. "What do you think she means?"

"I honestly don't know."

And the funny thing was, even after everything that had happened, I believed him.

"That's it, everyone. Show's over!" The guard waved his arms as if flagging down a semi. "Either get on the train or go home."

Dante turned to Agent Crisp. "That's it? We can take Timmy home?"

Crisp beamed. "Take your son home, Mr. Shemansky."

CHAPTER 21

When I peer through the plastic sleeve that con-tains my Baltimore *Sun* as it makes the short trip from my front stoop—or the nearby bushes—to my kitchen table each morning, I rarely see good news above the fold, but Saturday's paper was the happy exception.

Madonna and Child. That's what ran through my mind as I smiled at the picture of Emily and Tim with a heart so full of joy that it was in real danger of bursting. Emily wore a beatific smile, and her son? The photographer had captured him just at the moment he'd thrown back his head and laughed.

When I got to the kitchen, Paul already sat at the table, shoveling a bowl of cold cereal a spoonful at a time into his mouth. With Chloe and Jake back home with their parents, their family once again complete, it was our first morning without a trace of Froot Loops littering the floor.

"Look at this," I said, laying the newspaper on the table in front of my husband. Paul swept his empty bowl aside, picked up the paper, and read the article aloud.

The *Sun* had most of the facts straight—that Timmy had been spotted by his own mother at the train station, that the kidnapper had been about to flee on a southbound Amtrak train. But they made Emily's presence at New Carrollton seem like a happy coincidence—better copy—and the FBI, to their credit, didn't set them straight on the matter.

That afternoon, *The Capital* carried a similar spread—front page pictures of Emily and Tim's joyful reunion. A photo of Joanna Barnhorst in police custody, her head bowed, also accompanied the article.

I spread the paper out flat on the table and went to fetch the scissors to cut the article out.

When I returned with the scissors, a headline below the fold made me gasp: PASTOR'S HUSBAND ALLEGED PEDOPHILE FOUND DEAD.

The scissors fell from my fingers and clattered to the floor. I dropped into a kitchen chair and pulled the paper toward me, almost afraid to read any further, because if I did, the fact that Roger Haberman was dead could only be confirmed.

> The body of Roger Haberman, 51, was found by a fisherman early this morning, floating in the water under the Spa Creek Bridge. Haberman, a convicted pedophile, and the husband of the Reverend Evangeline Haberman, pastor of St. Catherine's Church in West Annapolis, had recently been featured on an NBC television special, where he and a dozen other men were caught in a sting operation . . .

The article went on and on and on, dredging up every detail from Roger's sordid and despicable past.

According to the reporter, suicide had not been ruled out.

Poor Roger, I thought, and then, *poor Eva.*

Leaving the newspaper lying open on the table, I

rushed into the hallway to fetch my car keys. I had to go see my friend.

The picket lines were gone. That was a plus.

I parked my car near the deli on the corner of Melvyn and Annapolis Street. I circled the block around St. Catherine of Sienna Episcopal Church on foot, tearing down posters about Roger from telephone poles and fences, crumpling them up and stowing them in a plastic grocery bag I'd retrieved from my trunk.

It didn't give me as much satisfaction as the first time I saw FOUND written across the top of one of Timmy's posters on the *America's Most Wanted* website, but at least I was doing something constructive.

When I telephoned her earlier, Eva said she'd be home that afternoon and she'd like to see me. We met at St. Catherine's, in the garden, as arranged, and hugged each other, hard.

Eva spoke first. "I'm so happy that our prayers about Timmy were answered."

"Yes. I don't believe I'll complain about anything ever again."

I stepped back from the embrace, held my pastor at arm's length and stared deep into her eyes. "But Eva, how about you?"

"Roger didn't kill himself, Hannah."

I thought Eva was living in a dream world but couldn't admit it. I appealed to her logic. "But even after he was exposed on that television show?"

Eva clamped her lips together, her jaw set and determined. "Never. Not even for that."

Thinking about Roger's missing gun, I gritted my teeth and asked, "Was Roger shot?"

"No."

"What did the medical examiner say, then?"

"Roger's up in Baltimore now." She glanced at her watch. "They should be calling me shortly with information."

"Do you think it was an accident, Eva?"

"You saw the picket lines, Hannah. The hate in those people's eyes."

I sucked air in through my teeth. "You think Roger was *murdered*?"

"I'm saying it's a possibility."

"What makes you think it wasn't a suicide, Eva?" My friend was in serious denial.

Eva indicated the garden bench, and we sat down on it. Once we were settled, she continued. "Roger had recently taken out a sizable life insurance policy. If he killed himself the policy would be worthless."

"That may well be true," I said. "But perhaps Roger wasn't thinking very clearly."

"It wasn't suicide, Hannah. I'm quite sure of that. Roger wouldn't do that to me. As screwed up as he was, that man still loved me."

Butterflies flitted around us, touching down with delicate feet on marigold after marigold. "But the paper said that the police had found a suicide note."

Eva sniffed. "That's true. Cassandra had asked Roger to come over to EYS and collect his things, and the note was found there." Eva rolled her eyes. "They tell me it was a printout, for heaven's sake! If Roger had killed himself, he'd at least have had the decency to write me a note. By hand."

"What did the note say, Eva?"

She wrapped her arms around herself, and in spite of

the heat in the garden, Eva shivered. "I don't know. The police haven't shared it with me."

I reached out for Eva's hand. "Roger was under tremendous pressure, Eva."

She wagged her head vehemently. "Doubtless. But suicide wasn't the answer."

As if to end discussion on the matter, Eva abruptly changed the subject. "What's happening to the woman who kidnapped Timmy?"

"She'll be arraigned sometime this afternoon." I shuddered. I remembered how it felt to be hauled off by the FBI, turned over to a pair of humorless U.S. Marshals, and arraigned at the Federal Courthouse in Baltimore. But I had been innocent. Joanna Barnhorst, in my opinion, deserved every hour in that cold, cold cell, and every rotten box lunch.

"Do you think the Barnhorst woman is sick, like Roger was?"

"I don't think she's playing with a full deck," I answered cautiously, "but, no, I don't think she's mentally ill, at least not in the legal sense."

I offered to buy Eva lunch. We walked the short two blocks to Regina's Deli, where I bought a club sandwich for us to split, then we walked back to the parsonage and ate it in her sunny kitchen.

We had just slotted our plates into the dishwasher, and I had returned to full reversal mode, comforting my pastor and friend instead of vice versa, when the police called Eva with the medical examiner's report.

Her ear to the receiver, Eva listened for a while, incomprehension written all over her face. "My attorney's here," she fibbed, with a sideways glance at me. "Do you mind if I put you on the speakerphone?"

Eva punched a button, and everything the officer was saying suddenly poured into the kitchen, as if through a child's tin megaphone. I recognized the voice. Officer Ron Powers. "We first thought it was suicide, Mrs. Haberman, but evidence found at the scene is suggesting otherwise."

"What evidence?" Eva demanded to know.

"A search of your husband's former office, near where his body was found, has uncovered a bottle of Jim Beam, laced with Prozac."

"But Roger didn't drink," Eva insisted.

"Maybe he didn't normally drink, Mrs. Haberman, but his bloodstream was full of antidepressants and alcohol."

"He died of an overdose?"

"We found water in his lungs. Your husband drowned, Mrs. Haberman."

Eva plucked a tissue out of the box she kept next to the telephone and dabbed at her eyes. "But you told me there was a suicide note," she continued.

"There was. When we searched your husband's office, we found the note still up on his computer screen, but he'd printed out a copy, too. The office has networked their printer. Your husband's note was in the printer tray near the photocopying machine."

"So, what makes you think it wasn't suicide, then," Eva whispered. She sounded exhausted and drained.

"I can't go into any details, of course," Powers continued, but we've arrested your husband's boss, Cassandra Matthews, and charged her with his murder."

"*Cassandra?*" Eva's face told the whole story. She didn't believe in Cassandra's guilt, not for a single minute.

But apparently there was enough evidence to satisfy the police, and that was the end of that.

Eva prodded Powers for details, but none were forthcoming.

"Don't worry, Eva," I said after she hung up the phone. "My brother-in-law is a cop. Maybe I can find out something from him."

That's how we found out sometime later that only two sets of fingerprints had been found on the whiskey bottle—Roger's and those of his former boss, Cassandra Matthews.

And to put the icing on the cake, Cassandra's were the only fingerprints on Roger Haberman's keyboard.

CHAPTER 22

Several days later I was sitting in my living room, catching up on some knitting I'd neglected since the winter Olympic Games—the ones in Nagano, not Salt Lake City—when somebody knocked at my door.

With a sigh, I laid down my knitting, and peeked out through the curtains. Eva Haberman stood on my porch. Incredibly, Cassandra Matthews was with her.

"Hannah," Eva said after I'd opened the door and ushered the women into my entrance hall. "You remember Cassandra Matthews."

"Roger's boss?" I said cautiously, extending my hand. "We met at St. Cat's, as I recall."

"Former boss," Cassandra corrected.

"I bailed her out," Eva explained.

Normally, I trusted Eva's judgment, but bailing out the woman who may have murdered her husband was a bit too forward-thinking, even for me.

Nevertheless, I invited them in.

It was a beautiful spring day, so I seated the women out on the patio, leaving them to commune with nature and make small talk while I brewed a fresh pot of coffee and wondered why they'd come to see me. While water gurgled through the Mr. Coffee machine, I hauled some sugar cookies out of the freezer and arranged them on a plate to thaw, thinking how appalled François Lesperance would be if he caught me doing it.

"What I don't understand, Cassandra," I said as I emerged from the kitchen with the coffeepot in one hand and three empty mugs in the other, "is what motive you had for killing Roger." I raised a finger. "Hold that thought."

I popped back into the kitchen for the cream, sugar, and cookies, then continued our conversation. "Seems to me that Roger had a much stronger motive to murder *you*, and not the other way around. You fired him, after all."

Cassandra blushed to the tips of her multi-blond roots. "Apparently you've been missing the evening news for the past several days, Hannah."

"I guess I have."

"That was me, front and center, on one of Erika Rose's picket lines. I was the blonde holding the sign that said, 'The Only Good Pedophile Is a Dead Pedophile.' "

In spite of the seriousness of the situation, I grinned. "Do you actually believe that, or did you simply glom on to the first sign Erika handed you?"

"No, it was my sign, my sentiment. I truly believe that pedophilia is incurable, but I'm certainly not glad that *Roger* is dead."

She sipped at her coffee. "Roger Haberman was a generous guy, and a hard worker. I never had any complaints—*ever*—that he was messing with the children at the sailing school. But after the news broke, I just had to let him go."

"Roger managed to control one thing, it seems," his widow muttered. "He was able to keep his addictions out of the workplace."

"True," Cassandra agreed.

"You're probably wondering why we're here today," Eva continued, dramatically shifting gears.

"My reputation for excellent coffee?"

"That, too." She'd been holding her coffee mug in both hands, but she set it down on the table. "We're hoping that you can help, that by putting three heads together, rather than two, we can sort this thing out."

I was wondering what thing they wanted sorted when Cassandra spoke, clearing up any confusion. "I didn't kill Roger."

"And I believe her," Eva said. "The police are basing the case against Cassandra on the most circumstantial of evidence," she continued. "The suicide note, which appears to have been written in her style, and her fingerprints on the bottle."

"It's circumstantial evidence like that that can do you in," I commented, remembering my own sorry plight when the hammer that had been used to bash in Jennifer Goodall's skull had turned up with my ridges and whorls all over the handle. "Was the Jim Beam bottle yours?"

"Oh, yes. I kept it in my desk drawer. For medicinal purposes." She blushed again. "I know it sounds lame, but every once in a while I'd have one of those days, and it'd come in handy. It wasn't the kids so much," she explained, "but their parents can certainly drive you to drink."

"Everyone knew where she kept the bottle," Eva added.

"And the Prozac?" I wondered.

Cassandra shrugged. "There must be half a dozen people to-ing and fro-ing in our office every day, exhibiting every sort of phobia and anxiety you can imagine. Any one of them could have had access to Prozac."

Thinking about the contents of my own daughter's medicine cabinet, I had to agree. "If the police think *you* murdered Roger," I continued with unrelenting logic, "they must believe that you faked his suicide note, too."

"I haven't seen it yet," Cassandra complained. "It was on Roger's computer."

Eva smiled at Cassandra sympathetically. "They took his CPU, didn't they? Looking for evidence? They've still got the PC Roger used at home."

Cassandra nodded.

Eva frowned. "Then that's it, then."

I raised a cautionary finger. "But wait! Cassandra, all your files are backed up every night to the mainframe computer, right?"

Cassandra nodded, comprehension dawning. "We should be able to find a copy of Roger's note if we restore it from backup!"

I shoved my coffee mug aside. "Brilliant! Well, what are we waiting for?"

Eva drove the three of us to the Eastport Yacht Sales offices near the intersection of Second and Severn in Eastport. We parked next to the sailmaker's shop.

It was still early, so the office was locked, but Cassandra let us in with her key.

The reception area of EYS looked like a photo layout for *Yachting* magazine. Comfortably upholstered chairs were arranged in a neat square around a glass-topped table, where back issues of *Yachting, Sail*, and *Cruising World* were arranged in neat cascades.

Roger's office, too, seemed ready for the photographers. Except for the dust bunnies marking the empty spot under his desk where Roger's CPU had so recently sat, the room was immaculate. The police had done a careful job, it seemed. Nothing appeared to have been disturbed—the papers in his outbox, his telephone, his monitor, his keyboard, mouse, and mouse pad. A customized mouse pad, I noticed with a twinge, with a picture of Roger and Eva smiling out from it, standing on the rim of the Grand Canyon.

Because Roger's access to the mainframe had disappeared along with his hard drive, Cassandra escorted us to her office, stopping along the way to turn the printer on in the photocopying room and to remove a laptop from a locked cabinet.

The state of Cassandra's office would have sent Mr. Monk, the obsessive-compulsive TV detective, into cardiac arrest. The rampant disorder made even me catch my breath. Catalogs, brochures, and business papers of all kinds littered every available surface. Sailing posters hung crookedly on the walls. The cord on the venetian blinds was a tangled mess, three slats in it were broken, and a sticky puddle marked the spot where coffee had recently spilled on Cassandra's desk. Either the Annapolis police had different searching standards from the FBI, or Cassandra was, quite simply, a slob.

"Sorry for the mess," she apologized, confirming my slob theory.

With a broad sweep of her arm she reclaimed the work space, sending a stack of papers cascading onto the floor. She set the laptop down and plugged in the

ISDN cable that snaked out of the wall. "They took my CPU for evidence, too," she explained. "But they didn't think about the company laptop. We use it mostly for boat shows."

I watched as Cassandra powered up the laptop and prepared to access the centralized office files. She tapped away with confidence, while Eva and I looked over her shoulder, bristling with nervous tension.

"Files, backup, restore," Cassandra was saying. The light on the front of the laptop blinked, and the hard drive whirred. "Word, file, open . . ." *Tap tap tap.* "Print!" she exclaimed at last, stabbing at the Enter key with a flourish.

"Wait here while I get the file," she said.

Cassandra returned a few minutes later with three copies of Roger Haberman's so-called suicide note.

It has come to my attention that people are conspiring against me. They will never rest until I am dead. I didn't mean to harm anyone. For the trouble I've caused, I'm desparately sorry. I'm a mess. I'm out of control. I see no other way than to quickly end it.

"It is rather generic," I observed, looking up from my copy of Roger's note. "And it doesn't mention you specifically, Eva, which I find pretty curious."

"It certainly doesn't sound like Roger." Eva tapped the note with her index finger. " 'It has come to my attention that' is just a bit stuffy, even for Roger."

"The police analyst has determined *I* wrote it," Cassandra said. "They've got all my word processing files, so I suppose they can prove it in a court of law. Apparently I use phrases like 'it has come to my attention' with a statistical probability of twenty-seven percent over samples of writing chosen at random from among the general population, or some such nonsense. But their analyst is dead wrong."

"This troubles me, though," Eva interjected. "Roger never learned how to spell 'desperately,' and he's misspelled it here, too. But this, I think, is the clincher."

"What?"

" 'To quickly end it,' " she quoted. "Roger was a stickler for grammar. The poor man couldn't split an infinitive if his life depended on it."

Eva grimaced, as if realizing that the tired old cliché had sudden meaning. She looked from Cassandra to me, tears glistening in her eyes. "Roger wrote this note himself, didn't he? For whatever reason, Roger wrote the note."

"I'm afraid so," I said.

"But why?" Tears rolled down her cheeks and splashed, unheeded, on her blouse.

"You gave me the answer yourself a couple of days ago, Eva."

"I did?" she sniffled.

From the chaos on her office shelves, Cassandra managed to unearth a box of tissues and hand them to her.

"Yes. You told me that Roger had recently taken out a life insurance policy, and that if he committed suicide, it would be worthless."

Dabbing at her nose with the tissue, she nodded.

"So try this on for size. Suppose that Roger, in his distress over being outed on national television, in fear of being branded as a kidnapper, thereby heaping more disgrace on you, even threatening your job and your calling to the priesthood . . ." I paused to take a breath. "Suppose Roger decided to kill two birds with one stone."

From her desk chair Cassandra muttered, "I don't get it."

"Okay. Roger has two problems." I held up a finger. "First, he wants to make sure the wife he loves and who he has so grievously wronged gets the money that's coming to her." I held up two fingers. "And second, he wants to punish the boss he believes wronged him, by firing him without provocation."

"I still don't get it."

"I believe Roger faked his own murder, then tried to frame you for it."

"My God," Cassandra said.

Next to me, Eva closed her eyes. Her lips moved and I knew she was praying.

I waited until Eva had opened her eyes again before I said, "And I think I can prove it."

"How?"

"All the time you were typing, Cassandra, I kept looking at your desk and thinking that something's not quite right."

I pointed out the spot where a coffee stain, dried up but still sticky, had spread across Cassandra's blotter and onto the metal surface of the desk itself. Brownish splatters from the spill extended to her monitor and her mouse, but her keyboard was suspiciously clean.

"How did you manage a coffee spill the size of the *Exxon Valdez*," I asked her, "and not get a single drop of coffee on your keyboard?"

Using my fingers, I picked the keyboard up carefully by the edges and displayed it for them. "See? Pristine."

Eva's eyes grew wide. "So you think Roger . . . ?" She paused. "Sweet Jesus, that's monstrous."

"I believe that Roger typed the note, then, probably wearing gloves, switched Cassandra's keyboard for his own."

I looked at Eva, Eva looked at me, and we both looked at Cassandra. We practically stumbled over one another in our haste to get back to Roger's office and check out my theory.

As I suspected, the keyboard now sitting on Roger's desk bore telltale specks of dried-up coffee. "Don't touch it," I warned. "The cops will want to test it for DNA."

"DNA?" Cassandra looked puzzled.

"When we type, we leave behind skin cells, bits of hair, particles of fingernail. DNA analysis will prove that the keyboards were switched. Much more conclusive than coffee stains."

Eva fell back against the wall, grabbing the door frame for support. "If Roger wanted to take his own life, that was certainly his prerogative," she said. "But it was very, very wrong of him to try to place the blame on somebody else." Eva winced, as if in pain, and I knew she was probably worrying about the state of Roger's immortal soul.

"Roger was mentally ill, Eva. He can't be held accountable, at least not in that way."

"I wouldn't have kept the insurance money, anyway," she muttered.

Cassandra brightened. "You could have given it to charity."

I glared. I'd just saved the woman's ass, and she was being glib.

"Well," Cassandra said, picking up on my unspoken

message. "I was simply suggesting that it would be nice if *some* good were to come out of all this."

"Shut up, Cassandra," I said.

From across the room, for the first time in many, many days, Pastor Evangeline Haberman actually smiled.

CHAPTER 23

Roger's death was ruled a suicide. Cassandra was cleared.

Featured in the July issue of *Spa* magazine, Paradiso continued to thrive, but the same wasn't true of the Shemansky marriage.

To be fair to my son-in-law, he was as clueless, I believe, as the rest of us. It took an article in the Sunday supplement of the Philadelphia *Inquirer* to clear up some of the mystery surrounding the Barnhorst case. While remaining mute for the cops, Joanna Barnhorst had spilled all for a reporter who showed up at the federal prison, serious cash inducements in hand.

Dante's college relationship with Joanna had been common knowledge. No one disagreed with that. Then Dante had ended the affair and abandoned her—Barnhorst's words, not Dante's—for a life in Colorado with my daughter.

What nobody knew, except Joanna and her gynecologist, was that Joanna had been three months' pregnant at the time.

Barnhorst claimed in the article that she'd informed Dante of the pregnancy, but he'd dropped out of school and fled, rather than face up to his responsibilities and a shotgun marriage to a woman he no longer loved.

She'd had no choice (the reporter wrote that Joanna sobbed uncontrollably for some twenty minutes at this point) but to terminate the pregnancy. Later, when Joanna Kerr married and became Joanna Barnhorst, she found she could no longer have children. When her husband divorced her for that, the article claimed, it had sent the poor girl reeling right over the edge.

"That's bullshit!" Dante exploded when he learned about the pregnancy. "She never said a word to me, not a fucking word." He shook his head, his ponytail flopping. "Besides, I always used a condom. Always."

Emily glowered. "Condoms don't always work, you bonehead."

The Pennsylvania State Police, we learned from the article, had confirmed the surgical procedure, but she'd not named the child's father at the time. After all these years, there was no way to prove whether the child Joanna aborted had been Dante's.

"If she had only told me," Dante continued, "all this, uh, unpleasantness might never have happened."

Dante was making a good point. Why hadn't Joanna told him about her pregnancy? I wondered. I thought back to my own college days, trying to put myself in Joanna's shoes. Either the child wasn't Dante's, as he so clearly wanted to believe, or she had been *afraid* to tell him about the baby.

"What kind of man would abandon his pregnant girlfriend and elope with another woman?" Emily asked me during a quiet, and increasingly rare, mother-daughter moment as we worked side by side in her utility room, catching up on the laundry.

"You don't know that he did, Emily."

Emily seemed to have aged ten years in the past week. Worry lines had deepened on her brow, and not all of them, I thought, could be blamed on Timmy.

"How can I live with him now?"

"A marriage has to be based on trust," I reminded my daughter as I added a scoop of soap powder to the washer. Then I gave her some advice my mother had given me when Paul and I had been going through a rough patch.

"I don't suppose we'll ever know the truth. The only people who do are Joanna and Dante. You'll have to make up your mind one way or the other: either he fathered and knowingly abandoned that child, or he didn't. Then, you decide if you can live with that."

"What do *you* think, Mom?" Emily asked, tears pooling in her eyes.

"What I think isn't important. It's what you think."

"But Dad never cheated on you."

"No, but I didn't find that out, not for certain, until years later. What it all comes down to, Emily, is trust." I gathered her hands in mine. "Do you trust your husband?"

The tears spilled over and rolled down her cheeks. "I don't know, Mom. I just don't know."

Emily was wrestling with personal demons, too. "I helped hound a man to his death," she confessed to me later that same afternoon. "Roger was guilty of pedophilia, that was true. But, I know now that he never would have harmed Timmy. Oh my God, Mother, I feel so terrible about that. Roger was a creep, but he didn't deserve to die."

"Nobody deserves to die," I said. "But we all do. Some of us sooner, some of us later."

"Mom," Emily said with a sudden smirk and a reassuring sarcastic twinkle in her eye. "Sometimes you are *so* profound."

CHAPTER 24

On the seventh Sunday in Easter, Paul and I at-tended Morning Eucharist at St. Catherine's with Emily and Dante in tow. At first I thought we'd come at the wrong time. The pews were virtually empty.

"What's going on?" I whispered to Paul as we slid into our regular pew on the right side of the sanctuary, three rows from the back.

"I hear we've lost some families to St. Anne's," Paul explained. "And St. Margaret's picked up a few members of the We Hate Roger Club, too."

"It seems wrong to punish Eva for something her husband did," I whispered back as I opened my hymnal, thumbing through it, looking for the number of the first hymn.

In the pew beside me, Emily stirred. "I'll need to be praying about that myself," she said.

"The concern isn't over what Eva did, it's what she didn't do," her father said. "Some of our parishioners feel betrayed. In spite of the advice Eva got from the bishop, the congregation should have been informed about Roger's, um, proclivities."

"And he certainly should have registered with

Maryland's sex offender registry," Emily reminded us. "Pastor Eva should have made sure that was done."

Dante scurried in from delivering the children to Sunday school, just in time to join in the opening hymn. With so few people in the congregation, Dante's fine tenor was a standout. I caught Emily looking up at him with pride as he soared into the upper reaches of "Crown Him with Many Crowns," and I felt a wave of relief wash over me. Perhaps their marriage was on the mend after all.

The service was what I expected, being the Sunday following Ascension. A reading from John. Full-blown Easter hymns. It's that time in the liturgical year where Jesus has gone up to heaven, but the Holy Spirit hasn't arrived. Humankind is adrift, so to speak, and Eva had told me that under the circumstances, she thought it'd be the perfect time to preach about feeling alone, when we're not actually alone.

So I was shocked and surprised when in place of the usual sermon, Eva announced she was leaving St. Cat's, removing herself from the midst of the devastating conflict so that the church she so loved could begin to heal. She'd requested, and the bishop had granted, six months of "spiritual renewal" leave. An interim would fill in during her absense.

I saw her after the service at coffee hour, of course, but she was mobbed, so I didn't get to ask her about it until the following day, when I simply showed up at St. Cat's, uninvited.

I found Eva sitting in the sterile wreck of what had once been her office. Packing boxes, large and small, were scattered everywhere, some already sealed with packing tape and marked STORAGE.

"Eva, at services yesterday, you didn't say where you were going."

"Until this morning, I hadn't really decided."

"I'd like to stay in touch while you're away."

"It won't be easy." She smiled wanly. "I don't know how long I'll be able to stand the solitude of my own, rather sorry company, but I inherited a cabin from my parents some years ago, up in the Sawtooth Range of Idaho. No phone, no TV, and back then, no electricity, either, although I'm happy to say that particular deficiency was remedied a few years back. We've got indoor plumbing now, too."

"What about Roger?" I asked.

"I sent his body back to Medina, Ohio," she said. "He'll be buried there in the family plot."

"No service?"

She shook her head. "Roger didn't want any service. He felt he didn't deserve it, after all the wicked things he'd done."

Eva put the books she was holding into a box, nestling them along the sides among some embroidered cushions that had once sat out on the window seat in her office. I'd often seen her sitting there, watching the birds. "I did hear from Roger, you know."

"You did? I'm so glad."

"He mailed me a letter, confessing to everything. You know Roger's handwriting."

I smiled, although I didn't have a clue what Roger's handwriting looked like.

"The post office couldn't read one of the numbers, so they first sent it to the wrong zip code. It didn't find me until yesterday."

I was dying to know what the letter said, but unless

Eva volunteered the information, I would respect my friend's privacy.

"The letter came in one of those videotape boxes," Eva added. "Do you know what else was in the box?"

I shook my head.

"Roger's gun." She smiled ruefully. "He wrote that he didn't have the courage to use it."

Eva wrapped a ceramic pencil cup holder in newspaper and placed it carefully in the box. "It was good to see Dante and Emily at church yesterday. How are things going with them?"

I had no secrets from Eva. "On the mend. I'm taking the children for a week so that Emily and Dante can have some time to themselves." I paused. "Besides, it will give me time to take Chloe in hand and teach her a little bit about Internet security. Do you know what I found out?"

"No, but I'm sure you'll tell me."

"That little scamp, and her best friend, Samantha, had profiles on Myspace.com. It's a social networking website," I added before Eva could ask me. "Thanks to Sam's older sister, who's all of fourteen, anybody in the world could see a picture of Chloe, know her name, what zip code she's from, and that she likes to go to Ben and Jerry's. Hello?

"I made sure she erased her profile," I added.

"And that woman who kidnapped Timmy?"

"Awaiting trial," I said. "God only knows when. Connie was slated to get the reward money, you know."

Eva smiled. "I didn't know, but how wonderful."

"She turned it down. Told Phyllis to give it all to NCMEC. So she did."

"I can't think of a better place for it."

Eva walked to the wall, took down two of the crosses, wrapped them in newspaper and tucked them into the packing box along with the pencil holder. "I saw that psychic on CNN again this morning."

"You did?" If Montana Martin had been on TV, I was surprised nobody had told us about it.

"You won't believe what she was saying."

I handed Eva a couple more books. "Try me."

"It seems she's added the Timothy Shemansky case to her portfolio of cases solved."

"I don't believe it! Montana's predictions about Timmy's whereabouts didn't even come close."

Eva dumped the books I'd handed her unceremoniously into the box. "She predicted 'on or near water,' right?"

I nodded.

"Did you notice the decorative fountain near Barnhorst's apartment complex?"

I groaned. "That fake Victorian monstrosity? Okay. I'll give her points for that. But she also said that Japanese people had taken him."

"Chinese," Eva corrected. "Isn't the Joy Luck Restaurant right across the street?"

"This is seriously spooky." I stared at my friend. "Maybe my mother really did want me to have her emerald ring."

"Maybe we need to perform an exorcism," Eva joked. "But let's wait until your father gets back and you've had time to ask him about the ring."

"Oh, Eva," I cried, leaping to my feet and giving her a bear hug. "I am going to miss you so much!"

After I'd let her go, Eva rattled on, changing the subject. "I've got an ATV I can drive in Idaho. That way I won't have to hoof it up and down the mountain when I need to get into town."

"Do they have Internet cafés in your Idaho town?" I asked.

She shrugged. "Never thought to look, but if they do, I'll be sure to e-mail you from time to time."

"I'd really like that, Eva."

Eva closed the box she was packing. I held the flaps closed with both hands while she sealed it with tape. "Would you like some tea?" she asked after we had finished with the box. "I've got a kettle on in the church kitchen."

"That would be nice."

"I'll be back in a minute, then."

I helped Eva stack several boxes on a rolling library cart and watched as she pushed the cart down the hall in the direction of the storage closet.

While I waited for Eva to come back with the tea, I puttered. Picking up a book here, a stray piece of paper there. As I moved to toss a dried-up tea bag into the trash, I noticed a tiny, shapely leg sticking out of the jumble of items in Eva's trash can. I bent over and plucked it out. It was Eva's Barbie doll. She'd been thrust down, head first, into a pile of crumpled-up sermons.

I smoothed Barbie's robe over her body, adjusted her surplice, dug around in the mounds of trash until I located her missing stole, and settled that around her shoulders again, too.

Out in the hall, Eva was still pushing the cart with the squeaky wheel down the hallway. I dashed after her, clutching the Barbie. "Eva! You left this! Don't you want to take your Barbie?"

With a tiredness born of disappointment and regret,

Eva slowed. She brushed at her cheeks before turning around, trying, without much success, to hide her tears from me. She raised her voice slightly so that I could hear. "No, I don't think I'll need it."

Still holding Barbie, I hustled down the hall, catching up with my friend near the door to the kitchen. "But Pastor Barbie was a gift from your sister."

"Yes, but every time I look at her now, she reminds me of my failures. I failed myself, my husband, and my church. But most painfully of all, I've failed my God."

"You're too good a priest to leave the Church for good, Eva. Maybe after you've been away for a while, you'll see your way clear to come back."

"Maybe," she said, but she didn't sound convinced.

Eva reached out and smoothed Barbie's hair. Then, just as suddenly, she snatched her hand back as if she'd been burned. "Just throw it away," she said.

I watched Eva, stooped, slump shouldered, and defeated, as she turned away from me and continued pushing her cart down the hall.

Holding her by her feet, I brought Barbie's face up to meet mine. "Well, Barbie, what do you say?" I opened my handbag and tucked Pastor Barbie toes first into the pouch that normally contained my cell phone.

Eva might never return to St. Catherine's, I thought with an ache in my heart, but someday Pastor Eva would come back to God. And when she did, Pastor Barbie would be at my house, waiting for her.